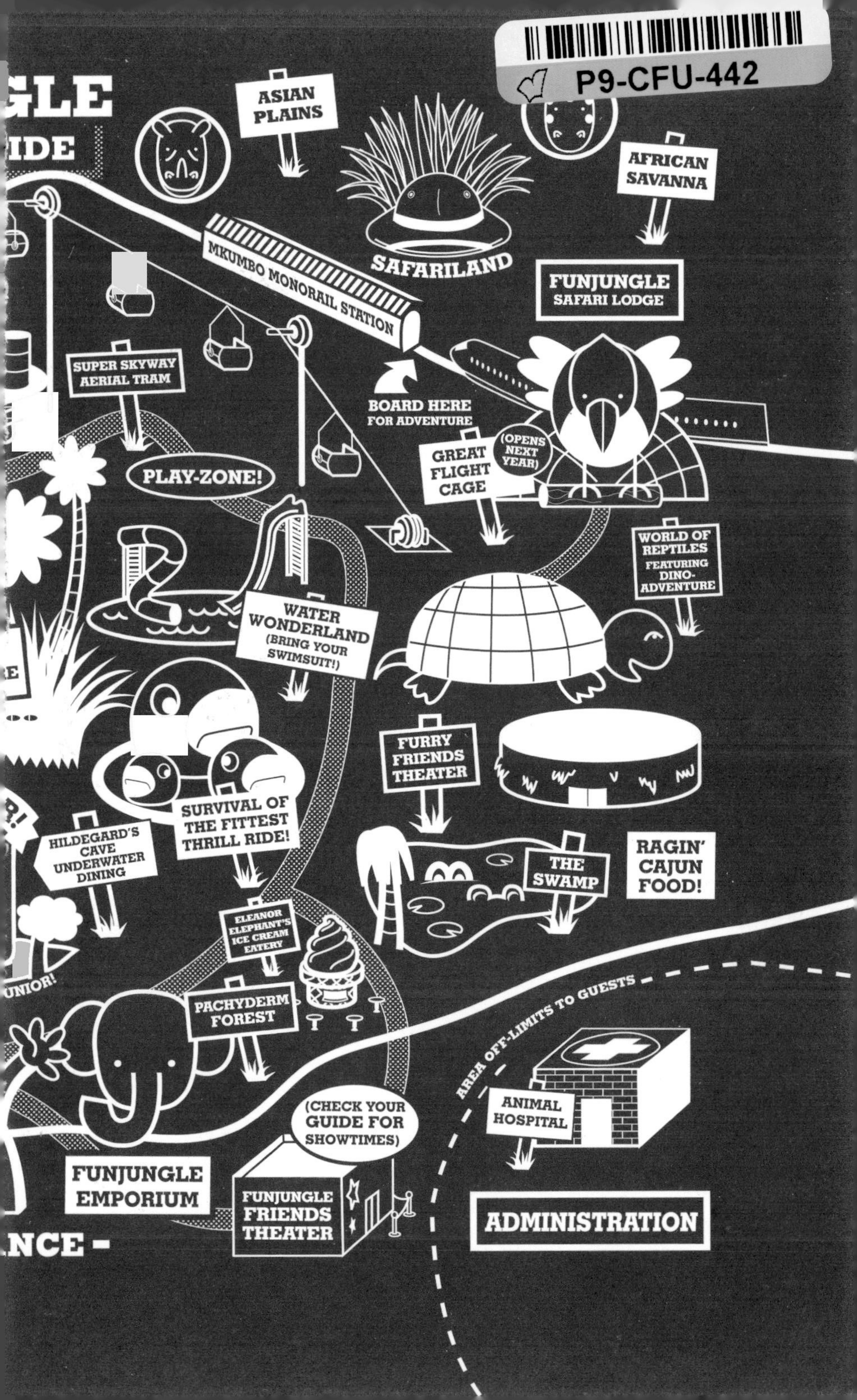
GLE
IDE
ASIAN PLAINS
SAFARILAND
AFRICAN SAVANNA
MKUMBO MONORAIL STATION
FUNJUNGLE SAFARI LODGE
SUPER SKYWAY AERIAL TRAM
BOARD HERE FOR ADVENTURE
GREAT FLIGHT CAGE
(OPENS NEXT YEAR)
PLAY-ZONE!
WORLD OF REPTILES FEATURING DINO-ADVENTURE
WATER WONDERLAND (BRING YOUR SWIMSUIT!)
FURRY FRIENDS THEATER
SURVIVAL OF THE FITTEST THRILL RIDE!
HILDEGARD'S CAVE UNDERWATER DINING
THE SWAMP
RAGIN' CAJUN FOOD!
ELEANOR ELEPHANT'S ICE CREAM EATERY
UNIOR!
PACHYDERM FOREST
AREA OFF-LIMITS TO GUESTS
ANIMAL HOSPITAL
(CHECK YOUR GUIDE FOR SHOWTIMES)
FUNJUNGLE EMPORIUM
FUNJUNGLE FRIENDS THEATER
ADMINISTRATION
NCE -

big game

Also by Stuart Gibbs

The FunJungle series

Belly Up

Poached

The Spy School series

Spy School

Spy Camp

Evil Spy School

The Moon Base Alpha series

Space Case

The Last Musketeer

STUART GIBBS

big game

A funjungle NOVEL

Simon & Schuster Books for Young Readers
New York London Toronto Sydney New Delhi

SIMON & SCHUSTER BOOKS FOR YOUNG READERS
An imprint of Simon & Schuster Children's Publishing Division
1230 Avenue of the Americas, New York, New York 10020

Book design and principal jacket illustration by Lucy Ruth Cummins
Endpaper art by Ryan Thompson
The text for this book is set in Adobe Garamond Pro.
Manufactured in the United States of America
0915 FFG
10 9 8 7 6 5 4 3 2 1
Library of Congress Cataloging-in-Publication Data
Gibbs, Stuart, 1969–
Big game / Stuart Gibbs. — First edition.
pages cm
Sequel to: Poached.
Summary: "Someone is trying to hunt FunJungle's Asian greater one-horned rhinoceros, and twelve-year-old Teddy Fitzroy is on the case."—Provided by publisher.
ISBN 978-1-4814-2333-5 (hardcover) — ISBN 978-1-4814-2335-9 (eBook)
[1. Mystery and detective stories. 2. Zoos—Fiction. 3. Zoo animals—Fiction.
4. Rhinoceroses—Fiction. 5. Endangered species—Fiction. 6. Poaching—Fiction.]
I. Title.
PZ7.G339236Bi 2015
[Fic]—dc23
2014042145

To my uncle David Holtz and my cousin Albert Sukoff,
who both taught me how to think outside the box

Acknowledgments

I am extremely indebted to many people for helping me develop this story and for providing great insight into the complicated issue of rhino poaching:

The San Diego Zoo and San Diego Safari Park were a great help to me in researching this book. In particular, I'd like to thank rhino specialists Lance Aubery and Victoria Zahn—and veterinarian Jeff Zuba—for answering as many questions as I could ask. Also, thanks to Rachelle Marcon for giving me an amazing behind-the-scenes tour. (It was also an incredible treat to get a personal visit with Surat, the San Diego Zoo's Asian rhino, from whom I learned a great deal about rhino behavior.)

Speaking of incredible treats, Hayden Rosenauer and my dear friend Georgia Simon arranged for me to spend several hours with two elephants, which was truly inspirational for the opening chapter of this book—and for me, personally, as well.

One of my oldest friends in the world, Mark Middleman,

introduced me to the world of exotic game ranching, while Joe Davidson was instrumental in helping work out the plot (though I can't say what he helped me with because it'll spoil part of the mystery).

My agent, Jennifer Joel, has been a tireless champion of my work, while my wonderful editor—and fellow animal enthusiast—Kristin Ostby, gave me thoughtful notes and clever insights.

Finally, I'd like to thank my wife, Suzanne, and my children, Dashiell and Violet, for their support, their suggestions, and their endless enthusiasm. I love you all more than words can say.

contents

THE STAMPEDE

I was helping walk the elephants when we all heard the rifle go off.

It was a little after seven o'clock on a February morning. We had to walk the elephants early, because it couldn't be done during normal theme-park hours. The elephants were walked *through* the park, and tourists would just get in the way.

In the wild, elephants walk a lot. They've been known to cover more than fifty miles in a day, although the average is around twenty. They're built for walking (they're the only animal with four knees), but even at a massive, state-of-the-art place like FunJungle Wild Animal Park, there couldn't be an exhibit big enough to let them roam that far. So, in the interest of keeping the elephants fit and happy, the staff walked them in the morning, the same way normal people walked their dogs—only, the pooper-scoopers were a lot bigger.

I wasn't really supposed to be walking the elephants because I was only twelve years old. Any animal that weighs eight tons and is capable of lifting a small car can be dangerous. But since I was the only kid who lived at FunJungle, I'd gotten to know lots of the keepers well, so they cut me some slack—as long as I kept a safe distance and one of my parents came with me.

That was easy to arrange. My father was always happy to bring me. As a professional wildlife photographer, he didn't mind getting up early; that was the best time to take pictures of animals in the wild. Plus, being with the elephants reminded him of life back in Africa. My mother was a famous primatologist, and before my folks had been hired by FunJungle, we'd spent ten years in a tent camp in the Congo while Mom studied chimpanzees. We'd all loved it, but a war had forced us to give up that life. Living in a trailer park behind the world's biggest zoo was probably as close to the African experience as we could get, but it still wasn't quite the same.

For starters, it was really cold that morning. The temperature in the Congo had rarely dropped below seventy degrees, while winters in central Texas could be bone-chilling. I had never even owned a sweater in Africa; Now I was wrapped in a ski jacket with three layers underneath. Our breath clouded the air in front of us, while steam rose off the elephants' warm bodies.

The elephants didn't seem bothered by the cold, though. The whole herd was there, twelve elephants ranging in age from two to sixty. Eleanor, the matriarch, was in the lead, while the younger mothers and their offspring followed. (The park's only breeding male, Tembo, had to be kept apart and did his walks late at night.)

It took five keepers to control the elephants. Two flanked the herd on either side, gently directing them along Adventure Road, the park's main concourse. The keepers were all armed with brooms with the bristles wrapped in towels, which looked kind of like giant Q-tips. These were used to gently prod the elephants along, or to nudge them back into line should they veer off and try to eat an expensive piece of landscaping.

Bonnie Melton, the head keeper, brought up the rear. Bonnie had forty years of experience in zoos and knew more about elephants than almost anyone on earth. She was wrinkled as a prune—caring for elephants meant you spent a lot of time in the sun—but she had the enthusiasm of a kindergartener. While none of her subordinate keepers seemed pleased to be working so early, Bonnie was chipper as could be, even though she had an industrial-size pooper-scooper slung over her shoulder.

"How's school going, Teddy?" she asked me, as we led the herd past the front gates.

"Pretty good," I replied.

"You making friends okay?"

"Yeah, I guess."

"You guess?" Dad repeated, then put an arm around me proudly. "Ever since Teddy knocked out the school bully, he's the most popular kid there."

Despite the freezing temperatures, I could feel my face grow warm with embarrassment. "No, I'm not, Dad."

"The head cheerleader came over for a date," Dad told Bonnie.

"It wasn't a date," I corrected. "She only wanted to see FunJungle behind the scenes."

"Sounds like a date to me," Bonnie said, stifling a smile.

I tried to change the subject. "If anyone's the most popular kid in my school, it's Summer McCracken."

Bonnie nodded knowingly. "She would be."

Summer McCracken was the daughter of J.J. McCracken, the local billionaire who'd sunk a good deal of his fortune into building FunJungle. Summer was only a year older than me, and she was the first friend I'd made in Texas. Until recently, she'd attended prep school on the East Coast, but she'd asked to come home—so now she was the newest student at Lyndon B. Johnson Middle School.

"Is that why she transferred from that fancy-schmancy school?" Bonnie asked. "So she could be belle of the ball here?"

I shrugged. "Summer said life was more exciting here."

Bonnie laughed. "Here? We're thirty miles from the nearest city." She suddenly turned and yelled, "Kwame! Don't eat that!"

Kwame, a three-year-old elephant, sheepishly unwound his trunk from an oleander bush like a kid who'd been caught with his hand in the cookie jar.

"There *has* been some excitement here," Dad pointed out. "A murdered hippo. A stolen koala. An escaped tiger. Those kinds of things don't happen too often at prep school."

At that moment, Eleanor Elephant lifted her tail and deposited a large pile of poop on the concourse.

"Oh yeah," Bonnie said. "This place is a thrill a minute." Then she hoisted the pooper-scooper off her shoulder and hurried off to clean up after Eleanor.

According to Summer, poop had always been J.J. McCracken's biggest concern about letting the elephants walk around the park in the morning. "Oh sure, he'll *say* he's worried about safety," she'd told me, "but really, it's the poo. He's terrified the keepers will somehow overlook a big old elephant poop one morning and that some poor guest will step in it."

I could understand J.J.'s concern. Elephants make nearly two hundred pounds of poop a day—as well as enough pee to fill a bathtub. A janitorial team armed with industrial-strength cleansers had to follow the elephant parade around the park every morning. To that end, J.J. had looked for an alternative way to exercise the elephants—and had even considered building jumbo-size treadmills at one point. Nothing had panned out, though, so for the time being, the elephants were still walking.

"I'll bet that cheerleader *thought* it was a date," Dad said.

I turned away from the elephants and looked at him, surprised. "What?"

"She spent over four hours with you," Dad told me. "I don't think she would have done that unless she liked you."

"Or she likes animals."

"What's her name again?" Dad asked. "Daisy?"

"Violet," I corrected. "Violet Grace."

"You should ask Violet to the movies sometime."

"No." I looked back toward Bonnie. I would have rather watched a person clean up elephant poop than have this conversation.

Dad wouldn't let it go, though. I got the sense this was a talk he'd been wanting to have for a long time. "Why not? She's the head cheerleader and she likes you. Back when I was in middle school, I prayed that would happen to me."

"I just don't want to ask her—that's all." Normally, I didn't like the idea of lying to my father, but at the same time, I didn't feel like telling him the real reason I didn't want to ask Violet out.

However, Dad was savvier than I realized. "Is this about Summer?" he asked.

I turned back to him, caught off guard. But before I could answer—or figure out how *not* to answer—Athmani Okeke came along.

Athmani was a wildlife security specialist from Kruger National Park in South Africa, where he'd worked to protect the animals from poachers. FunJungle had been open only six months, but already its hippo mascot had been murdered and a popular koala bear had been stolen, so J.J. McCracken had decided his animal security needed to be greatly improved. He'd hired Athmani as a consultant right after New Year's, and Athmani had been working so feverishly since then, he'd barely left the property. He was wearing a camouflage uniform from Kruger, because he still hadn't made it to town to buy any new clothes yet.

"Good morning, gentlemen!" he called, waving to both of us. Athmani spoke with a lilt in his voice, the way many native Africans did, which made his words sound a bit like a song. His skin was so dark that the whites of his eyes seemed to glow against it. "What brings you out here so early this morning?"

"Getting a little exercise." Dad shook Athmani's hand. "How about yourself?"

"I'm making sure my elephants are safe." Athmani held up his hand to me for a fist bump. Fist bumps were new to him, and he seemed to find them amusing.

I knocked my knuckles against his. "Do you think they're in danger?"

"Well, they're not while I'm around." Athmani grinned, but it didn't last long. "To be honest, I'm not crazy about them walking around the park like this. Lots of things could go wrong."

"We've got them under control," Bonnie said, trotting back over. Her pooper-scooper was considerably heavier and smellier now, though neither she nor Athmani seemed bothered by the stink. Their years around the elephants had made them immune. "And they love the exercise. They can't just sit in their exhibit all day."

Athmani frowned. "I'm not that crazy about their exhibit either. I have concerns about security in that part of the park."

"Like what?" I asked.

Before Athmani could answer me, a rifle shot rang out. It sounded like it was coming from close by, loud and clear, shattering the morning quiet.

I know what a rifle sounds like. There were lots of hunters in that part of Texas. Our trailer sat right on the edge of the woods, and I'd heard plenty of rifle shots from there.

But I'd never heard one this close to FunJungle before.

Dad, Bonnie, and the rest of the keepers instantly went on alert. So did all the animals. By now we were close to Monkey Mountain, and the air was suddenly filled with startled whoops and cries from the primates. Elsewhere, birds squawked, zebras brayed, and big cats roared.

But the elephants responded most dramatically of all.

It's not a myth that elephants never forget. They have tremendous memories, particularly of emotional moments. Eleanor had been born in the wild and orphaned by poachers. When the rifle sounded nearby, she panicked. She trumpeted loudly and ran, leading her herd toward safety. The other elephants dutifully followed. They veered away from their keepers, off Adventure Road, stampeding in the opposite direction from the gunshot.

Unfortunately, Dad and I were right in their path.

"Look out!" Dad yelled, as though maybe I hadn't noticed twelve elephants bearing down on me and trumpeting at the top of their lungs. He grabbed my arm to drag me away, though I was already moving.

An elephant can run twenty-five miles an hour. Dad and I dove out of the way just in time. The herd thundered past us, then plowed right through some decorative landscaping.

A group of topiary animals was flattened into mulch within seconds. One of the bigger females sideswiped a large oak tree, which toppled as though it had been hit by a truck, crushing a souvenir kiosk.

"Eleanor, stop!" Bonnie shouted, but her words were drowned out by the ruckus the elephants were making. Bonnie and the other keepers ran after the herd, but keeping up with it was hopeless. The elephants were too fast, and to make matters worse, they—like most animals—responded to fear by emptying their bladders.

The evolutionary reason animals (and in many cases, humans) do this is that it's hard to run with a full bladder. Plus, all that pee and poop weighs quite a lot—especially when you're an elephant—and when you're fleeing for your life, every last bit of weight you can leave behind helps. Within seconds, the ground was a minefield of elephant poo, with an ocean of pee around it. Understandably, the keepers were in no hurry to run through it.

Ahead of them, the panicked elephants stampeded onward—even though the Gorilla Grill, one of the most popular restaurants at FunJungle, sat right in their way. In the wild, there's not much that elephants can't plow through, except for the occasional baobab tree, so when they're on the run, they tend to go in a straight line, flattening anything in their path.

The restaurant was no match for them. The front of it was floor-to-ceiling windows. The herd smashed right through them, shattering the glass and splintering the support beams, then stormed through the dining area, crushing tables and chairs as though they were made of paper. They crashed through the far wall, trampled the outdoor furniture, and raced off toward Monkey Mountain.

I picked myself up off the ground and surveyed the wreckage. The restaurant was totaled. The service counter had been pounded into toothpicks. The grills had been upended and jets of flame flared from where the gas lines had snapped. Geysers of soda erupted from the previous site of the soft-drink dispenser. Then, with a shriek of rending wood, the roof caved in.

Bonnie and the other keepers kept after the herd, desperately yelling commands at them as though they were Labrador retrievers. "Stop! Stay! Bad elephants! Bad elephants!"

My father and Athmani both looked extremely concerned—although they weren't watching the elephants. In fact, neither seemed to be aware the restaurant had collapsed. They were staring off in the opposite direction, the way the rifle shot had come from. Both started running that way.

"Wait!" I called, chasing after them. "Shouldn't we help with the elephants?"

"Bonnie will get them under control," Dad told me.

"Right now I'm more worried about whoever fired that shot."

"You don't think it was only a hunter?"

"No," Dad said. "Whoever fired that gun was too close to FunJungle. I don't think they were going after deer or rabbits."

"You mean . . . ?" I began.

"Yes." Dad looked back at me, and I could see the worry in his eyes. "I think someone just tried to kill one of our animals."

THE RHINO

I kept right on the heels of my father and Athmani as they raced through FunJungle. Somewhere around World of Reptiles, it occurred to me that maybe running *toward* someone with a gun wasn't the brightest idea in the world. But then, if I stopped running, I'd end up alone in the park with a herd of stampeding elephants on the loose, which wasn't exactly safe either. I decided to stick close to my father, figuring he wouldn't let any harm come to me.

Dad and Athmani both thought that the gunshot had come from the SafariLand section of FunJungle, so we headed that way. FunJungle wasn't a traditional zoo. It was designed more like a theme park, but instead of rides, it had innovative animal exhibits—and SafariLand was one of the most impressive. It consisted of several enormous open-air paddocks where dozens of different species could coexist together, giving guests a decent idea of what the wild might look like in certain parts of the world. For example, the African Savanna section had giraffes, zebras, Cape buffalo, waterbuck, impala, kudu, eland, flamingos, ostriches, and crowned cranes—more than four hundred animals in all—in an area larger than most entire zoos. SafariLand was so big, there wasn't any way to see it all from one spot, but Kololo Lookout offered the best vantage point for much of it. It was right at the place where the African Savanna and the Asian Plains met, so we went there first.

While I could still hear elephants trumpeting from elsewhere in FunJungle—as well as the occasional crash of another souvenir kiosk being trampled—life at SafariLand looked exactly like it usually did. The animals were grazing calmly. Unlike the elephants, they either hadn't been upset by the gunshot—or they'd already forgotten about it.

The humans in the area were doing considerably worse. Five people had already gathered at Kololo, and they seemed far more freaked out than the animals. Two of them were keepers, two were security guards, and one was a maintenance man. They were all arguing about what should be done. Everyone looked relieved to see Athmani arrive, pleased that someone in authority was there to make decisions for them.

"Were any of the animals hurt?" Athmani asked.

"We don't know," admitted one of the keepers. The name patch on her uniform said SANDRA, and she had short blond hair. "We haven't seen anything, but we haven't had a chance to search the whole exhibit yet."

"Did anyone see the shooter?" Dad asked.

Everyone started talking at once. None of them had seen the shooter, but each had a completely different idea of where they might have been.

Athmani had to whistle to get their attention. "We need to do a thorough sweep of this exhibit right now, end to end, before the park opens. The Fitzroys and I will start in the Asian Plains." He pointed to the keepers and told them, "You start at the north end of Africa and work your way across." He then turned to the security guards. "You two get a rover and go check the outside perimeter of the park. See if there's any breaches in the fence—or, who knows, maybe you'll even spot our hunter out there."

Everyone nodded and ran off, except the maintenance man, who asked, "Need anything from me?"

"Stay up here," Athmani told him. "Keep your eyes peeled. If you see a wounded animal or someone down in the exhibit who doesn't look like they're supposed to be there, radio me."

The maintenance man saluted as though Athmani were an army general, then went to the railing and stared vigilantly across the exhibit.

Dad and I started toward the employee entrance to the Asian Plains, but Athmani held up a hand to stop us. "Wait," he said. "Can you see all the rhinos?"

Dad and I turned back to the exhibit. It might seem odd that, out of the dozens of species of animal in Safari-Land, Athmani was concerned about only one, but the Asian greater one-horned rhinos were among the most endangered animals in all of FunJungle. There were fewer than twenty-five hundred of them left in the world. Sadly, there are rhino species that are even more endangered—the Javan and Sumatran rhinos are extinct in the wild, and there are only five African northern white rhinos left on earth—but still, every Asian greater one-horned rhino is extremely precious. We had five at FunJungle.

Luckily, the rhinos were also the biggest animals in the Asian Plains and thus the easiest to spot.

"There's two," Dad said, pointing. From where we stood, the rhinos were merely dark lumps in the distance, but I could still tell they were up on their feet and grazing, alive and well.

"And there's two more," Athmani reported, pointing at another pair of lumps under a distant tree.

"That just leaves Rhonda," I said.

Dad and Athmani looked at each other, suddenly worried. "Rhonda!" they exclaimed, and took off running as fast as they could go.

I did my best to keep up with them, aware why they were so concerned. Rhonda was even more precious than any of the other rhinos. She was pregnant.

The public didn't know this yet. FunJungle was keeping it a secret. An Asian rhino is pregnant for almost sixteen months, and the publicity department feared that the public's interest would fade if the news was released too early. It was better for park promotion—and luring tourists—to make a surprise announcement once the baby was born. In truth, no one was exactly sure how long Rhonda had been pregnant. It's not that easy to tell when a four-ton animal is getting a little heavier, and unlike pregnant humans, pregnant rhinos don't suddenly start feeling nauseated. A pregnant rhino behaves exactly like a nonpregnant rhino. However, it was now evident that Rhonda was in the later stages of pregnancy. Her belly was swollen and dipping so far down, it was only a few inches above the ground.

Normally, Rhonda was allowed out with all the other animals in the Asian Plains, where rhinos were the most popular species on display. While all rhinos are fascinating, Asian ones are surprisingly docile and can be quite friendly. You could pay extra at FunJungle to feed them apples, which was fun—as long as you didn't mind ending up with a hand covered in rhino slobber. However, to keep Rhonda safe and relaxed during the end of her pregnancy, she had been taken off exhibit. She was now living in a special building inside the Asian Plains, rather than out in the open.

Dad, Athmani, and I ducked down a path behind the SafariLand Snack Shack, slipped through a gate marked EMPLOYEES ONLY into the backstage area of FunJungle, then arrived at a far more secure gate that led into the Asian Plains. This one was topped with barbed wire and had an electronic lock with a keypad entry. Athmani entered that day's code, and the lock clicked open.

The Asian Plains was the second-largest animal enclosure at FunJungle, after the African Savanna next door. It was two hundred and fifty acres of grassland, dotted with a few groves of trees and populated by more than three hundred and twenty separate animals. Despite this, it was one of the most ignored exhibits at the park. The Asian Plains residents were mostly antelope and deer, and for some reason, tourists didn't seem nearly as interested in them as they were in the giraffes, zebra, and Cape buffalo in the African Savanna. Sure, they rode the SafariLand monorail around the exhibit, but that was only because they had to do that to get to Africa. There were rarely ever crowds at the viewpoints unless an Asian rhino happened to be close by.

This was a shame, because all the other animals were really fascinating: nilgai antelope as big as oxen, sambar deer sporting dense manes of hair, saiga antelope with freakish noses that looked like lopped-off elephants' trunks, not to mention chital deer, hog deer, muntjacs, Przewalski's horses, and oryx. At the very least, I would have expected people to be interested in the gaurs, wild cattle that were some of the largest, and most dangerous, land animals on earth—but the gaurs usually got lumped in with the rest of the hoofstock and ignored. The guests would look right past male sambars butting heads or frolicking chital fawns to get a glimpse of a sleeping rhino, which essentially looked like a rock.

A herd of muntjacs that had been browsing close to the gate scattered as we entered the exhibit. Muntjacs bark when they're frightened, which was always a little disconcerting. The noise seemed bizarre coming from an antelope. They sounded like a pack of dogs as they bounded away.

Rhonda Rhino's temporary home was only a short walk from the entry gate: a squat cement building with a walled yard attached. It was designed to give her privacy during her pregnancy; tourists couldn't visit it—or even see over the wall from the monorail. The yard had a tree for shade and a pool for wallowing—when it's hot, Asian rhinos really like the water—along with a hay trough and a large pile of poop. Rhinos often poop communally, creating large piles known as middens, which act as olfactory message boards. Rhinos can tell which other rhino has been there from the smell. It's like an extremely disgusting form of texting. Even when alone, rhinos form middens, so the keepers always had to leave some poop around, rather than cleaning it all out.

Given the cold weather, Rhonda was still inside. There were heaters in there, keeping her nice and warm while she was pregnant. The main door had another security keypad. Athmani was about to enter the code when his radio buzzed.

"Athmani! This is Chief Hoenekker. Where are you?"

Chuck Hoenekker had been hired by J.J. McCracken to replace Marge O'Malley as FunJungle's head of security after Marge had botched the investigation of the stolen koala. (Sadly, Marge hadn't been fired; she'd merely been demoted, which meant she was still around to cause trouble for me.) Park Security was FunJungle's police force—although originally, no one had expected they'd have to handle any crime more serious than shoplifting. But now, after a murdered hippo and a poached koala, J.J. had brought in Hoenekker. Neither of them would say what Hoenekker's background was—only that it was "in security"—but my parents suspected he'd either been in the military or had worked as a spy. Whatever the case, he *acted* like he was in the military, always insisting that we call him "Chief Hoenekker" and parading around the park in his uniform.

Athmani frowned before answering the radio, as though he didn't like Chief Hoenekker much. "I'm about to check on Rhonda Rhino, Chuck."

"I'd appreciate it if you'd address me as 'Chief Hoenekker.' Has the rhino been harmed?"

"I don't know," Athmani replied. "We haven't gone inside her quarters yet."

"Then don't. That's a potential crime scene and, as you are not official FunJungle Security personnel, I would prefer that you not compromise it."

Dad and Athmani both rolled their eyes at this. Then Athmani got back on the radio. "Rhonda's life could be in danger. And I *am* official security personnel. . . ."

"J.J. McCracken hired you as a consultant, not as an enforcement agent."

Athmani sighed with exasperation. "We only want to check on Rhonda and make sure she isn't injured."

"If she is, then it's my job to investigate," Hoenekker said. "Not yours. Do not enter that building."

I looked to my father, confused. "What's going on here?"

"J.J. hired Athmani without asking Hoenekker first," Dad explained. "Hoenekker wasn't happy about it. He claimed he didn't need any help protecting the animals."

I frowned. It sounded to me like Hoenekker cared more about zoo politics than Rhonda's safety.

Luckily, Athmani had hatched a plan to deal with him. He winked at Dad and me, wanting us to play along, then spoke into the radio. "I'm sorry, Chief. I didn't quite catch the last thing you said. The muntjacs are making a lot of noise. Could you repeat that?"

Dad instantly started barking the way the muntjacs had, making a big racket. I followed his lead and joined in too.

"I said that you are not to enter the building," Hoenekker replied.

"Enter the building?" Athmani asked. "Okay. Will do."

"Do not enter!" Hoenekker screamed. "Do not!"

Dad and I barked even louder.

"I can't hear you," Athmani told Hoenekker. "I'll call back in a bit, after I enter the building." Then he turned off the radio and entered the key code for the rhino house.

Dad turned to me. "Stay back here, Teddy. This could be dangerous."

I was pretty sure this was a lie. Rhonda was one of the friendliest animals I'd ever met. She was like a four-ton golden retriever. I think my father was really concerned that she might be dead and he didn't want me to see it. I didn't really want to see a dead rhino either, so I held back.

Athmani slid the door open, then heaved a sigh of relief. "She's okay."

Dad slipped inside behind him. "Are you sure?"

"Doesn't look like she's hurt," Athmani replied.

I peered around the door. The room was a cement box divided in half by a thick metal fence. One half was the “bedroom”—the place where Rhonda lived—while the other half was for the keepers. The fence was only four feet high, which meant Rhonda could easily poke her head over it, as she was six feet tall. Because the room was cement, it wasn’t exactly pretty—but then, cement is extremely easy to clean; you simply hose it down—and rhinos aren’t very picky about home decor.

Rhonda stood by the fence, directly below the heat lamps, like she was one of the burgers in the warming tray at the Gorilla Grill. Asian rhinos differ from other rhinos in that their thick skin has folds, which kind of makes it look like the rhino is wearing a suit of armor. Rhonda was big for a female—and she had an unusually large horn as well, a spike rising more than a foot from the tip of her nose. It wasn’t a perfect cone, as Rhonda had banged it up over the years; it was covered with scrapes and gouges, revealing some of the fibrous keratin it was made of—but it was still impressive. Meanwhile, Rhonda’s swollen belly hung so low that, if she’d been a car, she could have gotten stuck on a speed bump. She didn’t seem to be in any pain, or upset in any way. If anything, she looked happy to see Athmani, snuffling excitedly and wagging her thick tail.

“Sorry. I don’t have any treats for you,” Athmani told her. “I just came here to see if you were all right.”

Rhonda didn’t seem to believe him. Instead, she sniffed

him carefully, trying to see if he was hiding food in his pockets. When she didn't find anything, she snorted in annoyance, nailing him in the face with a big glob of rhino snot.

Dad and I both laughed at this. Even Athmani recognized it was funny. "Thanks a lot," he muttered, wiping the goo off his cheek. "That's what I get for checking on you?"

I stepped inside the rhino house. Some big animals can be skittish or aggressive around people they aren't familiar with, but Asian rhinos will take food from almost anyone, and they love to be petted. Rhonda stuck her giant head over the rail to see if I had anything to eat, but I gave her a scratch behind the ears instead. She enjoyed that and sidled up against the bars so that I could pat her whole body. Her skin was thick and rough, like she was covered by one giant callus, but inside the folds, it was soft and warm, like a well-oiled baseball mitt.

"We ought to go check the rest of the exhibit," Dad said. "Make sure none of the other animals were hit."

"Yes," Athmani agreed. "See you later, Rhonda." He gave the rhino a final pat, then started for the door.

I was about to follow them when something caught my eye in the window closest to Rhonda's yard. All the windows in the building were very small, as windows were expensive and animals never complain about their view. The windows were all set rather high in the wall, near the ceiling, designed to let light in rather than let Rhonda see out. One of them was broken, but in an odd way. Cracks were radiating out from around a small circle.

"Is that a bullet hole?" I asked.

Athmani and Dad froze on their way to the door, then looked the way I was pointing. Up to that moment, there had been a noticeable sense of relief at finding Rhonda was unhurt. Now it instantly vanished.

"It definitely *looks* like a bullet hole," Dad observed, concern in his voice. Then he told Rhonda, "Turn around."

The rhino obeyed. Like many of the large mammals, she had been trained to follow some simple commands to aid the keepers and vets in taking care of her. It's easier to ask a rhino to lift her leg than it is to try to lift it for her. Dad and Athmani quickly examined Rhonda's other side. Thankfully, there wasn't a bullet wound anywhere.

"She wasn't hit," Athmani said gratefully.

"Then where'd the bullet go?" I asked.

Before anyone could answer, a FunJungle safari rover roared up outside. The muntjacs we'd startled before scattered once again, barking up a storm. The rover skidded to a stop next to the rhino house, and Chief Chuck Hoenekker clambered out.

Even though it was still well before eight a.m., Hoenekker was dressed impeccably in his security uniform. His shoes were polished. His tie was crisply knotted. His pants and jacket were ironed. Hoenekker also sported a military crew cut, and his muscles bulged beneath his starched shirt. He gave me a hot stare as he entered the building and said, "It's a violation of security protocol for you to be in here."

"We have bigger problems," Athmani told him. "Someone fired a shot into this room."

Hoenekker's eyes widened in surprise. "Was the rhino hurt?"

"No," Dad said, then added, "Looks like she got lucky."

Annoyance crept back into Hoenekker's gaze. "I told you both not to enter this room. This is now a crime scene, and you have compromised it."

"We were worried that Rhonda might be wounded," Athmani said. "Or worse. We didn't have time to wait for you." Rather than facing Hoenekker, he was staring at the bullet hole in the glass. Keeping his eyes locked on it, he walked around the room as though imagining the path the bullet had taken.

"Well, as chief of security, I'm now in charge," Hoenekker said. "My men and I will handle this investigation. So if you'd kindly leave the premises . . ."

"J.J. McCracken hired me to advise you on security issues," Athmani interrupted.

"I didn't ask him to do that," Hoenekker growled. "I know how to run an investigation. I don't need your help."

"You might," Athmani countered. "I've dealt with rhino poachers in Africa too many times to count."

"Well, this isn't Africa." Hoenekker stepped into Athmani's path. "I'm in charge here, and you are interfering with my job. Don't make me pull rank on you."

Athmani didn't answer him. Instead, he pointed at a divot in the cement wall, near Rhonda's side of the metal fence. It was down by the floor, and there was a round hole in the middle of it. "That's where the bullet hit."

"Am I going to have to physically remove you from these premises?" Hoenekker asked.

Now Athmani met his gaze, glaring angrily. "Maybe you ought to care a little bit less about your job and a little bit more about this rhino."

Hoenekker started toward Athmani angrily. "I care plenty about this rhino. . . ."

Dad quickly stepped between them. "We're leaving," he said, then took Athmani by the arm and led him toward the door.

"Wise move," Hoenekker told them. He snapped his radio out of his holster and spoke into it. "This is Chief Hoenekker. All available security personnel report to Rhonda Rhino's quarters in the Asian Plains at once. We have what appears to be an assassination attempt."

Dad walked Athmani out of the building, then turned

back to Hoenekker and said, "If I were you, I'd have your men seal off the park exits first."

Hoenekker gave him an annoyed glance. "And why's that?"

"The window the bullet came through faces FunJungle, not the exterior fence," Dad explained. "Whoever fired that shot did it from *inside* the park."

Hoenekker's annoyance was quickly replaced by surprise. He stared at the broken window, realizing Dad was right. "Oh, crud," he said.

"You mean an employee of FunJungle did this?" I asked.

"I'm afraid so," Dad replied.

THE ROYAL TABLE

I wanted to stick around FunJungle to see if I could help with the investigation, but I had to go to school.

Not that I'd have been allowed to help anyhow. Chief Hoenekker didn't seem to want anyone who wasn't an official member of his security forces involved in the investigation, and my parents wanted me to keep my distance too. "The last two times you've investigated crimes at FunJungle, you've ended up in serious danger," Mom explained.

"But I survived," I argued. "*And* I solved the crimes."

"Chief Hoenekker's a professional," Mom replied. "Let someone else face the danger for once."

And so, at eight a.m., my parents loaded me onto the bus and I set off for Lyndon B. Johnson Middle School.

That didn't mean I left the troubles at FunJungle behind,

though. The first thing Xavier Gonzalez, my best friend, said when he got on the bus was, "Why'd those elephants stampede this morning?" Xavier was a budding biologist and a FunJungle fanatic; he knew almost as much about animals as I did.

"You heard about that?" I asked, surprised. "How?"

"It's all over the news." Xavier slid into the seat next to me. "Pete Thwacker was being interviewed."

This was surprising to me. Pete was the head of public relations at FunJungle. He went on television a lot, but usually to *deny* that bad things had happened.

"I thought Pete would try to cover that story up," I said.

"It's an elephant stampede!" Xavier exclaimed. "They trampled the Gorilla Grill! You can't cover that up!"

"That doesn't mean Pete wouldn't *try*," I countered.

"Well, he wasn't telling the *whole* story," Xavier said. "Or at least, I don't think he was. He said the elephants stampeded because they were frightened by a mouse, but that's something that only happens in cartoons, right?"

I groaned. "Right." Even though Pete was being strangely open about the stampede, it seemed he was still trying to keep the fact that someone had shot at Rhonda a secret. Thus the mouse story. Pete probably thought it was true that elephants were afraid of mice; despite working at the world's biggest zoo, he didn't know squat about animals. In previous interviews, he'd mistakenly claimed that dolphins were fish (they're mammals), that chimpanzees were monkeys (they're apes), and that woolly bears were bears (they're caterpillars). His real talent was looking good on television.

"So what *did* scare the elephants?" Xavier asked.

"I don't know," I lied. If Pete was keeping the gunshot a secret, then I figured I'd better keep quiet about it myself.

"You're lying," Xavier said accusingly. "Knowing you, you were probably there."

"What do you mean?"

"Because you walk with the elephants every morning. And besides, whenever anything crazy happens at FunJungle, you're always there."

"That's not true."

Xavier ticked things off on his fingers. "You were there when Henry died, when the mamba got out, when the tiger escaped, when the shark tank collapsed . . ."

"Okay," I admitted. "I've been there for a lot of crazy stuff. But I wasn't there this time."

Xavier pouted, turning away from me. "I thought you were my friend."

"You know I am."

"Friends don't keep secrets from each other."

I sighed. The truth was, I *wanted* to tell Xavier the truth. I wanted to discuss what was going on with Rhonda with someone. But it would have been nearly impossible to do that on the bus without someone else overhearing, and once word got out that somebody had tried to shoot Rhonda, it would spread like crazy through the school. Then the parents would find out and share the news, and pretty soon the entire country would know about it and I'd end up in trouble for not keeping my mouth shut. So I tried to change the subject and talk about our math homework. Xavier wouldn't take the bait, though. He spent the rest of the ride to school pretending to read a book, making a point of ignoring me.

It turned out, I could have saved myself all the trouble. Because Summer McCracken accosted me the first chance she got. Summer already knew about Rhonda because her father had been informed and Summer had been there when he got the news. She'd already texted me a dozen times that morning, wanting to know more, and I'd shared the little information I had, but that wasn't enough. Since Summer was a grade ahead of me, we didn't see each other until lunchtime. The moment I walked into the cafeteria, she ambushed me. "So, who do you think tried to shoot Rhonda?"

I cased the room to see if anyone was watching us. Of course, almost everyone was. Summer was famous, even though all she'd ever done was be born rich, and the whole school was always riveted to her every move. Including the teachers. It didn't help that Summer always wore pink from head to toe and had brilliantly blond hair, so she stuck out in any crowd like a flamingo surrounded by penguins. Plus, she had bodyguards. Today, her newest one, a hulking mass of muscle named Hondo, was tailing her. Luckily, it didn't seem that anyone had been close enough to overhear her.

I headed for our usual table, keeping my voice as low as I could. "I don't think we should talk about this here."

"Why not?"

"Because I'm pretty sure your dad wants it to be a secret."

"That doesn't mean it *should* be one. If one of our animals is in danger, the public ought to know."

"Know about what?" Xavier asked, dropping in beside us.

"Nothing," I told him.

"Someone tried to shoot Rhonda this morning," Summer said.

Xavier's jaw dropped open so wide, he looked like an angler fish. "Is she okay?"

"Yes," I said. "The shooter missed."

Xavier scowled suddenly, remembering he was supposed to be angry at me. "I knew you were lying about something this morning! Why didn't you tell me?"

"Because it's supposed to be a secret," I said, more to Summer than Xavier, as we arrived at our table.

Violet Grace was already seated there, along with my

friends Dash Alexander and Ethan Sokol and half a dozen other kids. "What's supposed to be a secret?" Violet asked.

"Someone tried to kill Rhonda Rhino," Xavier replied.

"Oh my God!" Violet gasped, horrified. "Is she one of the sixth graders?"

Not everyone at school knew the names of the animals at FunJungle as well as Summer, Xavier, and I did.

"No," Xavier explained. "She's a real rhino. At FunJungle."

Our friends were relieved to hear that someone wasn't trying to kill our fellow students and extremely concerned about the rhino.

Those days I always sat at the center table in the cafeteria, along with the athletes, like Dash and Ethan; the cheerleaders, like Violet; and a couple of kids who weren't either, like Summer and Xavier. The group was known to most of the other students as the Royals, because they seemed cooler than everyone else, but now that I'd become friends with them, I had trouble thinking of them that way. For the most part, they seemed like all the other kids in middle school, with the same concerns and worries.

The only person who was really different was Summer. Although she'd decided to transfer from boarding school so she could have a "normal education," she hadn't completely embraced everything at public school. Lunch, for example. In her defense, the cafeteria food was disgusting, but while

I avoided eating it by bringing a lunch from home, Summer had her staff deliver a hot meal to her every day. Summer didn't want to appear too privileged, so she had her staff put the lunch in a plain brown bag, but she wasn't fooling anyone.

"What happened with the rhino?" Dash asked Summer as she and I sat down. Hondo hovered a respectful distance away.

Summer shrugged. "Ask Teddy. He's the one who was at the crime scene."

Everyone's gaze shifted to me.

"I knew it!" Xavier cried. "Every time something crazy happens, you're there!"

"We're not supposed to talk about this," I said.

I was pelted with wadded-up napkins in response. "C'mon!" Ethan taunted. "Don't be a dork!"

Several people echoed this. I shot a disgruntled look at Summer, but she avoided my gaze and dug into her meal. It was some kind of steak with fancy gravy, steamed potatoes, and sautéed green beans. She had a homemade napoleon for dessert. My tuna sandwich and carrot sticks looked pathetic in comparison.

I gave in to peer pressure. I didn't want to be a dork, and if I didn't say anything, Summer probably would have told everyone anyhow. "I'll tell you, but you all have to keep quiet about this, okay? It doesn't go any further than this table."

Everyone nodded eagerly and swore they wouldn't spread the word, crossing their hearts and zipping their lips.

"I really don't know that much," I reported. "Someone shot at Rhonda while she was inside her house in SafariLand this morning. She wasn't hurt, though. The bullet missed her and hit the wall." I purposely left out the parts about Rhonda being pregnant and the shot having been fired from inside the park. Thankfully, Summer either didn't know this information herself—or she realized it shouldn't be shared and didn't correct me.

"Did this happen while the elephants were stampeding?" Dash asked.

"It's what *caused* the stampede," I explained. "The elephants heard the gun and freaked out."

"They went right through the Gorilla Grill," Summer reported. "The whole place is trashed."

"Aw, man." Ethan groaned. "That's the best place to eat at FunJungle."

Violet shook her head sadly. "Why would someone try to kill the rhino?"

"Probably for the same reason people kill them in the wild," Xavier said, taking a bite of his sandwich. "For their horns. A lot of people think powdered rhino horn cures cancer—even though it's only made of keratin, which is basically the same stuff as our fingernails. They're willing to pay tons of money for it. Rhino horns are actually worth more per ounce than gold."

Several people gasped in surprise at this—although Violet didn't. "I know all about the poaching," she said. "My parents donate to the International Rhino Foundation. But the rhinos in the zoo are surrounded by walls and fences and stuff. Even if you can shoot one, that doesn't mean you can get its horn afterward, right?" She looked to me for confirmation.

"Right," I agreed. "Rhonda was locked inside her house when the shot was fired. There's a keypad entry to get inside the building—and *that's* inside SafariLand, which has a different keypad at the gates. So stealing the horn from there would have been almost impossible."

"Then why would someone shoot Rhonda?" Violet repeated.

There was a moment of silence while everyone mulled that over. Then Ethan said, "Sometimes people like shooting things just to shoot them."

Summer laid down her silverware, looking disgusted. "You mean they do it to be cruel?"

"That's probably not the way *they* think of it," Ethan

explained. "It's more like, sometimes around here, guys go out with guns looking for stuff to shoot. Rabbits and birds and such. Not to eat or anything. It's only for fun."

"It doesn't *sound* fun," Summer replied. "It sounds horrible."

Several of the cheerleaders chimed in agreement.

"Hey, I've never done it," Ethan said quickly. "When I hunt, it's only for ducks or deer, and we eat what we shoot. I'm only saying there are other people who aren't like that. And maybe, if someone thought it was cool to shoot a rabbit for fun, they'd think it was *really* cool to shoot a rhino."

Everyone nodded sadly. As distasteful as the idea was, I had to admit it made more sense than someone trying to poach Rhonda for her horn when the horn would be impossible to recover. "Do you know any of these people who like to shoot things for fun?" I asked.

Ethan sighed. "Lots of people do it. Half the people in town hunt, and I'll bet plenty of them have shot something just to do it at least once."

"Even kids do it sometimes," Dash added. "They get a new BB gun for Christmas, and the first thing they do is go out in the woods looking for snakes or blue jays."

"That's disgusting," Summer said. "Why would anyone ever want to kill anything?"

"You're eating a steak!" Ethan exclaimed. "Where do

you think that came from? You think the cow committed suicide?"

Summer's cheeks flushed in embarrassment. "That's different."

"Not really," Ethan shot back.

"Vance Jessup used to shoot things for fun," Xavier said quickly, before the argument got out of hand. "All the time. He was always carrying a rifle around in the woods."

"Maybe," Violet said. "But Vance is locked up in juvenile hall right now for stealing the koala, thanks to Teddy. So I don't think he's the one who shot at Rhonda."

"I know," Xavier replied. "But Vance almost never did anything without TimJim, and they're still free."

TimJim was actually two people—the Barksdale twins—but they were almost always together and no one could tell them apart, so everyone just called them TimJim. Even their parents. Back when Vance Jessup had been bullying anyone he could, TimJim had been his accomplices. Now that Vance was gone, they didn't bully nearly as much, but they weren't exactly angels, either.

I glanced over my shoulder at them. They were sitting in a corner of the cafeteria, taking the baloney from their sandwiches and throwing it at the ceiling, then laughing when it stuck.

"Those guys are so dumb, they need to team up to count

to twenty," Summer said dismissively. "You think they're smart enough to go after a rhino?"

"You don't *need* to be smart to shoot at a rhino," Xavier replied. "All you need is a gun."

Dash nodded. "Even TimJim could manage it. There's a ton of places along the back of FunJungle where someone could shoot into the park."

"How do you know that?" Summer asked suspiciously.

"Because I'm evil," Dash replied sarcastically, then said, "You can see the back fence from inside the park when you're on the SafariLand monorail. It's only chain link the whole way around. There's barbed wire at the top, but that doesn't mean you can't shoot through it."

"He's right," I agreed. "I once even found a place where I could get over the fence by climbing a tree."

"Really?" Xavier polished off the last of his sandwich. "It's that unprotected?"

"I think they cut the tree down," I replied. "But yeah, it's pretty unprotected."

Xavier said, "Given how much people like to hunt around here, I'm surprised no scuzzball's taken a shot at an animal before this."

"Yeah," Violet agreed, looking at Summer somewhat accusingly.

Summer glared back at her. "My father does everything he can to keep those animals safe."

"Where's the rhino house?" Dash asked. "Near the fence?"

"No," I told him. "In fact, it's pretty far away. Maybe a couple hundred yards."

"Plenty of rifles could shoot that far," Ethan said. "But you'd have to be a pretty good shot to make it pay off."

"The hunter didn't," Xavier pointed out. "He missed."

"Anyone find the bullet yet?" Dash asked.

"Maybe by now," I replied.

"Well, if they have, then they should know what type of gun was used," Dash said. "That'd be good to know."

"Yeah," I agreed. Even though Dash and Ethan mistakenly believed that the shooter had fired from outside the zoo, they still had some good points. If I had figured out how to jump the fence into SafariLand, someone else could, too, which meant that whoever had fired the shot from inside FunJungle wasn't necessarily an employee. And if they'd had a good enough gun, they wouldn't have had to shoot from anywhere near the rhino house.

"Maybe whoever did it wasn't even shooting at the rhino," Violet suggested.

"What do you mean?" I asked.

"My little brother has a B-B gun, but he's never used it to shoot animals. He shoots things like bottles and cans. And once he thought it'd be funny to shoot the windows out of this house they were building down the street from us. My parents were royally angry and they took the gun away for three months, but that's what kids do sometimes, right? You said whoever did this shot through the window. Maybe they just wanted to shoot a window."

Everyone nodded thoughtfully.

"Good point," Dash said, then turned to me. "Would whoever did this have been able to tell there was a rhino in that building?"

I considered the rhino house. "Maybe not. The windows are pretty high up. It would've been hard to see Rhonda in there."

Ethan slapped his knee happily. "Well, there you go. There's a good chance this wasn't some psycho rhino killer after all. It was only a stupid vandal."

Everyone eagerly agreed with this, not necessarily saying it *was* vandalism, but that it was possible. They all seemed a bit relieved to have found a solution that didn't involve a rogue rhino hunter, and I couldn't blame them. I felt a bit of relief too, hoping that what Violet had proposed was the truth.

Only Summer seemed unconvinced. Plus, she appeared to

have lost her appetite for her steak during our conversation.

"If it was vandalism, I'll bet there's a good chance Tim-Jim was behind it," Xavier said. "Remember last year, when the cops busted them for throwing rocks at the windows of the old gas station?"

"And they tagged the school gym with graffiti," Violet added.

The others at the table chimed in, recalling more incidents of TimJim's misbehavior or suggesting other possible vandals. They quickly compiled quite a list; a surprising number of kids had done things like shoot holes in road signs, drape trees in toilet paper, or leave flaming bags of dog poo on people's front porches.

Meanwhile, Summer shoved her unfinished steak away, pulled her phone out of her pocket, and checked her messages. You weren't supposed to have phones at school, but Summer often acted as though rules were for other people. Then she tucked her phone away, grabbed her lunch bag, and carried it toward the garbage, pausing for a second to give me a glance that said I ought to join her.

Even though I wasn't quite done with my lunch, I got up and followed her.

"They're fooling themselves," Summer said, tossing her uneaten food into the trash. "This wasn't vandalism. Someone wants Rhonda dead."

"How do you know that?" I asked.

Instead of answering, Summer said, "Hondo's taking me to FunJungle today after school. I'll give you a ride so you don't have to take the bus."

"I can't," I said. "I've got soccer practice after school today."

"Not anymore," Summer told me. "Daddy wants to see you."

ACCUSED

J.J. McCracken wasn't the kind of person you could say no to. He was rich and powerful, and half the town worked for him. All I had to do to get out of soccer practice was tell Coach Redmond that J.J. had asked to see me. Coach released me immediately, then told me to ask J.J. if he'd buy the school a new soccer field.

Even though Summer was rich, she didn't use a limo. J.J. McCracken didn't like limos; he considered them snooty and impractical. There was a lot of stuff that J.J. dismissed as too fancy for his tastes. The McCrackens could have had a mansion in Beverly Hills or a penthouse in Manhattan, but they had a ranch in the Texas Hill Country instead. The road to their front door was dirt; a limo never would have made it. Instead, Summer's chauffeur drove her around in a rover

SUV. It was just like any other rover on the inside—except it was a bit longer and there was a glass partition between the front and back seats that could be closed to give the people in the back privacy.

The chauffeur didn't dress very fancy, either. He was a recent college grad named Tran, and instead of a suit, he usually wore jeans, a button-down shirt, and cowboy boots. Which was basically how J.J. dressed too.

The one thing that J.J. didn't skimp on was security. He was terrified that Summer might be a kidnapping target. The rover's windows were tinted and bulletproof. The doors looked normal, but they were armored. And as we rode back to FunJungle, Hondo was stationed in the front seat, right next to Tran.

Summer chafed at having a bodyguard at all times—it put a crimp in her ability to act like a normal teenager—so Hondo did his best to be unobtrusive. It wasn't that easy, though, since he was the size of a refrigerator. Plus, he was covered with tattoos, which made him look like a walking comic book. Like many of Summer's bodyguards, Hondo had a rough background; he'd been in a gang as a teenager and had done some jail time. But he'd straightened himself out and was surprisingly friendly. While some of Summer's previous guards had been gruff and cold with me, as if I were a potential threat to her safety, Hondo was always kind and trusting. He even let us put up the glass between us and the front seat so we could talk in private.

"Any idea why your dad wants to see me?" I asked Summer.

"No," she replied. "But I'm sure it has something to do with Rhonda."

"Like what?"

Summer only shrugged in response. I got the idea she knew more than she was letting on, but I couldn't pry anything else out of her. Instead, she spent the rest of the ride trying to come up with possible rhino killers, but since we didn't have any more information about the case, we simply ended up with a long list of people Summer didn't like. She even insisted we consider Mrs. Crowley, her history teacher, a suspect because Mrs. Crowley had recently sent Summer to the principal's office and Summer figured this meant Mrs. Crowley had a grudge against the McCrackens.

"Maybe you got sent to the principal's office because you weren't behaving in class," I said.

Summer rolled her eyes. "I don't need to pay attention in class. I know twice as much history as Mrs. Crowley."

I didn't bother arguing that, as there was a chance it was true. Summer was one of the smartest kids in school, although a lot of people assumed she was dumb because she was beautiful. This never made sense to me; she was J.J.

McCracken's daughter, after all, and no one ever thought J.J. had gotten so successful by being stupid.

We finally arrived at FunJungle. Tran pulled up to the front employee entrance closest to the administration building, where J.J.'s office was. As we climbed out of the car, we could see the main entrance of the park. Despite the cold weather, there was a good-sized line of tourists waiting to get in.

Summer watched them, intrigued. "That's a big crowd for a school day in February," she said. "Is something special going on here today?"

"Not that I know of," I replied.

"Let's go see what's up." Summer started toward the front gates.

Hondo immediately stepped into her path. "Sorry, ma'am. My orders are to deliver you directly to your father's office." He had a voice so low and deep, I imagined it was how a hippopotamus would sound if it could talk.

"We're only making a slight detour. It'll take two minutes." Summer tried to sideslip Hondo, but he caught her arm and held it tight.

"I'm afraid I can't allow that," he said. "Crowds are a significant risk of danger to you." He then steered Summer toward the guard booth at the employee entrance.

Summer tried to dig her heels in and resist, but she

was like a flea fighting an elephant. "C'mon," she pleaded. "They're tourists, not terrorists."

Hondo didn't reply. He swung open the guard booth door and swept Summer and me through it.

The booth was a very small room, only ten feet square. Inside it there was an X-ray scanner for bags, like at an airport security checkpoint, a walk-through metal detector, and a small desk for a security guard to sit at. The guard on duty didn't look a whole lot older than we did. According to his badge, his name was Kevin. When he saw Summer, he gasped, starstruck. But then he reacted with even more surprise when he saw me, which was odd. He did such a double take, he almost fell out of his chair. "Uh, hi there, Miss, uh . . . Summer," he stammered. "I'm afraid I have to, um, ask you folks to wait here for a, er, a moment."

"Why?" Summer asked.

"It's a, uh, security issue." Kevin picked up a phone and dialed a number scrawled on a Post-it note. "Hi," he said to whoever answered. "This is Kevin at the front guard booth. The, uh, person you're looking for is here. . . . Okay, yes. I'll, uh, hold him."

Hondo tensed, growing concerned. "What's this all about?" he asked.

Kevin shrank from him fearfully. "I, um, I . . . I'm not supposed to say. But you won't be waiting long." His eyes flicked toward the metal detector. There was a piece of paper taped to the side of it, where Kevin could see it but we couldn't.

Summer snatched it and immediately started laughing at what she saw. "Oh my gosh, Teddy. Check this out. You're a fugitive!" She held it up.

It was a photo of me.

Above it was the word "Wanted." Below, it had my name, height, date of birth, and other distinguishing characteristics, followed by the words, "If you see this boy, detain him for questioning and call Officer Marge O'Malley immediately."

"Oh no." I groaned.

Summer laughed even harder.

"It's not funny," I said.

"Yes, it is," Summer told me. "Look at you! You're Fun-Jungle enemy number one!"

Outside, there was a screech of tires, followed by Large Marge's all-too-familiar bellow. "Get out of the way, you moron! Security coming through!"

I looked through the window of the security booth. Marge was speeding toward us in a golf cart emblazoned with a FunJungle Security symbol. Instead of watching where she was going, she was shouting at a poor maintenance worker whom she'd nearly run down.

Marge had been a thorn in my side ever since the moment

I'd met her. A tourist had been trying to feed a monkey a hot dog, even though there was a sign right nearby saying not to feed the animals, so I'd shot him with a squirt gun. No one got hurt, but Marge had decided I was trouble and had spent much of her time at FunJungle trying to prove that to everyone else. Admittedly, I had played practical jokes on her now and then, but those were all to get her off my back. I would never have tied tin cans to her car's bumper or replaced her hair spray with green spray paint if she had simply left me alone.

Marge's hatred of me had been her own undoing. She'd been so convinced that I had stolen Kazoo the Koala that she'd never bothered to look for the real thief. Which was why J.J. McCracken had demoted her from her job as chief of security. Of course, Marge didn't see things that way. She blamed *me* for her demotion and was even more determined to get me now.

J.J. had given Marge the golf cart to soften the blow of demoting her. Marge loved it a little *too* much. She almost never got out of it, driving everywhere she could, which was a shame because if anyone could have used more exercise, it was Marge. Plus, she had turned out to be as bad a driver as she was a chief of security. She was constantly speeding around the park, nearly running people over and yelling at them for getting in her way.

Marge skidded to a stop outside the security booth and slammed into a trash can, which toppled over, spilling garbage everywhere. Ignoring this, Marge pried herself out of the golf cart, brushed some powdered sugar—most likely from the funnel cake stand—off her uniform, and marched into the booth. "Well, well, well," she said, looking at me the way a lion looks at a baby wildebeest. "It appears the suspect has returned to the scene of the crime. Kevin, search his backpack for evidence."

"Yes, ma'am!" Kevin saluted obediently, grabbed my pack from the X-ray scanner, and dumped everything out on the conveyor belt.

"Spread your arms and legs, Theodore," Marge demanded.

"Why?" I asked.

"Just do it!" Marge snapped.

I did, and to my surprise, Marge began frisking me. "I didn't have anything to do with Rhonda," I said.

"Rhonda?" Marge asked blankly.

"The rhino," Summer told her.

"Oh, that," Marge said dismissively. "Please. I couldn't care less about some wacko taking potshots at one of our buildings. I'm here about a far more serious crime: theft of FunJungle property." She got right in my face as she said this, so close I could smell the chili she'd had for lunch on her breath.

I recoiled, wrinkling my nose. "What are you talking about?"

"Don't act dumb with me," Marge warned. "I'm not buying it."

"Yeah," I said. "When it comes to being dumb, you're an expert."

Marge's eyes flared in anger. She lashed a hand out to grab me, but Hondo moved like a cobra, catching her arm in midstrike.

"I don't like to see people picking on kids," he growled. "Now, I have orders to get these two to J.J. McCracken's office ASAP, and you're holding us up. So either state your case or stop wasting our time."

Marge glowered at Hondo, then wrested her arm away from his grasp. "Early this morning, there was a crime committed on these premises that I'm positive Teddy here was a part of: the burglarizing of Carly Cougar's Candy Corner."

"That's what this is about?" Summer asked, incredulous. "Some stolen candy?"

"No. It's not only some stolen candy," Marge mimicked rudely. She fished out her phone and brought up a photo on it. "There was also felony breaking and entering and wanton destruction of FunJungle property."

She showed us the photo. It was of the Candy Corner, which was a small store near the park entrance. To my surprise, it hadn't merely been robbed; it had been trashed. The front window was shattered and the candy bins had been ripped open. The floor was covered with thousands of pieces of broken glass.

Summer gasped. "What happened there?"

"Your friend Teddy here threw a trash can through the window," Marge replied, "and then made off with approximately twenty-five pounds of assorted chocolates, jawbreakers, and gummy bears."

"*Twenty-five pounds?*" I repeated. "You actually think I'd steal that much candy?"

"Oh, I don't *think*," Marge sneered. "I *know*. The crime was perpetrated early this morning, when no one was near this park except for the people who live in employee housing. You're the only child who lives in employee housing—and children like candy."

I waited for more to come, then realized there wasn't any. "That's it? That's your whole case?"

"What more do I need?" Marge demanded. "You have a history of troublemaking at this park."

"I've only played pranks," I replied. "This is stealing. And vandalism. I didn't have anything to do with it."

"Sure you did," Marge snarled.

"Do you have any proof?" Summer asked. "Like surveillance video showing Teddy destroying the candy store?"

"No," Marge admitted sullenly. "There's no footage of the crime."

"Really?" I asked. "Because there's, like, ten thousand security cameras in this park."

"Those are to protect the animals," Marge told me. "That's why they're around the exhibits. Unfortunately, no one installed them to watch the candy store. Rest assured, though. I'll get my evidence one way or another. So why don't you save both of us a lot of trouble and just own up to it?"

"Um," Kevin said meekly. "I've, uh, completed my search of the backpack."

Marge turned to him expectantly. "And?"

"There was no candy inside," Kevin reported. "Although there *was* a wrapper from a granola bar, if that means anything."

"It doesn't," Marge said, annoyed.

I was about to argue my innocence again when a thought suddenly occurred to me. "Did the break-in happen before someone shot at the rhino this morning?"

"You know exactly when it happened," Marge snapped. "Because you did it."

Summer quickly reminded her, "The last time you thought Teddy committed a crime here, you were completely wrong. In fact, you were so wrong, you didn't bother looking for the real thief and he almost got away. Which is why Daddy demoted you."

Marge swung toward Summer, livid, but she actually had enough sense not to lash into the boss's daughter. "Just because I was wrong about Teddy once doesn't mean he's not trouble," she argued. "In fact, this would be the perfect time for him to pull off a caper like this. Because he knows no one would believe me after what happened last time. But he's not going to get away with it. I'm smarter than he is."

"I highly doubt that," Summer said.

Marge had to bite her lip to rein in her anger. Her eyes bugged, and she turned red as a hummingbird's throat. For a moment it looked as though her head might explode, but she somehow managed to regain control. "All right," she said. "For your sake, let's assume Teddy is innocent." She turned back to me. "What's the point of asking when the theft took place?"

"I was thinking, it's kind of weird that two crimes happened here this morning, so maybe they're connected somehow."

Marge screwed up her face, trying to make sense of this. "What do you mean?"

"Maybe someone broke into the candy store to create a diversion from the fact that they were shooting at the rhino," I said. "Or maybe they shot at the rhino to divert everyone from the candy store."

"I don't know when the candy store was broken into," Marge admitted. "Only that it happened this morning sometime. I know the store was intact at closing time last night—but I didn't discover the burglary until right before the park opened today."

Summer asked, "Is it possible that one of the elephants smashed into the store during the stampede? One of them could easily have eaten twenty-five pounds of candy."

Marge shook her head dismissively. "The stampede didn't pass the candy store. And I think I can tell the difference between the work of an elephant and a twelve-year-old boy." She narrowed her eyes at me suspiciously once again.

"I didn't do it," I told her. "You can search my whole house if you want. You won't find any candy there."

"We'll see about that," Marge said. "But wherever that candy is, I'll find it. You won't be able to hide it forever."

She came toward me, but Hondo stepped between us. "Ma'am, I have some experience with the law myself. And right now you have no proof against Teddy—only speculation. So, if you'll excuse us, I really need to get him to J.J. McCracken's office."

"I haven't finished my interrogation," Marge protested.

"Yes, you have," Hondo told her. "We've wasted enough time here." With that, he shepherded Summer and me through the metal detector.

Kevin handed my backpack to me. "Sorry for the inconvenience."

"Don't apologize to criminals!" Marge shouted, and Kevin cowered like a scolded puppy.

Then Marge yelled after me, "I'm warning you, Teddy! You won't get away with this! I'm going to stay on you like glue until I finally prove to everyone that you're no good!"

"What a screwball," Hondo muttered.

"You haven't seen anything yet," Summer told him.

I shivered as we passed outside again, though I wasn't sure if this was because of the cold air or the fact that, once again, Marge was determined to bust me for a crime I hadn't committed. Plus, the candy store theft worried me as well. I knew I hadn't done it—but who had? And why?

MY ASSIGNMENT

J.J. McCracken was currently serving as the director of operations at FunJungle. Tracey Boyd, the previous director, had stepped down after only a few months on the job. The official story was that Tracey had decided running the park wasn't the best fit for her; the unofficial story was that, after the dual crises of a stolen koala and a collapsed shark tank, Tracey had suffered a nervous breakdown. (J.J. had come into Tracey's office one day and found her curled in the fetal position under her desk, gibbering about wombats.) J.J. owned a lot of other businesses, but FunJungle was his pride and joy, so he had put all his other work aside to take over the job until a new director of operations could be found.

Pete Thwacker was in J.J.'s office when Summer and I arrived. Both men were staring through the giant windows behind J.J.'s desk, which looked out over FunJungle. The office was on the seventh floor of the administration building—the very top—and on a clear day, you could see almost to San Antonio from there. However, some low-slung gray clouds were blocking the view. I could barely make out SafariLand at the far end of the park.

The main entrance was still visible, though, as it was right below us—and that was all Pete was interested in. "Look at those crowds!" he exclaimed. "And on a weekday in February, no less! I'm telling you, this elephant stampede is going to be a gold mine!"

J.J. didn't look convinced. "You really think that's what brought them in?"

"Oh, I'm sure of it. Look down there!" Pete pointed toward the shattered remains of the Gorilla Grill. "There must be fifty people looking at the wreckage!"

I went to the window and looked myself. Normally, when disaster had befallen FunJungle, wooden barricades were quickly erected to hide the damage from the public. But today there was only a single strand of yellow ribbon cordoning off the destroyed restaurant, allowing guests to see it easily. "That's why you're not covering up the story?" I asked. "To make the disaster an attraction?"

"Exactly!" Pete cried. "I realized that every time we try to cover up something around here, it doesn't work. The public finds out and we get savaged for lying to them. So I ran some numbers." He triumphantly waved a report he'd printed in the air. "It turns out the public doesn't care if something bad happens here. In fact, their interest in the park increases! And these so-called bad stories get much more attention than the good ones. When we announced that the tiger cubs had been born, we got moderate press coverage from a few media markets around the country. But when the tiger escaped, that was international news. Same thing when Henry's funeral went wrong. Or when the koala got stolen. So I figured, why try to cover up the elephant stampede? After all, those things don't happen every day. And I was right! The story's gone viral. It's trending at the top of the news. That's already generated interest in the park, and interest generates ticket sales. That small crowd down there isn't merely a one-day blip. It's the beginning of a trend. By the end of the week, I guarantee you fifty times that many people will be gathered around the scene of the stampede." He turned to J.J. "We really shouldn't clean up that wreckage. People want to see it."

"I can't leave a smashed-up restaurant in the middle of my park!" J.J. protested. "It's a health hazard! And besides, I need that restaurant up and running again. Our guests need places to eat."

"So put some hot-dog carts around the stampede site in the meantime," Pete said.

"I'm rebuilding the grill," J.J. told him.

"Then what's the chance that we could stage another stampede?" Pete asked. "Unfortunately, there was no video taken of this one, which would have given the story even better play. So imagine that we have it happen again, during park hours, and get a little footage of it this time?"

"Have an elephant stampede during park hours?" J.J. gasped, incredulous. "With tourists around? Are you insane? We're lucky no one was hurt this time! And I lost an entire restaurant, which I now have to pay to rebuild."

"Insurance is covering that," Pete said dismissively. "But okay, I see your point. The elephant stampede is too risky. Is there any way to fake some other disaster? Giraffes trend very well. Especially with the tween girl demographic. Do they stampede? Maybe we could have a few of them 'escape.'"

"No!" J.J. exclaimed. "I've got enough problems with all the real disasters we have around here. The last thing I need is to create fake ones."

"All right." Pete raised his arms in surrender. "I hear you. But at least *think* about it. I really think these disasters have some serious publicity potential."

"Yeah, I'll think about it," J.J. said, in a way that meant

he wouldn't. "Now, if you'll excuse me, I have other things to deal with."

"Of course." Pete headed out of the office, pausing to nod to me and flash Summer a trademark grin. "Teddy, Summer, always a pleasure to see you two."

Once he was out the door, Hondo shut and locked it, then positioned himself to the side and stayed there, silent, like a piece of furniture.

"Sorry to keep you waiting," J.J. told Summer, giving her a hug. Even with cowboy boots on, he was only a few inches taller than her. "How'd you do on your science quiz today?"

"Aced it." Summer pulled the exam, marked with an A-plus, out of her backpack as proof.

"That's my girl! The apple doesn't fall far from the tree!" J.J. turned to me and extended a hand. "And how are your studies going, Teddy?"

"Very well, sir." I shook his hand.

"That's what I like to hear." J.J. waved Summer and me to his couch, then perched on the edge of his desk. "I didn't get where I am today by slacking off in school. In fact, that big old brain of yours is exactly what I wanted to see you about, Teddy."

"So . . . I'm not in trouble or anything?" I asked.

J.J. burst into laughter. For a small man, he had a very big laugh. "Lord, no! Why would you think that?"

"Summer wouldn't say why you wanted me here. And the last time I got called into your office, I was in trouble. . . ."

"Well, this time you're not," J.J. said. "In fact, you're here because I could use your help taking care of some trouble."

"What's that?" I asked.

"This Rhonda Rhino business. I understand you were there this morning when Athmani and your father found evidence of the attack."

"Yes."

"I won't kid you," J.J. said. "I'm extremely concerned about this. I want to find whoever fired that shot before they try again—and I think you might be of considerable assistance in doing that."

"You mean, you *want* me to help investigate?" I asked.

"I'd like you to aid in the inquiry, yes."

I glanced over at Summer, wondering what to make of this. She was smiling from ear to ear, apparently thrilled by what her father was saying.

I turned back to J.J. "Last time there was a crime here, you warned me to stay away."

J.J. gave a small, apologetic shrug. "You're right. I did."

"You even said you'd fire my parents if I got involved."

Summer's smile faded. She gaped at her father. "Daddy! You didn't!"

J.J. held up a finger, and Summer fell silent. "I might

have implied there'd be consequences, but I never threatened anyone. And let's not forget, Teddy, at the time there was ample evidence that you were actually the criminal in question." I started to protest, but before I could, he continued. "Anyhow, that's all water under the bridge. I apologize for any misgivings I might have had about you in the past. And, given that you have proven your deductive skills in solving two crimes at this park, it would mean a great deal to me if you'd lend your assistance on this investigation as well."

"You mean work with Chief Hoenekker?" I asked, remembering how crusty he'd been with Athmani that morning. "He's okay with this?"

"Of course he is," J.J. said, a little too quickly. "I've told him about your talents, and he's smart enough to accept any help he can get on this. I mean, you're like our own personal Encyclopedia Brown. It doesn't make sense to keep you on the sidelines."

"And I'll be able to help too, right?" Summer asked.

"Sure," J.J. said. "You can't have Encyclopedia Brown without Sally Kimball."

Summer grinned, so excited she bounced up and down on the couch. "C'mon, Teddy! This will be great! It'll be like when we investigated Henry's death, only we'll have permission this time!"

I considered the offer. Although I didn't trust J.J.

McCracken much, I couldn't help being flattered by his comments about me. The truth was, I *wanted* to help. And not just because it would give Summer and me a chance to hang out together. I was concerned about Rhonda. And yet there was one major issue holding me back. "I don't think my parents would approve," I said.

"You don't think they want to find out who tried to kill the rhino?" J.J. asked.

"No. I'm sure they do. They just don't want *me* doing it. The other times I investigated crimes here, I ended up in danger."

"Well, that's not gonna happen this time," J.J. said. "In those other cases, you were investigating on your own, which forced you into those dangerous situations. This time you'll have the full support of my security staff. If any trouble arises, you call them, and *they're* the ones who'll face it, not you. Plus, I'll have Hondo keeping an eye on you, too. I'm not about to put a young man's life in jeopardy."

"Still," I said. "I don't think my folks will agree."

J.J. chewed his bottom lip for a moment, then said, "You wouldn't necessarily have to ask their permission."

I sat back, startled. "You mean lie to them?"

"Whoa. Hold on now." J.J. raised his hands, signaling me to calm down. "My number one consideration here is for that rhino and her calf. I'll admit my reasons for building this park were entirely financial at first, but in the process I have developed great concern for the animals here—and I've become particularly fond of the rhinos. I'm sure you're aware of how endangered those animals are?"

Summer and I nodded.

"It's a travesty!" J.J. hopped off his desk and began pacing around his office. "That an animal so wonderful and majestic should be hunted down for such idiotic reasons. There's not a whit of proof that rhino horn has any medicinal value at all, and yet entire subspecies have been wiped out in the wild—while the others are barely hanging on. Do you realize that more than a thousand rhinos a year are being poached in the world?"

"No," I admitted.

"They are," J.J. said. "And sadly, those numbers just keep going up. So I'm doing my part to help. I got FunJungle signed up with the international rhino breeding program. There's no profit in that. In fact, I'm losing money hand over fist on it. But I'm doing it anyhow, because I care about rhinos. The keepers and the vets and I have all sunk a great deal of time and energy into this. And now here we are on the threshold of our first success—we've got a baby rhino on the verge of being born—and some crackpot decides to take a shot at the mom. I don't know if it's a poacher going for her horn or a hunter who wants her head on his wall, or some knucklehead just trying to cause trouble, but I'll be cussed if I'm gonna let them succeed. I'll use whatever means I have at my disposal to see that they are found and brought to justice. And one ace I have up my sleeve is *you*." J.J. pointed a stubby finger directly at my nose. "That rhino's life is at stake, Teddy, and I want to save her. So what'll it take to bring you aboard?"

I thought about that for a bit. J.J.'s concern for the rhinos seemed genuine. And so was mine. "I guess *you* could talk to my parents and see if you can convince them this is all right."

J.J. nodded. "I suppose I could." He checked his watch, then looked to Summer. "Sweetheart, could you do me a favor? This rhino business has thrown a big old wrench into my plans today, and we're gonna be home later than expected. Could you step outside to call your mother and give her the news?"

"Sure." Summer stood, then smiled at me and said, "Thanks for agreeing to do this, Teddy."

"I haven't," I said, but she didn't seem to hear me as she slipped out the door. Hondo followed her, leaving J.J. and me alone.

The moment the door clicked shut, J.J. returned his attention to me. Although he was still smiling, something seemed to have changed about him. I suddenly had the same eerie feeling as when I'd discovered I was alone in the reptile house with a poisonous snake. "I have to be honest with you, Teddy," J.J. said. "I don't think my talking to your parents will do much to sway them. I doubt either of them likes me all that much."

"You did try to have me arrested for stealing the koala," I said.

J.J. shrugged, as if this were the type of mistake people made all the time. "Whatever the case, you're right about them. There's a good chance they'll tell you not to get involved with this. But should that happen, well . . . I still want you involved. It'd be in everyone's best interests if you agreed to help." There was something menacing about how he said this last bit, like it was a threat rather than a request.

"What do you mean?" I asked.

"There are other people out there who do what your parents do," J.J. said. "It'd be hard to find a primatologist as good as your mother, but then, I could probably find someone a little more cooperative."

I felt my stomach sink. "So . . . if I don't help you, you'll fire my parents?"

J.J. smiled. Only, it wasn't a genuine smile. It was the kind of smile you got from a crocodile. "I didn't say that. I'm simply asking for your help."

"But—" I began.

"Hoenekker's at the rhino house right now," J.J. said,

interrupting me. "From what I understand, he hasn't made a whole lot of headway yet, so it'd be nice to have another pair of eyes down there."

"Hoenekker won't want me there," I argued. "He doesn't even want Athmani there, and Athmani's your security consultant."

"That's all water under the bridge," J.J. told me. "I had a little chat with Hoenekker this morning and let him know I want Athmani's input on this too. I don't want ego getting in the way of solving this crime. And as for you . . ." He plucked an envelope off his desk and handed it to me. It was sealed and said "Hoenekker" on the outside in what I assumed was J.J.'s handwriting. "Give this to the chief when you get there. It ought to take care of any issues he might have."

I noticed that J.J. hadn't asked me to go to the rhino house. Nor had he ordered me. He was simply acting as if my working on the investigation were a done deal. It felt like saying no to him would be a very bad idea. Although the fact was, I didn't want to say no anyhow. I wanted to help—and it was kind of exciting that J.J. trusted me enough to do it. I only wished it felt more like it had all been my decision.

"Okay," I agreed.

"Great! It's good to have you aboard. I look forward to hearing your thoughts." J.J. motioned me to the door, indicating our meeting was over. Before I even knew what was happening, I was standing in the room outside his office as he shut the door behind me.

Summer was hanging up with her mother. She turned to me, her eyes wide with excitement. "So? Are you doing this?"

"I guess so," I said.

"Awesome!" Summer exclaimed. "Let's get started!" She grabbed my hand and led me down the hall, toward the elevators.

I couldn't help but feel excited myself. Maybe it was having permission to investigate a case for the first time, or maybe it was having Summer excited to work with me, or the thrill of having my hand in hers. And yet underneath that, I felt worried, too.

The last time there'd been a crime at FunJungle, J.J. had threatened to fire my parents if I got involved. Now he'd threatened to fire them if I didn't. He hadn't actually *said* he'd fire them—which meant he could always deny it—but the threat was definitely there. It was unsettling to be manipulated like that, and I found myself fearing what J.J. McCracken might do if I failed him.

For the time being, though, I had a mystery to solve.

SCENE OF THE CRIME

With Hondo tailing us like a stray dog, Summer and I set out for the rhino house. We swung by the Gorilla Grill on the way. Or rather, we swung by what was left of it.

It turned out Pete Thwacker wasn't merely leaving the wreckage out in the open for the crowds to see; he was advertising it. Starting at FunJungle's front gates, makeshift signs had been posted to direct tourists along the "Elephant Stampede Route." Guests could see where landscaping had been trampled and trees had been uprooted, but the collapsed restaurant was the main attraction. Despite the fact that it was a cold and raw day, a large group of tourists was gathered there, snapping pictures of their friends in front of the wreckage. Kristi Sullivan, whom Pete considered the most attractive and personable member of his PR staff, had been posted there as well. Officially, she was supposed to be answering questions about elephants, although a lot of the male guests were doing their best to flirt with her. Kristi always worked hard to learn everything she could about the animals, but she attracted men the way a dead animal attracts vultures.

As we arrived, Kristi was telling one of the male guests, "To answer your questions: One, in the wild elephants can eat up to three hundred and thirty pounds of food per day—and two, sorry, but I already have plans on Friday night." Before the guy could press for another date, she told him, "Excuse me, but I think those children have a question," then scooted over to us. "Hey, guys! What brings you this way?"

"Just thought we'd check out FunJungle's newest amazing attraction," Summer replied, with a lot of sarcasm. "How's it going?"

"I'm freezing." Kristi clapped her gloved hands together to warm them up. "You'd think the elephants could've waited until April to stampede. But no. Pete's got me stuck out here in the cold while he gets to stay inside dealing with the rhino hunter." The moment she said this, Kristi grimaced, then looked around to see if any of the tourists had heard her. Luckily, none had. She lowered her voice to a whisper and asked, "Have you heard any news on that?"

"No," I said. "But we're heading that way now."

"Daddy asked Teddy to help investigate," Summer said.

"Really?" Kristi's big blue eyes lit up. "Well, if anyone can figure out who did it, it's you," she told me. "You caught that koala-napper when no one else could."

"Thanks," I said, wishing I had the same confidence in myself that Kristi did.

Another young man approached Kristi with a question, although it was pretty obvious he was only looking for an excuse to talk to her. "Excuse me, but I wanted to know something about elephants," he said.

"I'll be right there," Kristi told him, then sighed to us. "Back to the old grindstone. Good luck. And if you see Pete, ask him to get some heaters out here for me."

Summer and I continued on to SafariLand, using the same route to the rhino house that I had taken with Athmani and my father that morning. Normally, we wouldn't have been able to get through the security gates with the keypad entries, but J.J. had texted the day's codes to Hondo, who opened them for us. We entered the Asian Plains to find a large herd of sambar deer grazing close by. They watched us warily as we passed, ready to flee at the slightest provocation.

As we walked among them, Hondo grew as skittish as the antelope.

"Is something wrong?" I asked him.

"No," he said quickly. "Everything's fine."

Summer leaned in close to me and whispered, "Hondo's afraid of animals."

"*All* animals?" I asked.

"Pretty much. A few days ago, my guinea pig got out and ran over his foot. He almost had a conniption."

I glanced back at Hondo. It was hard to imagine that a man who was so tough around humans would be frightened by a bunch of deer, but he was definitely on edge. Every time one of them so much as flicked its ears, he would tense in fear.

"Why's he so scared by them?" I asked.

"City boy," Summer told me. "No pets as a kid. The only animals he ever saw were rats."

"Hmm," I said thoughtfully.

Summer started laughing.

"What's so funny?" I asked.

"You're already going into Sherlock Holmes mode, aren't you? Hondo didn't shoot at Rhonda."

I looked back toward Hondo again, worried he'd overheard this, because that was exactly what I'd been thinking. Thankfully, he hadn't; he was too distracted by a few muntjacs. He was regarding them warily, like they were lions, rather than deer. "How can you be so sure?" I whispered. "He has a criminal background. And he doesn't like animals."

"First of all, he's a *reformed* criminal," Summer said, a

little louder than I would have liked. "Daddy wouldn't have hired him otherwise. Second, not liking animals is a lame motive. And third, Hondo has the perfect alibi: me."

"Oh. You were with him this morning?"

Summer nodded. "We were having breakfast when the shot was fired. So he couldn't be our guy."

"Guess not," I said. We continued on across the Asian Plains to the rhino house.

Security had been greatly beefed up there. Hoenekker had stationed three new guards, one on each side of the building, while the third patrolled the roof. None of them was carrying a gun—that would have freaked out the tourists—and they were all dressed like keepers, rather than security, but they were definitely on the alert, scanning in all directions for any sign of trouble. Rhonda was in her yard, happily devouring a trough full of hay, seemingly unaware anything unusual was going on.

The gate that would have allowed Rhonda back into her house was closed, keeping her in the yard. However, the door that led into the house from the Asian Plains was wide open. I could see Chief Hoenekker inside, on Rhonda's side of the metal fence, taking measurements around the point where the bullet had impacted the wall.

The guard posted at the door of the rhino house didn't seem surprised to see Summer and me. He held up his hand, signaling us to wait, then called out, "Chief! They're here!"

Hoenekker looked up and sighed heavily. Then he pointedly went back to his measurements without saying anything to us.

"Hey!" Summer yelled to him. "My dad sent us to see you."

"I know." Hoenekker jotted something on a small notepad, then climbed out of the rhino pen and came to the doorway. "I understand you have a letter for me?"

I handed him the envelope J.J. had given me. Hoenekker tore it open, read the message inside, then crumpled it angrily and threw it on the ground. "Apparently it's official," he growled. "In addition to conducting an investigation, I now have to babysit both of you."

He was so disdainful that, if I'd been there by myself, I might have given up the investigation. But Summer stood up to him. "Daddy wouldn't have sent us here if he didn't think we could help."

"Yeah, your daddy's very proud of his little girl." Hoenekker waved us into the rhino house, then pointed at a corner. "Stay over there and try not to mess anything up."

Summer reacted, offended. She wasn't used to people treating her like this. "What could we possibly mess up? There's nothing in here but cement and rhino poo."

"This is a crime scene," Hoenekker told her. "Anything in here could be evidence."

I dutifully moved to the corner he had indicated, trying my best not to antagonize him. However, Summer had a point. Save for a few chalk marks that had been made around the spot where the bullet had hit the wall, the rhino house seemed exactly the same as it had that morning. It didn't look very much like a crime scene. "Have you learned anything yet?" I asked.

Even though I'd asked as nicely as I could, Hoenekker still seemed annoyed by the question. "What do you think we've been doing here all day? Playing tiddlywinks?"

"Y'know," Summer said, "this would work out much better if you'd answer our questions instead of being such a jerk."

Hoenekker glared at her. I got the sense that if anyone else had spoken to him that way, he would have tossed them out the door—or at least chewed them out—but since Summer was the boss's daughter, she could get away with more than most people. So the chief swallowed his pride and reported what he'd found. "We dug the bullet out of the wall. It had flattened on impact, but we were still able to determine the caliber. It was from a .375 Holland & Holland Magnum, which is relatively rare in this country. It's a big gun, for big animals with tough hides. Use something like that on a white-tailed deer and you won't have anything left but the hooves. But it's very popular with big-game hunters in Africa."

"Does that mean it's hard to get here?" I asked.

"In Texas?" Hoenekker laughed. "You can pretty much get any hunting rifle you want here. I checked around. There's quite a few stores in the area that carry them."

"Even though they're too powerful for deer?" I asked.

"Oh, there's plenty to kill here that's not local," Hoenekker told me. "There's hunting ranches throughout Texas stocked with exotic animals. They've got all kinds of big game: kudu, eland, water buffalo."

I was completely startled by this. "You mean, people are raising all those animals around here just for people to hunt?"

"Oh yeah," Summer said sadly. "They're all over the state. Go a hundred miles from here in almost any direction and you'll find one. Daddy got a lot of our animals from them." She pointed out the door toward all the antelope grazing on the Asian Plains.

I leaned against the wall, trying to comprehend this. When I'd first moved to America from Africa, plenty of things had caught me by surprise, but by now, after two years, I felt pretty westernized. Every once in a while, though, something would still seem almost incomprehensible to me. "So . . . they're places like this, only instead of raising all these animals to conserve them, they're killing them?"

"Not exactly."

The voice startled me, as it came from behind us. I spun

around to find that Athmani had entered the rhino house. "Hunters are usually big supporters of wildlife conservation," he explained. "After all, if all the animals are gone, there's nothing left for them to hunt. There are many conservation areas in Africa that allow carefully managed hunting, as it brings in a great deal of money. And many game ranches in the United States have helped breed endangered species. . . ."

"Which they then kill," Summer said pointedly.

"Sometimes it's a necessary compromise," Athmani said. "You might think it's cruel, but then, there are people out there who think zoos are cruel. No matter how much great conservation work is done here, they still look at this place as a giant animal prison."

"It's not!" Summer protested.

"I'm only saying there are many sides to the conservation issue," Athmani told her. "So, I understand that the two of you are now helping our investigation?"

"Yes," I said.

"First J.J. forces me to work with you," Hoenekker muttered to Athmani, "and now he sticks us with the Bobbsey Twins here."

Athmani ignored him and smiled at Summer and me. "I'm glad to have your help. The more minds we have on this, the better." He gave Hoenekker a pointed glance. "Have you learned anything new?"

"I was just bringing the kids up to speed," Hoenekker grumbled. He sounded even more annoyed to have to share his information with Athmani than with me, but he seemed aware it was pointless to defy J.J. McCracken's orders. "You already know the bullet is from a .375 H&H. I've checked state sales records. Those rifles aren't plentiful, but there's still a couple thousand in Texas, so that doesn't narrow our suspects down very much. Especially since the records probably aren't very accurate."

Athmani sighed, seeming disappointed by this, then pointed to the chalk marks around the bullet hole. "And what's all this?"

"Ballistics," Hoenekker replied. "By calculating the angle of the shot from the impact point in the wall and the hole in the window, we've determined the shooter fired from the roof of the monorail station. That's more than a hundred yards away, which makes this a difficult shot, especially with a gun that size. Whoever did this wasn't an amateur."

Now that Hoenekker was distracted by Athmani, I left the corner he'd assigned me, climbed into the rhino pen, and examined the spot where the bullet had hit the wall. Since the bullet had been dug out, the impact point was only a jagged spot of busted concrete. I turned and looked through the hole the shot had left in the window. Night was falling outside, but I could still see the monorail station clearly in the distance, silhouetted against the glowing glass dome of World of Reptiles. Sure enough, the roof of the station was in a direct line from where I stood.

In the rhino yard, lights had come on automatically, so it still looked like it was broad daylight out there. Rhonda kept munching her food happily, ignoring everything else around her. I suddenly felt worried for her. "Should we maybe bring Rhonda inside?" I asked. "If the poacher comes back, she's an easy target out there."

"Relax," Hoenekker told me. "There's no way that poacher got back into the park today. We greatly increased security at all the entry gates."

"But that wouldn't stop someone who works here, would it?" I asked. "Maybe the poacher never even left FunJungle. If so, they wouldn't have to come back through the gates."

"I have my men patrolling the park," Hoenekker said. "No one's going to take a shot at Rhonda with them around."

"Even so," Athmani said, "Teddy has a point. We shouldn't be taking *any* chances with Rhonda. Why not bring her in now?"

Hoenekker glowered at me, annoyed I'd second-guessed him, but then gave in. "Fine. I'm almost done here anyhow."

Athmani turned to me. "You need to clear out of Rhonda's space."

I nodded understanding. Humans weren't ever supposed

to be on the same side of the fence as a rhino. Even though Rhonda was gentle, an animal her size could still cause a lot of harm by accident. If I got caught between Rhonda and the wall, she could crush me flat.

As I started to climb back over the metal fence, something on the floor caught my eye. It was a tiny hot pink globule, wedged into a crack in the cement where the metal fence post was bolted down. I knelt and tried to pry it out, but the crack was too thin for me to even get a finger in.

"What's that?" Summer asked. "Rhino poo?"

"If it were rhino poo, do you think I'd be trying to pick it up with my bare hands?" I asked.

Athmani and Hoenekker both came over to see what I was looking at. "Step aside," Hoenekker ordered me. "That could be evidence you're tampering with."

I did what he'd asked.

Hoenekker pulled out a Swiss Army knife and pried the pink object out of the crack. It was a misshapen clod, not much bigger than an army ant. Hoenekker scrutinized it carefully, then frowned. "Looks like dried mud."

"It's *pink*," Summer pointed out.

"Mud comes in plenty of colors," Hoenekker shot back. "Pink, red, orange, you name it. Usually when it's clay, rather than dirt."

I nodded at this, thinking back to my life in Africa. There

were lots of mud wallows in the jungle that had different colors. The rhinos loved to roll in them. Occasionally, you'd come across one smeared red, orange, or yellow, like a preschooler's art project. I'd never seen a pink one, though that didn't mean it wasn't possible. However, there was another problem with Hoenekker's suggestion. "There's no pink mud in the Asian Plains, though, is there?" I asked.

"This exhibit's a couple hundred square acres," Hoenekker growled. "I haven't analyzed every bit of mud in it."

"Mind if I see that?" Athmani asked, holding out his hand.

Hoenekker dropped the pink glob into his palm, and now Athmani took his time scrutinizing it. "Looks like mud to me, too," he announced. "Rhonda probably wallowed in it somewhere out in the Asian Plains, then it dried on her and she rubbed it off in here."

"But Rhonda hasn't been out in the plains for weeks," Summer pointed out. "She's been in here, being pregnant."

"There's no way to tell how old a piece of mud is," Athmani countered. "This could have been wedged down there for a year."

"Can I look at it?" I asked.

"For Pete's sake," Hoenekker growled. "It's a piece of mud. It doesn't have anything to do with our shooter." He turned to Athmani. "You bringing that rhino in or not?"

"I am," Athmani said. He dropped the pink glob in my

hand, then motioned for me to get out of the rhino pen.

I climbed over the rail, then took a look at the pink object myself. Summer leaned in as well. The pink thing certainly *felt* like clay. It was grainy enough that a little bit crumbled off in my hand. I even tried smelling it, but if it had a smell, it was overwhelmed by the odor of rhinoceros in the room.

"Could be old gum," Summer suggested.

"I doubt it," I said.

"Taste it," she suggested.

I recoiled in disgust. "*You* can taste something off the floor of the rhino house if you want. I'll pass."

Meanwhile, Athmani opened the food-storage closet. There was a great deal of hay inside, as well as a large plastic trash can filled with rhino kibble and some smaller bins with fresh fruits and vegetables in them. Athmani selected a carrot, then flipped a switch on the wall.

The gate between the rhino house and the rhino yard slid open.

Rhonda's ears swiveled toward the sound, and she perked up immediately.

Athmani waved the carrot in the air. "Want a treat?" he asked.

Rhonda quickly abandoned her trough—she appeared to have licked it clean—and trotted into the rhino house. She probably hadn't been able to see the carrot at all; instead, she had most likely smelled it. Rhinos have lousy eyesight, but their nostrils are big enough to inhale cue balls. In addition, Rhonda's upper lip was prehensile; it wasn't quite as useful as an elephant's trunk, but she could still grab things with it. Rhonda rested her enormous head atop the fence and extended her lip, reaching for the carrot, revealing her whole mouth. Her upper palate was almost as pink as the mysterious glob in my hand.

"Good girl," Athmani told her, handing over the carrot.

The rhino happily gobbled it down, creating a staggering amount of slobber. Enough drool to drown a Chihuahua spilled out of her mouth and pooled on the floor.

Hondo shuddered and took a few steps back from the rhino, toward the door.

Athmani laughed at his reaction. "You're not afraid of Rhonda here, are you?"

"No," Hondo said, way too defensively. It was an obvious lie.

"Come here and meet her," Athmani offered. "She's gentle as a kitten."

"I got scratched by a kitten once," Hondo replied. "Needed fifteen stitches."

"Rhonda doesn't even have claws," Summer pointed out.

Hondo shrugged this off and edged closer to the door.

I held up the pink blob to give it one more look. Rhonda

immediately mistook my movement, thinking I was handing her food. She suddenly lurched my way, thrusting her head over the rail as far as it would go and grabbing my hand with her prehensile lip.

Hondo shrieked in fear. "She ate his hand!"

"She didn't," I told him. I'd actually been startled by Rhonda's sudden movement—it's always disconcerting to find your hand in a rhino's mouth—but I did my best to remain calm so Hondo wouldn't freak out. "Look. I'm okay." I held up my hand to show him. It was slimed with rhino drool, but it was still there.

The pink blob was gone, though. Rhonda had eaten my evidence.

"Is there something I can dry my hand on?" I asked.

"Come anywhere near my dress with that slobber and I'll kill you," Summer warned.

"I always use my shirt," Athmani said.

There didn't seem to be any other option. While I was wiping my hand clean, Vicky Benbow entered the rhino house. Vicky was one of the evening keepers, responsible for making sure all the animals were housed and fed for the night. While she was great with the animals, she tended to be reserved and quiet around humans. She seemed startled to find so many people in the rhino house. "Um," she said, sounding embarrassed, "I need to get Rhonda settled for the night."

"I guess we should clear out of here, then," Athmani said graciously. He looked to Summer and me. "Teddy, if you'd like, I can give you a ride home. And then take you back to your father, Summer."

"That'd be great," Summer said.

On a warm summer night, I usually would have opted to walk home through the zoo myself, but the temperature had plummeted with the darkness. "Sure," I said.

We all headed for the door, except Chief Hoenekker, who hung back with Vicky. "I'd like to discuss the new rhino security protocols with you," he told her.

Vicky looked like this was pretty much the last thing in the world she wanted to do, but she nodded acceptance. "Okay. I guess."

I waved good-bye to them as we left the building. Vicky gave a meek little wave back. Hoenekker ignored me completely. "I don't expect we'll have any more trouble with this hunter," I heard him tell her. "But just in case, I'm going to have two armed guards patrolling the park tonight."

Athmani's safari rover was parked close to the rhino house. Hondo pointed both Summer and me to the backseat, then climbed into the front, where he could keep a better eye out for threats. Once we were buckled in, Athmani slowly drove through the Asian Plains. It was now dark, and he didn't want to run over any antelope.

As we jounced along, I asked Athmani, "Do you have any idea why the bad guy shot at Rhonda?"

Athmani met my gaze in the rearview mirror. "Based on my experience in Africa, I'd say they were after her horn. Right now Rhonda's would be worth around half a million dollars on the black market."

"Half a million?" Summer gasped, stunned. "Holy cow."

"But Rhonda was locked inside her house," I pointed out. "So the hunter wouldn't be able to get her horn."

"Unless whoever shot at her knew the entry code," Summer suggested. "We already know they could get into FunJungle. So why not the rhino house, too?"

"Then why didn't they enter the house to shoot Rhonda?" I asked. "Why shoot from way over by the monorail station instead of doing it from close by?"

"Or why'd they go after Rhonda at all?" Summer added thoughtfully. "Why not one of the other rhinos that *wasn't* locked up last night?"

Athmani sighed. "Those are good questions," he admitted. "I don't know the answers."

I looked from the monorail station to Rhonda's house. The distance between them was almost the length of a football field. The shot wouldn't have been easy.

"Do you think Hoenekker's right?" I asked Athmani. "That we won't have any more trouble from the hunter?"

"No," Athmani replied. "I don't think Hoenekker believes that himself. If someone took a shot at Rhonda once, there's no reason to think they wouldn't do it again. And you're right about our other rhinos. They need to be protected too. I've arranged for *all* of them to be housed indoors this evening. . . ."

"Where?" Summer asked.

"There are several other facilities like Rhonda's house in SafariLand. The other rhinos are all locked up safely inside them."

"But the hunter shot at Rhonda while she was inside last night," I pointed out.

"And they missed." Athmani pulled up to the gate for vehicles to leave SafariLand. A sensor triggered it to open automatically. "Unfortunately, we don't have any better place to put the rhinos. The best I can say is, it'd be a very difficult shot to hit them through one of the windows—as we saw last night. They're certainly much safer indoors than outside. And the extra guards will hopefully frighten off our poacher."

There was a large space to pull into beyond the auto gate with another gate on the other side. This was to ensure that, should one of the animals slip through the first gate along with the rover, it wouldn't be able to get past the second gate and escape into the park.

Athmani pulled into the space and waited for the first gate to close behind us.

"So all the rhinos now have as many guards as Rhonda?" Summer asked.

"Er . . . no," Athmani admitted. "FunJungle doesn't have the staff to handle that. Your father is trying to hire more men, but it's not easy to find people we trust with weapons around the animals on short notice."

The first gate clicked shut and a green light came on ahead of us to tell us it was safe to activate the second. Athmani pulled forward, and that gate began to open.

I asked, "You mean, you're worried the guards themselves might go after the animals?"

"If they're not carefully selected," Athmani said. "Though I believe we can trust the men we have here tonight."

The second gate opened fully, allowing us to drive into the employee area of the park. Hondo relaxed visibly now that we were away from the animals and surrounded by things he seemed more familiar with, like people and cement. Instead of staying in the employee area, Athmani veered through another gate, ending up on Adventure Road.

Although this was the main pedestrian route around the park, cars could drive on it after visiting hours. And they did. It was the best way to transport the enormous amount of food the animals needed each day—or to remove the enormous amount of garbage the visitors generated. At times it could be as crowded as a highway. Athmani weaved around a flatbed truck full of hay bales and headed for the employee housing area, where I lived.

"Will these new guards be permanent?" Summer asked.

"I'm not sure," Athmani replied. "Why?"

"Because if they're only here for a few days, or weeks, maybe the poacher will just wait for them to stop working and then come back," Summer explained. "And what protects the rhinos then?"

"Yeah," I agreed. "We can't keep them inside forever, can we?"

"You're right," Athmani said. "Ideally, the best scenario would be to catch this poacher quickly, but if we don't . . . I've suggested an alternative way to protect the rhinos, but I can tell you, it will be an uphill battle."

"What's that?" I asked.

"We cut the horns off," Athmani said.

Summer and I both gasped at the idea. My own reaction surprised me. After all, a rhino in the zoo didn't *need* its horn, but the idea of removing it seemed like a horrible act.

"That'd be like wiping the smile off the Mona Lisa," Summer said.

"The difference is, no one is going to kill the *Mona Lisa* for her smile," Athmani countered. "I didn't say it was a great solution, but it's a solution. It has been done many places in

Africa. If you get rid of the horn, there's no reason for anyone to poach the rhinos."

"Unless someone's going after Rhonda for some other reason," I said.

"Like what?" Athmani asked.

"Wanting a dead rhino head to put on their wall," I replied.

Athmani sighed. "I suppose that's possible, but I think someone wanting the horn is more likely. It'd be easier to steal the horn than a whole head."

"Would taking the horn off hurt the rhino?" Summer asked.

"No," Athmani replied. "There are no nerves in the horn itself. But it is still not an easy job. A veterinarian would have to do it." Athmani pulled over by the rear employee exit from FunJungle. "Here you go, Teddy."

"See you tomorrow?" Summer asked me.

"Sure," I said. Normally, the idea of Summer asking to spend time with me would have been thrilling, but everything about the rhino was wearing me down. I climbed out of the rover and waved good-bye.

Summer waved back as Athmani drove away.

I left FunJungle and headed into the trailer park that served as employee housing, my mind full of questions. Was the hunter going after the horn, or another trophy from

Rhonda—or, as my friends had suggested, were they looking to kill only for fun? But if it was for fun, why go after a rhino rather than any other animal? And if it was for the horn, why had the hunter gone after the one rhino that was locked up rather than any of the others that weren't? Was this tied to the candy store theft in any way—or was that an entirely separate crime?

As I wove through the trailers toward home, a thought nagged at me. I had the feeling there was something strange about the attempt on Rhonda that I'd missed, but I couldn't figure out what it was.

I rounded the final trailer and froze in astonishment. In addition to all the other mysteries of the day, there was now one more.

My entire house had disappeared.

HOMELESS

At first, I thought I'd made a mistake. It didn't seem possible that an entire house—even if it was only a trailer home—could vanish. I looked around, wondering if maybe I'd wandered the wrong way through the trailer park. I'd walked this way hundreds of times before, but that night I'd been distracted.

I hadn't made a mistake, though. Everything else was exactly where it should have been. All the neighbors' trailers were there. But where ours had been that morning, there was only a bare rectangular cement slab.

I immediately called Mom at her office at Monkey Mountain. She answered on the fourth ring. "Hey, kiddo. . . ."

"Mom, our house is gone!"

"Theodore, that isn't funny."

"I know it's not. It's true."

Mom sighed, still not believing me. "I don't have time for any pranks right now. One of the apes is sick, and Doc's here to check on her. . . ."

"I'm not joking!" I yelled. "I promise! I'm standing right where our house is supposed to be, and it's not here!"

My tone convinced my mother I wasn't messing around. "Teddy, how could a whole house disappear?"

"I don't know, but it did."

"Stay where you are. I'll be right there," Mom said, then hung up.

I tried calling Dad, but it went straight to voice mail. I figured leaving a message that our house had vanished might panic him, so I just asked him to call me when he could.

It was now very cold. I hadn't worn my warmest jacket or my gloves that day; both were in my bedroom, which was in my missing house. So I looked for a warm place to wait. Unfortunately, none of our neighbors were home. This wasn't rare. None of them had kids and most had offices that were far cozier and more comfortable than the cheap trailers FunJungle had given us. I had to settle for trying to move as much as possible. I jogged in place and waved my arms around, trying to get my blood flowing, then searched the area for clues as to where the house could have gone.

It was a moonless night, and we lived far from civilization and the light pollution that came with it, so it was very dark outside. Using the light from my phone, I tried to scan the ground around the cement slab for tire tracks or drag marks but couldn't find any. None close by, at least. So I widened my search, spiraling out around the slab. I'd done only two circles before Mom arrived. She raced up, then froze the same way I had and gasped, "It's gone."

"I told you," I said.

Mom shook her head, trying to make sense of everything. "This isn't possible. The house was right here this morning. Homes don't just get up and walk away."

"Mobile homes can be moved. Maybe someone stole it."

"Out of all the mobile homes in the world, why would someone steal *ours*?" Mom asked. "It's not even the nicest one here."

I shrugged. "I tried calling Dad."

"So did I," Mom said. "Let's try again."

She pulled out her phone, but before she could start dialing, a pair of high-beam headlights lit us up. I'd been in the dark so long, they were blinding. I had to shield my eyes as the approaching vehicle thumped along the trailer park's dirt access road.

As it got closer, I realized it wasn't a car at all. It was a souped-up golf cart. It was also tilting sharply to one side due to the weight of the driver. Marge.

To my surprise, Mom sighed with relief. "Thank goodness. Security's here to help us."

"I wouldn't bet on it," I said under my breath.

There was only one bush anywhere near the cement slab, but somehow Marge still managed to hit it. She plowed right into the poor plant, then clambered out and glared at it angrily, as if somehow it were at fault. "You ought to have that bush removed," Marge told us. "It's a driving hazard."

"Yeah," I said. "It jumped right in your path, didn't it?"

Mom signaled me to not start anything. "Marjorie, thanks for coming so quickly. . . ."

"I need to talk to your son," Marge interrupted rudely, then turned on me. "I didn't get the chance to finish my interrogation this afternoon."

"Interrogation?" Mom asked. "Wait. Why are you here?"

Marge proudly removed a piece of paper from her jacket and dramatically unfolded it. "This is an official warrant to search your home for stolen candy."

"What are you talking about?" Mom demanded.

"Teddy here is the number one suspect in a heist perpetrated this morning at Carly Cougar's Candy Corner. I suspect the stolen items may have been concealed within your domicile."

"Be our guest," I said. "Feel free to search the house."

"Oh, I will," Marge sneered. She turned toward the previous location of our front door—and only then did it occur to her that something was seriously wrong. Her expression went blank. "Where's your house?"

"That's what *we* were wondering," Mom said.

Marge scowled and wheeled on me. "You think you're so clever, don't you? Hiding your whole house so that I can't search it?"

"You actually think I did that?" I asked. "Moved an entire house?"

"It's a *mobile* home," Marge pointed out. "'Mobile' means you can move it."

"Why would I hide the candy in my house and then move the house?" I asked. "Why wouldn't I simply move the candy?"

Marge screwed up her face as she tried to make sense of that. "How am I supposed to know how a little deviant like yourself thinks?"

"Teddy isn't a deviant," Mom said sternly. "And he didn't move our house. Someone else did. It's been stolen!"

Marge looked to Mom. Understanding slowly seeped

through her thick skull, and she finally seemed to comprehend what was going on. "Hold on. Someone stole your whole house?"

"Yes!" Mom yelled, exasperated. "That's what we've been trying to tell you!"

Marge burst into laughter. "And you don't know where it is? There's finally a crime that Teddy the genius can't solve?"

"You think this is funny?" Mom asked, nearing her wit's end. "Everything we own is in that house!"

Marge held up both hands, signaling Mom to calm down. "Keep your britches on, Charlene. I'm on the job." She snapped her radio from its holster on her belt and called in. "HQ, this is O'Malley. I'm out in the employee housing area, and the Fitzroy family trailer appears to be missing. Thieves suspected. Backup requested."

There was a moment's pause on the other end. Then the dispatcher replied, "Uh, Marge . . . Today was the first day of the employee housing relo project."

"It was?"

"Yes. I'm looking at the schedule right here."

"Gotcha. Cancel that request for backup, then." Marge reholstered her radio, then turned back to us, grinning proudly. "Good news. I've solved the case. Your home wasn't stolen. It was moved."

This didn't make me feel any better. Mom still seemed

upset as well. "Where?" she demanded. "And why?"

The smile quickly faded from Marge's face. "No one told you anything about this?"

"No," Mom said. "What's the employee housing relo project?"

"Um," Marge replied, "I think you should talk to J.J. McCracken about that."

NEW PLANS

A half hour later, I was back in J.J.'s office. This time both my parents were there with me. Dad had been at Carnivore Canyon, installing some cameras in the tiger exhibit. Much of the Canyon was carved into solid rock, so cell phone service was nonexistent there. After being around tigers all afternoon, Dad smelled like them, a combination of musk and cat pee. Because of this, Mom was keeping her distance from him, sitting at the opposite end of the couch.

Summer was in J.J.'s office as well. She and her father had been about to head home when word of our misplaced trailer came through. Now she was sitting at his enormous desk, doing her homework while he paced the room.

For the first time since I'd met him, J.J. seemed embarrassed. Normally, J.J. was full of confidence, but at that moment, he looked as uneasy as a man in a rattlesnake nest. "I want you all to know how dreadfully sorry I am about this," he said. "I'm going to find out what went wrong and fire whoever was responsible."

"You mean our house wasn't supposed to be moved?" Mom asked.

"Er, no," J.J. admitted. "That was supposed to happen, all right. But you should have been notified *weeks* ago."

"Why was our home supposed to be moved?" Dad demanded.

"Actually, *all* the homes are supposed to be moved," J.J. corrected. "Yours was merely the first."

"Why?" Dad repeated.

"I found a better location for them," J.J. said. "You're gonna love it. It's farther from the park, so you won't be downwind from the stench of antelope poop."

Mom gave J.J. a hard stare. "Know what stinks worse than antelope poop? That lame answer. Why are you *really* moving the trailers?"

J.J. glanced at his office door, as if hoping someone was going to come through it and bail him out of trouble. Then he sagged and admitted, "I need the space where the employee housing is."

Mom's annoyance turned to relief. "Why didn't you just say so? What do you need it for? A new animal exhibit?"

"Are you going to expand SafariLand?" I asked hopefully.

J.J. glanced at the door once more, then said, "Er, no. It's not for a new animal exhibit at all."

"Then what?" Dad asked.

J.J. hedged for a few more moments, then owned up. "I'm going to build a roller coaster. And some other rides."

All of us sat up in surprise at this. Even Summer. "Daddy!" she cried. "You promised you wouldn't ever build things like that here!"

J.J. flashed her a weak smile. "No. I promised I wouldn't build rides that would interfere with the animals' well-being. No river rafting through the hippo exhibits or coasters through SafariLand. But the fact is, this park has suffered some financial setbacks, what with Henry's death and the theft of Kazoo and all, and according to my research, if I want to bring more guests in, I need to build rides."

"But this is a zoo . . . ," I protested.

"It's a tourist attraction," J.J. corrected. "And for Pete's sake, even zoos have rides. San Diego's got a sky ride. The Bronx has a monorail. Every darn one of them has a carousel."

"But they don't have roller coasters," Mom pointed out. "Coasters are loud. They'll startle the animals every time they go past."

"I'm doing everything in my power to protect our animals," J.J. explained. "My engineers have made noise reduction a priority. And the whole reason I'm putting the rides out where your house used to be is to get them as far from the animals as I can."

"I don't like this," Dad said. "When you recruited us here, you swore that providing the best possible care for these animals was going to be the number one priority of this park, not making money."

"Well, if I don't make any money, there isn't gonna be a park!" J.J. shot back. "All these state-of-the-art facilities I built—Monkey Mountain and Hippo River and Carnivore Canyon and all that—they ain't cheap. High-quality care costs money. Our conservation and breeding programs cost money. All of sudden today I had to double my security expenses to keep some yahoo from picking off our rhinos. That costs money too. This park is a money pit. If you don't want the gates closed and all your precious animals shipped off to the circus, then you're all gonna have to cut me some slack here."

We all bit our tongues after that. I didn't like the idea of rides being built at the park, but I understood J.J.'s point.

The office door opened and Pete Thwacker rushed in. His arms were full of blueprints.

J.J. wheeled on him. This was obviously whom he'd been expecting. "Where the heck have you been?"

"I was halfway home when I got your call. And then I

figured I should stop by the planning room to get these." Pete set the blueprints on J.J.'s desk and began to unroll them.

J.J. asked, "Would you like to tell the Fitzroys here why they didn't find out about their home being relocated *before* it was relocated?"

"That's the communications department's snafu, not public relations," Pete said. "Apparently, they printed up all these nice notifications to hand deliver to employee housing weeks ago, but then failed to deliver them."

"What happened to them?" Mom asked.

"I'm still trying to find that out," Pete admitted. "It seems they were misplaced—or possibly eaten by a llama. Whatever the case, you and everyone else in employee housing weren't notified, and we here at FunJungle are extremely sorry for any inconvenience this might have caused. Rest assured, however, that the transfer of your home to its new location was handled by the finest mobile home transfer company in the state of Texas. . . ."

"Aw, lay off the PR snow job with us, Pete," Dad groused.

"I'm speaking the truth," Pete replied. "We spared no expense. Your home should be in exactly the same condition you left it in this morning—if not exactly the same *place* you left it."

"How'd you even move it?" I asked. "There weren't any tire marks or anything near the slab."

"We used a crane," Pete explained. "A big mobile one. Winched your home right off the base and onto a flatbed trailer. Then we trucked it out to Lakeside Estates."

"Lakeside Estates?" Mom repeated.

"The new employee housing community!" Pete dramatically unrolled one of the blueprints on the desk. "The previous site of your home was admittedly subpar. Not a whole lot of thought went into where to place the trailers."

"I'm surprised to hear that *any* thought went into it," Dad said. "It looked like the trailers were all just scattered by a tornado."

"I *liked* where our house was," I told them. "We were right by the woods. There were always deer outside."

"Well, you're gonna like Lakeside Estates even better." Pete thumped a finger on the blueprint.

I took a closer look. The blueprint showed the new plan for the mobile home park, with rectangles marking the homes themselves, surrounded by landscaped paths and trees.

"We'll have lighted pathways between the buildings for increased safety," Pete explained. "Plus better landscaping and a new Jacuzzi tub."

"What's this?" Summer asked, pointing to a blob shaped like a potato.

"That's the lake!" Pete crowed happily.

"Where is this?" Dad asked.

"On the far side of the employee parking lot," Pete replied.

"I've been over there," Mom said. "That's not a lake. It's a pond."

"True," Pete admitted. "But Pondside Estates sounds kind of weird."

"It's not even a pond, really," Dad put in. "It only has water after a big rain. The rest of the time, it's a mud pit. And a mosquito breeding ground."

Pete looked to J.J. "Er, I'm sure we could spring for some bug zappers at each residence."

"Why don't you put in a *real* pool there?" I asked. "Something to use in the summer when it gets crazy hot."

Now everyone looked to J.J. expectantly. "Pools are expensive," he grumbled.

Mom said, "I'll bet it'd be cheaper than hiring a whole bunch of new biologists. Because you're gonna have a lot of people quit once they hear you're moving their homes next to a sinkhole without their permission."

"It's not a sinkhole!" Pete argued. "It's a mud pit! I mean, it's a lake."

"Fine." J.J. sighed. "We'll put in a pool."

"And we could use nicer trailers," Mom said. "As opposed to those bargain-basement ones we have now."

"Those trailers are top quality!" J.J. proclaimed. "My own company makes them!"

"They're crap," Dad said. "The heaters barely work, there's no insulation, the walls are paper thin, and the kitchens are firetraps. I know your mobile home division makes far better products, so why don't you cut yourself a deal on some of them for us?"

"Double-wide," Mom added.

J.J. grimaced. "It doesn't work quite like that."

"I'm guessing you want to control the story about these new rides you're building," Dad said. "I bet you and Pete already have a whole PR campaign cooked up to whet the public's appetite. So it'd probably be really bad if the public first heard about all these rides some other way—like a news report about how you forcibly relocated all your biologists without any warning."

J.J. sat at his desk and rubbed his temples. "I need an aspirin. You folks are giving me a migraine the size of Dallas."

"It's only fair," Summer told her father. "I've seen the Fitzroys' trailer. It's smaller than Mom's closet."

J.J. shot Summer a look of betrayal, then turned to my parents. "If I give you folks a double-wide trailer, everyone else is going to want one."

"I bet they will," Dad said. "And I'm sure they'll be extremely thankful when they get them. Thankful enough not to complain to the press, I'd say."

J.J. stared at my parents for a long while, then sighed.

"All right. Fine. You'll get your new trailer. But you'll also sign an agreement saying you won't blab one word of all this to the press."

"Deal," Mom said, with a satisfied smile.

J.J. shook his head sadly. "Of course this had to happen today. As if an elephant stampede and a rhino poacher weren't enough to deal with."

"Any progress on that poacher?" Dad asked.

J.J.'s eyes quickly flicked to me, a warning not to say anything about the help I was giving him. Then they flicked back to my parents. "Chief Hoenekker is investigating. I'm expecting a report from him later tonight."

I averted my eyes from everyone, feeling guilty about keeping my parents in the dark. I looked down at the other blueprints Pete had unrolled on J.J.'s desk. These showed some of the theme-park rides slated for construction. There was a triple-loop roller coaster called the Beast and a log flume, which appeared to have a Canadian Rockies theme, filled with fake moose, wolves, and bears. At least, I hoped they were fake. I wasn't sure how much I could trust J.J. McCracken.

"What are you doing to protect the rhinos in the meantime?" Mom asked.

"Plenty," J.J. said. "I've got them all under lock and key, and I've souped up security in SafariLand. Right now those rhinos are better protected than the president of the USA."

"But you can't keep them locked up forever," Mom said.

"I know that," J.J. said, growing exasperated. "I'm gonna find the jerk who took a shot at Rhonda and send him up the river."

"And if you don't?" Dad pressed.

"Athmani says we should think about cutting the horns off," Summer said.

J.J. recoiled in shock. He obviously hadn't heard this yet. My parents did the same thing. Even Pete, who wasn't that big a fan of animals, seemed disturbed by the thought.

"You can do that?" he asked. "Doesn't it hurt?"

"No," Dad told him. "There's no nerves in the horn. It's like clipping a giant toenail."

"But it'd look weird, right?" Pete asked. "A rhino with no horn would be like an elephant with no trunk. Or a short giraffe. People won't want to see that."

"And they're not going to see it," J.J. stated. "I'm not having my rhinos defaced. Literally."

"Even if it might save the rhinos' lives?" Mom asked.

"We're gonna save the rhinos' lives by catching this hunter," J.J. declared. "End of story. Now, if you folks will excuse me, it's been a very long day. I'd like to get back to my home, and I'm sure you'd like to get back to yours."

"Now that we know where it is," Dad said under his breath. He and Mom stood up to go.

"You folks want a ride to your new place?" J.J. asked.

"No," Mom said. "We ought to be able to find it now."

"You sure?" J.J. pressed. "It's cold out there."

"We'll be fine," Mom told him. I got the sense that she was still angry at J.J. and didn't want to accept any favors from him.

"All right, then. Have a good night." J.J. shook hands with Dad as we headed to the door, then extended a hand to me, too. "Always a pleasure, Teddy." He gave me a sly wink as he said this, like we had a secret club or something. He seemed pleased that I hadn't spilled the beans about investigating the rhino situation for him.

"Let's talk at lunch tomorrow," Summer told me.

"Sure," I said.

As soon as we were out of the office, Hondo shut the door behind us.

Dad and I started down the hall to the elevators, though Mom hung back for a second, staring at the door.

"What's wrong?" Dad asked.

"Every time that man offers to answer our questions, I end up with a hundred more." Mom sighed. "He's hiding something from us."

"He always is," Dad said.

Mom followed us to the elevators. Despite the fact that my parents had just negotiated a brand-new home for us, I felt pretty terrible. After all, I was hiding something from them too. I was desperate to tell them the truth, but I feared what J.J. might do if I betrayed *his* trust.

I hoped we could find whoever had shot at the rhino and get the whole thing over with quickly. Unfortunately, I didn't have a clue as to who'd done it. Or who'd broken into the candy store. I'd been railroaded into investigating one crime and accused of committing the other. Overall, it had been an extremely crummy day.

And it was about to get worse.

THE HUNT

"What's all this about you robbing the candy store?" Dad asked.

We were walking back to our trailer through FunJungle, passing World of Reptiles, bundled up against the cold. The zoo was unusually quiet. Often, you would hear animals at night or see employees working the late shift, but everyone else seemed to have had the sense to stay inside.

"I didn't do it," I said.

"Oh, I know you didn't," Dad assured me. "But why does Marge think you did?"

"Because Marge hates me. I'm surprised she hasn't accused me of trying to kill Rhonda."

Dad laughed. "When did this happen?"

"Sometime last night," I replied. "Or maybe early this

morning. Whoever did it smashed the whole store up and stole twenty-five pounds of candy."

Mom turned to me, surprised. "*Twenty-five pounds?* Who on earth would want twenty-five pounds of candy?"

"Pretty much every kid I know," I said. "You think it could be related to the Rhonda thing somehow?"

"How so?" Mom asked.

"It seems strange, both things happening on the same night. I thought maybe the robber broke into the store to divert everyone from the rhino shooting—or vice versa."

Dad scratched his chin, considering that. "The rhino thing was definitely a distraction, I'll give you that. I didn't even hear about the candy store robbery until your mother told me about it tonight."

"And everyone's so focused on the poacher, Marge is the only one left to investigate the candy store," I said. "She's such a bonehead that it pretty much guarantees the thief will get away."

"It seems awfully extreme, though," Mom cautioned. "Who would take a shot at a rhinoceros simply to get away with stealing twenty-five pounds of candy?"

"Someone who really likes candy," I suggested.

Vicky, the keeper from the rhino house, passed us heading back from SafariLand, cocooned in a heavy winter jacket, her hands crammed deep into the pockets. We all waved to her, but she didn't wave back. Either she was too shy or she didn't want to expose her hands to the frigid air.

Mom said, "If someone was going to go through that much trouble to create a diversion, wouldn't you think they'd go after something more valuable? Or at least steal the money from the candy store's cash register?"

"Maybe they *did* rob the register," I replied. "I wonder if Marge even thought to check."

"She probably didn't," Dad said. "Maybe J.J. ought to hire *you* to run security here." He proudly put his arm around my shoulders.

I quickly wriggled free.

Dad faked a wounded look. "Don't tell me you're getting too old to get a hug from your father?"

"No. You just smell like tiger pee."

"I do?" Dad sniffed his arm, then wrinkled his nose. "Ugh. I do. Man, that stink really sticks around. As soon as we find our house, I'll shower."

"What were you even doing over there today?" Mom asked.

"This incredible new project." Dad's eyes gleamed with excitement. "You know how the public has been dying to see the new tiger cubs?"

Mom and I nodded. The cubs had been born a few weeks

before but were too young to go out on exhibit yet. This was driving Pete crazy. He had announced their birth with great fanfare, mistakenly believing the cubs would immediately be available for viewing. Now he was overwhelmed by complaints from angry tourists who'd come to the park expecting baby tigers only to find an empty exhibit.

"Well," Dad went on, "on the park's website we've had only one stationary camera in their enclosure, so if the cubs went offscreen or hid, that was that. But I rigged up four new cameras to give much better coverage and linked them all to the Internet. So now users can switch viewpoints or even pan or zoom in—and they can take high-resolution photos as well."

"So they'll be able to control the cameras through the Internet?" Mom asked.

"Yes," Dad said. "You can control pretty much anything remotely these days."

We were passing the SafariLand monorail station. I looked up at the spot on the roof where the poacher had shot from, half expecting to see someone there. It was empty, though.

My parents scoped things out as well. There was a viewing platform at the station, from which we could see Rhonda's house down in the Asian Plains. The heaters glowed red through the windows, making it stand out in the darkness.

"Where's the extra security?" Mom asked. "I thought there were supposed to be more guards protecting the rhinos."

"They're probably moving around," Dad replied. "There's a lot of area to cover."

Mom walked to the edge of the viewing platform and scanned the exhibit. "Someone ought to be *here*. There's a clear shot at Rhonda's house from here."

"There's a guard," Dad said, pointing. "See? He's down in the exhibit."

I looked the way he was indicating. At first, I couldn't make anything out in the shadows, but then I noticed some movement. As my eyes adjusted to the darkness, a shape took form, someone cautiously slinking toward Rhonda's house, a rifle slung across their back.

Instead of relief, however, I felt worry. "Um, Dad. Are you *sure* that's a guard? He looks like he's trying not to be noticed."

"And he has a gun," Mom said.

"The guards aren't armed?" Dad asked.

"I don't think so," I replied.

Dad stepped to the edge of the railing and yelled at the top of his lungs. "Hey!"

The person in the exhibit froze, turned our way . . . and ran.

"That's no guard!" Mom cried. "That's the hunter!"

Dad was already moving. He climbed over the railing of the viewing platform and leaped down into the Asian Plains. Without even thinking about it, I started to follow.

"No, Teddy!" Mom warned. "It's dangerous in there. Stay up here and alert security. Your father and I will handle this." Then she scrambled over the railing and dropped in as well.

The hunter was racing toward the far side of the exhibit, where the park fence was, blending into the shadows more and more as he got farther away. Many of the antelope in the exhibit were now running as well, startled by the hunter's sudden movement—and probably put on edge because Dad reeked of tiger, their number one predator. Antelope have acute senses of smell and hearing; even antelope on the far side of the Asian Plains were making calls of alarm.

I didn't have the direct number for park security, so I scanned the station for an emergency phone. There were red emergency phones all over FunJungle, but of course, now that I wanted one, I couldn't see one anywhere.

So I fished out my phone and dialed Summer.

She answered on the third ring. "Wow. You just can't get enough of me today."

"Are you with your father?" I asked.

"Yes." She sounded concerned by the tone of my voice. "We're still in the car. Is something wrong?"

"The hunter's back. My parents scared him off, but they need help."

There were some shuffling noises as the phone switched hands. Then J.J. McCracken got on. "I heard what you said. I'm notifying Hoenekker right now. Where's the hunter?"

"In the Asian Plains. My parents are chasing him."

There was a sudden pained cry from my mother in the darkness. It sounded like she'd been hurt.

"Where in the Asian Plains?" J.J. asked.

"I don't know," I admitted, scanning the darkness. I'd lost sight of my parents and the hunter and couldn't find them anymore.

"Charlene!" Dad yelled. "Are you all right?"

"I'll be fine!" Mom yelled back, though I could hear the hurt in her voice. "Stay after him!"

"Is the rhino all right?" J.J. asked.

"For now," I said. "I have to go." I jammed the phone into my pocket and jumped over the railing into the Asian Plains.

I wasn't even aware I was doing it until I was dropping into the exhibit. I was thinking only about my mom. Then I landed badly and tumbled through the grass. I could feel the ground trembling beneath me from the thunder of hoofbeats and only then realized that I may have made a big mistake.

I rolled to my feet quickly, scanning the grasslands for trouble. By now panic had spread through the entire antelope and deer populations. I could sense movement in the darkness throughout the exhibit, different herds scattering in different directions. The night air was alive with the rumble of their hooves on the ground. The loudest was coming from my left.

I turned that way to find three nilgai coming right for me. Nilgai are the largest Asian antelope. From the viewing area above, they had never seemed too imposing, merely slightly larger than normal deer. But now that they were bearing down on me at a full gallop, they were far more frightening. They were more than six feet tall, with sharp horns and thickly muscled bodies. Getting trampled by one of them would have been like getting hit by a car.

I scrambled out of their path toward a small tree, grabbing a low branch and hauling myself up as they ran by. They came so close, one's horns scraped my thigh, leaving two thin gouges in my skin.

Then they continued on, vanishing into the night, leaving only a cloud of dust behind.

None of the other stampeding herds sounded close by, so I dropped to the ground again and called out, "Mom! Where are you?"

"I'm all right!" she yelled. "Do not get into the exhibit! It's too dangerous!"

"Too late!" I yelled back. I'd gotten a good bead on her voice and headed that way. I went as fast as I could, but the ground was uneven and strewn with rocks, so I couldn't quite run at full speed for fear of wiping out. I crested a small hill and nearly slammed into a stampede of chital deer. The chital were pretty small compared to many of the other animals in the paddock, but they were still bigger than me. It was like I'd suddenly turned the wrong way onto a one-way street. I curled up, tucking my head into my arms to avoid being gored by antlers. The chital swarmed around me, bumping me from side to side as they passed, and then faded into the night behind me.

I continued onward, searching for a sign of either of my parents ahead. Unfortunately, it was hard to pick out their movements, because now *everything* was moving. All around me, the herds were on the run, giving the impression that the entire landscape was alive. There were so many hoofbeats, it was hard to separate them all, to tell which herds were running away and which were bearing down on me.

Ahead, toward the back fence of the park, I thought I caught a glimpse of two men running among all the other shadows, but then they melted away again.

"Teddy!" Mom's voice came from surprisingly close by.

I found her struggling out of the creek bed that rambled through the exhibit. In a month, after the spring rains, there would be two feet of water in it, but at the moment, it was almost dry, a mere trickle surrounded by steep banks. Mom was hobbling, putting as much weight as possible on her right leg, wincing every time she touched her left foot to the ground.

I ran to her side and put my arm around her, taking her weight. "What happened?"

Mom sagged against me, folding her left leg up under her like a flamingo. "I got knocked over by something. A sambar deer, I think. Then I fell down into the creek and twisted my ankle."

Though I wanted to follow after my father and the hunter, I had no choice but to turn back toward the exit. I could tell Mom was frustrated by this too, but she didn't complain. With her injured, we were sitting ducks out there.

We made our way back across the plains as quickly as we could, though that wasn't very fast, given that we had only three working legs between us. Mom wasn't very big, but she was still bigger than me, and it was tough to support her weight over the rocky, uneven ground.

Luckily, most of the antelope and deer seemed to be calming by now, perhaps because Dad, with his reek of tiger, was out of range. Not nearly as many were racing about, but they were still on edge. I could sense them around us in the darkness, watching us carefully, ready to run—or possibly attack—at the slightest sign of danger. Occasionally, I caught a glimpse of their eyes reflected in the distant park lights, riveted on our progress.

However, we didn't see the gaurs until we almost ran into them.

Gaurs are wild cattle from India. The ones in front of us were each more than six feet tall at the shoulder and weighed nearly a ton, with wide racks of horns set across their brows. Thanks to their dark fur, they had blended perfectly into the darkness. Mom and I might have slammed right into the lead female if she hadn't given us a warning snort.

We froze in fear.

In the wild, gaur are usually shy and timid, running away from humans rather than at them, but we'd come upon a small herd of females with young calves, and the mothers were determined to protect their young. They had formed a wall, keeping the calves behind them and aiming their thick, sharp horns our way, prepared to gore—or trample—us at any provocation.

"Back away slowly," Mom warned me, in a voice barely above a whisper. "No sudden noises or movements."

I knew this already, but I didn't bother arguing. Instead,

I did exactly as she'd ordered. I took a few steps back, and Mom hopped along with me.

The matriarch snorted again, letting us know she wasn't quite ready to back down yet.

We gingerly moved another few feet in reverse.

The gaurs remained motionless as a row of statues.

And then my cell phone rang.

A few bars of music suddenly blared in the night. It wasn't loud, but it was enough to startle the gaurs. They bellowed angrily, frightening a nearby herd of chital deer, which exploded out of the grass around us. Mom and I spun toward them in fright, a far-too-sudden movement, and the gaurs charged.

"Run!" Mom shouted, and before I knew what was even happening, she'd shoved me away from her, removing herself as a burden so that I could escape. There was no way she could hold off their attack, though. Compared to the enormous cattle, she might as well have been made of paper. She was obviously hoping they'd be distracted by her and ignore me.

The cattle charged toward her.

"No!" I yelled.

And then a pair of headlight beams swept across the plains, landing right on the herd. The cattle stopped at once, blinded by the lights but staring into them anyhow, trying to assess the new threat.

An engine's roar carried across the paddock. I was afraid to pull my gaze from the gaurs, so I couldn't see the car, but from the sound, I could tell it was one of the FunJungle safari rovers.

My phone was still ringing. Our confrontation with the gaurs felt like it had taken hours, but it had been only seconds. Now that I had a moment of calm, I recognized the ringtone. It was my father calling.

Things were still too dicey to answer it, though. The gaurs remained on alert. Mom stayed frozen on one leg beside me, watching the cattle carefully for any sign of what they were about to do.

The whole night seemed to light up as the headlights got closer. The rover skidded to a stop between us and the gaurs, kicking up a cloud of dust. The gaurs flinched but stayed put.

Chief Hoenekker was behind the wheel. "Get in!" he yelled.

Mom and I didn't need to be told twice. I started back to help her, but she was already hopping toward the vehicle. We both dove inside, her in the front seat, me in the back, and Hoenekker slammed the pedal down. The rover lurched across the grass.

The lead gaur bellowed angrily, then charged. The females behind her followed suit. One's horn clanged off the rear of the rover as it sped away.

Through the rear window, I watched the angry cattle follow us a few more steps, then pull up, convinced they had dispensed with the threat. They quickly hooked U-turns and returned to their calves.

Hoenekker kept the pedal down anyhow. Normally, park vehicles were supposed to stick to designated dirt roads in the paddocks. Hoenekker had gone cross-country to rescue us, and now the uneven terrain was bouncing us around like popcorn kernels. Neither Mom nor I had had a chance to buckle up. I was nearly thrown to the floor.

"Slow down!" Mom ordered. "Before you kill some innocent antelope!"

Hoenekker glared at her but braked anyhow. "A 'thanks for saving our lives' might be nice."

Mom held his gaze a moment, then gave in. "Thanks for saving our lives. How'd you find us?"

"Teddy called J.J. J.J. called me. Lucky for you, I hadn't gone home yet tonight."

I pried my phone from my pocket and called my father back. I didn't want him to worry about us.

Hoenekker spotted one of the dirt roads to the right and veered toward it. "Where's your husband?"

"I don't know," Mom replied. "Last I saw, he was chasing the hunter toward the back fence."

"That was him calling," I told them. "I'm trying him back now." I flipped the phone to speaker so they could hear it ringing.

Hoenekker glanced at Mom's ankle. "You need to go to the hospital?"

"I'll be fine," Mom told him.

Dad finally answered the phone. "Where are you?" he asked. "Is everything all right?"

"I'm with Mom in a rover," I replied. "Chief Hoenekker's driving. Where are *you*?"

"Outside the park."

"What?" Mom asked. "How'd you get past the fence?"

"Same way the hunter did. He laid a towel across the barbed wire and climbed right over."

The rover reached the dirt road in the exhibit and swerved onto it. It was a smoother ride than going over the grass had been, but not much. With every jounce over the ruts and bumps, Mom winced in pain.

Hoenekker snatched the phone from me. "Any idea where that shooter is now?"

"No," Dad replied. "By the time I found his access point, he was long gone."

"So you lost him." Hoenekker sighed, annoyed.

"Yes," Dad admitted. "I lost him."

"Meaning you just risked your dang fool lives for diddly-squat," Hoenekker growled.

"We saved Rhonda's life!" I snapped.

Hoenekker looked at me in the rearview mirror and narrowed his eyes. "Maybe," he muttered. "But only for a little while."

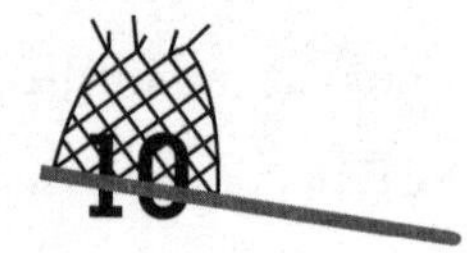

LAKESIDE ESTATES

My parents let me skip school the next day. After all the excitement in the Asian Plains, we'd had to spend hours relating what had happened to Hoenekker and a bunch of other security guys, so by the time we finally found the new location of our mobile home and got to bed, it was after midnight and I was exhausted. My parents were too. Dad thought maybe Mom should go to a hospital about her ankle, but she kept insisting she was fine; she took some painkillers and went right to bed. Dad said I deserved some rest after all I'd been through, so he told me to sleep in.

I did. I might have slept all morning had I not been awakened by someone pounding on our front door. Our trailer was so poorly built that the entire thing trembled with each knock.

I pried my eyes open and tried to find my alarm clock. Since we hadn't been notified about the move of our trailer, we hadn't packed our things beforehand. I didn't have much stuff, but what I did own was scattered all over my room. It looked like my closet had blown up.

"Answer the door, Teddy!" Marge hollered. "I know you're in there!"

I groaned and dragged myself out of bed. Our trailer's heater was so awful, it was freezing inside. The moment my feet touched the cold, bare floor, I snapped awake. It was like sticking my toes in ice water.

Marge started pounding on the door again. It felt like someone was jackhammering the house. "Teddy!" she roared. "Show yourself!"

"I'm coming!" I yelled back. I dug some socks out of a pile of clothes in the middle of the room and found my alarm clock buried beneath it all. It was almost nine o'clock. I couldn't believe I'd slept so late. At school, I'd have already been in second period.

I glanced out the window. I couldn't see Marge, but I could see her golf cart. There was only one bush anywhere near our front door, but Marge had managed to run into it.

This was the first time I'd seen the new location of my home in daylight. Lakeside Estates didn't look anywhere near as nice as Pete Thwacker had made it out to be. None of the landscaping or pathways he'd promised had been laid down yet. Our home sat in a large clearing, surrounded by bare slabs for the other trailers: a dozen cement rectangles looking bizarrely out of place in the woods.

The so-called lake barely had any water in it, and what little there was had frozen, so it was really only a patch of ice-encrusted mud.

Marge kept banging on the door, apparently convinced this was the way to get me to move faster. Instead, I decided to take my time, knowing it would aggravate her. Maybe I'd get lucky and her head would explode from frustration.

I slowly pulled on my jeans, shoes, and a sweatshirt. Through it all, Marge kept pounding away.

It occurred to me that my parents must not be home. I'd expected that they might sleep in too, but if either one had been there, they surely would have told Marge to can it by now. Sure enough, there was a note from Mom on the breakfast table. "Went to work. Don't try to shower. Water isn't hooked up yet. Call when you wake up."

My cell phone was still in my pocket, set to silent mode. I pulled it out and found twenty-five texts from Summer about the previous night's excitement. She'd texted me questions right up until midnight and apparently had thought of plenty more since then:

How's Rhonda?

Is UR mom OK?

Where R U 2day?

I thought about taking the time to answer them all, but the trailer was trembling so much from Marge's incessant thumping, I worried it might collapse. "I can hear you in there!" she yelled. "Open the door!"

"Who is it?" I asked sweetly, simply to get under her skin.

"You know darn well who it is!" Marge snapped, then added, "It's Marge!"

"What can I do for you?"

"Open. The. Door!"

"Why?"

"So I can search your house."

"No."

"Your house is technically the property of FunJungle," Marge growled. "I'm being nice, asking you to open it. If I wanted to, I could just kick the door down."

I didn't challenge her on this. The door was so flimsy, a grasshopper could have kicked it down. It already appeared dented from Marge's knocking.

So I opened the door. Marge stormed right in, barreling past me, her face flushed as red as a uakari monkey's. "You've really done it this time," she told me, going right to our freezer and yanking it open. She seemed surprised to find it empty, save for a few bags of frozen vegetables, then wheeled on me. "Where is it?"

"Where's what?" I asked. "The candy? I already told you I didn't steal that."

"This isn't only about candy anymore and you know it."

"Actually, I don't."

Marge fixed her piggy little eyes on me. "Eleanor Elephant's Ice Cream Eatery was broken into last night. Sixteen gallons of assorted flavors were stolen, including Cheetah Chocolate, Monkey Mint Chip, and Rhino Raspberry Swirl."

"And you think I stole that, too? What would I do with sixteen gallons of ice cream?"

"Eat it."

"I can't eat sixteen gallons of ice cream!"

"If I thought you could eat that much ice cream at once, I wouldn't be here looking for it, would I? I know you stashed it somewhere. But I assure you, I will find it. And when I do, you're getting shipped off to juvenile hall." Marge stomped down the short hallway and went into my bedroom.

I followed and found her tossing my clothes aside. "What are you doing?"

"Looking for the stolen merchandise."

"In my bedroom?"

"It's cold enough in here to keep ice cream."

I couldn't argue with that. "Marge, if you talk to Chief

Hoenekker, he'll tell you I was with him until midnight last night. . . ."

"I'm well aware of that."

"So you think that, after all that, I went back to FunJungle and robbed the ice cream stand?"

"I don't think anything."

"No kidding."

Marge tossed aside a handful of shirts and wheeled on me. "I *know* you did this. What better time to commit a crime than right after you've been with security? You might have everyone else here fooled with your goody-two-shoes act, but not me."

I sagged against the doorjamb. "Why are you so determined to get me arrested?"

"Because it's my job. I'm supposed to root out trouble at FunJungle—and you're trouble."

"No, I'm not."

"You're not the one who jammed porcupine quills in the seat of my security vehicle?"

"No," I said, although it was a lie. Not only had I placed the quills pointy-end up in her cart, but I'd also surreptitiously recorded her sitting on them and then posted it on YouTube.

Marge glared at me. "It took the doctor an hour to dig those out of my behind."

"Well, it probably took him a while to find them. He had a big area to search."

"That does it!" Marge pounded across the room toward me, as menacing as any of the gaurs had been the night before. She backed me into a corner and stabbed a thick finger into my chest. "I have had it with you, Fitzroy! One way or another, I am going to catch you one of these days, and when I do, I am going to wipe that smug little smile off your face for good! You are a nuisance, a pest, and an all-around bad egg!"

"And you're a bully," I said.

Marge reared back as though she'd been slapped. "What'd you call me?"

"A bully. You're even worse than Vance Jessup. He was only a dumb teenager trying to make himself feel good by picking on smaller kids. You're an adult and you're doing the same thing. You've always been after me." I'd never really thought of Marge in these terms until I'd said the words, but as I spoke, I realized I was right. "There's no evidence that I broke into that candy store or that ice cream shop, but you're determined to pin it on me anyhow, just like you were with the theft of the koala."

For a brief moment, it looked as though I might have actually gotten through to Marge. A glimmer of understanding flashed in her eyes. But then it was gone, replaced by anger again. "There might not be any evidence now, but if it's out there, I assure you, I'll find it." She turned away and went back to ransacking my room.

I started to protest, but as I watched Marge flinging my clothes about, I was struck by a thought. "Did you take pictures of the ice cream shop after the break-in?"

"Of course. Procurement of photographic evidence is standard procedure."

"Can I see them?"

Marge turned back to me. Somehow she'd managed to get a dirty sock of mine perched on her shoulder, but she didn't even notice. "You already know what it looks like. You did it."

"So?"

Marge considered that for a moment, then dug her phone out and brought up the photos. "Fine. Want to see the damage you did? Here you go." She slapped the phone into my hands. "You try to erase any of those pictures, though, and I'll arrest you for tampering with evidence."

I examined the photos closely. Like the candy store, the ice cream shop hadn't merely been burglarized; it had practically been destroyed. Once again, the front window had been shattered by having a trash can pitched through it. The floor was strewn with broken glass and garbage. The glass freezer cases that held the ice cream had been busted as well.

I found a photo that showed the garbage can lying on its side. It was one of the big metal ones that were all over FunJungle. (J.J. McCracken had insisted on having one every twenty feet; he had research stating that the basic theme-park tourist was so lazy, if they had to walk any farther to get to a garbage can, they'd end up simply dropping the trash on the ground.) The can was more than three feet tall with a solar compactor built into it.

A thought occurred to me. "Marge, this garbage can is huge. You really think that *I* could throw it through a plate-glass window?"

Marge began to argue, then stopped, her mouth half open, as she realized I had a point. "Maybe. It's only a trash can."

"I'll bet it weighs a hundred pounds. I can't lift a hundred pounds."

Marge narrowed her eyes. "Maybe you had help, then. Like that friend of yours who's always hanging around with you. Paco?"

"Xavier?"

"That's the one! He looks like he likes candy and ice cream. And that'd explain why the contraband isn't here: It's at his place!"

I gaped at Marge, stunned that she'd managed to take a solid piece of evidence that I was innocent and implicate my best friend with it as well. "Xavier didn't help me with this! No one did!"

"Aha!" Marge cried. "So you admit you did it!"

"No! Think about this!" I held up her phone, displaying her own picture of the destroyed ice cream store to her. "If I really wanted to get away with stealing all this ice cream, I wouldn't leave such a huge mess behind. In fact, I'd try to not make a mess at all so no one would even know I'd broken in. Here the ice cream hasn't only been stolen. All the furniture has been knocked over. And the freezer's been smashed open, even though there's no lock on it."

Marge chewed her lip, actually trying to think. It looked like it wasn't easy for her. But then, Marge didn't have much practice at thinking. "What's your point?"

"This wasn't about getting candy or ice cream. It was about vandalism."

"So, you and your pal vandalized the place. That's still a crime."

"Why would I do that?"

"Because you're trouble. Like I said."

"You think that, after all the commotion last night, I came back here and called Xavier, then had him come down to the park so we could trash the ice cream place, and then we both went home and pretended to go to sleep?"

"Maybe you decided to make it look like a bunch of

vandals to cover up the fact that you really wanted all the ice cream."

"Or maybe someone else did it besides me. An adult. Someone who could actually lift that giant trash can and throw it."

"And why would an adult do that?"

"I don't know."

Marge snorted in disgust, then returned to searching my room, opening the cabinets of my dresser, as if I might have actually hidden sixteen gallons of ice cream there.

I was annoyed at myself for not having a better answer for her. It felt like there was something important I was overlooking about the thefts, something that would help make sense of them, but to my frustration, I couldn't figure out what it was. I wondered if I was still tired from the events of the day before.

"Why don't you check the video from the park?" I asked.

"I already told you, there weren't any cameras aimed at the concessions."

"But there's cameras everywhere else, right? There are thousands in the park. If you look through the footage from around the ice cream place, you ought to be able to find someone heading there in the middle of the night."

"You think it didn't occur to me to check the other cameras?" Marge demanded. "I'm not an idiot."

That's news to me, I thought, but I didn't say it. I'd already antagonized Marge enough. Instead, I asked, "So why haven't you done it?"

"Because I don't have the authority, thanks to you. Now that I'm not in charge of security anymore, I have to file a requisition for someone to comb through the footage—and right now everyone's focused on this whole rhino thing instead. They're checking all the camera feeds for any sign of the hunter from last night, so I have to wait in line. Apparently, these rhinos are higher priority than my case."

"Well, someone *is* trying to kill them," I pointed out.

"And I'm dealing with the theft and destruction of official FunJungle property. Rest assured, though, when my time comes, I'm gonna give that footage a good, hard look. And if I find you anywhere even *close* to that ice cream shop around the time of the crime, I'm gonna have you in juvenile hall so fast, it'll make your head spin."

"And if you see someone else instead?"

Marge rolled her eyes. "That'll be the day."

Obviously, I wasn't going to talk any sense into her. And I didn't feel like waiting around for her to search the whole trailer. Our home wasn't big, but if Marge wanted to be thorough, she could still end up wasting a lot of my time. So when she got down on her hands and knees to search under my bed, I quietly backed out of my room and slipped out of the trailer.

The keys to Marge's golf cart were dangling in the ignition. I removed them and flung them into the woods. It was antagonistic and immature, but, I figured, you had to fight back against bullies any way you could. Besides, Marge could use more exercise.

I was twenty yards away from the house before Marge even noticed I was gone. Her voice suddenly boomed through Lakeside Estates, loud enough to startle birds into flight. "Teddy! Get back here! I'm not done with you yet!"

I didn't even look back. Instead, I picked up my pace, ducking through the woods toward FunJungle.

Behind me, I could hear the door bang as Marge stormed out of our trailer. "This isn't over, Teddy!" she yelled after me. "I'll get you if it's the last thing I ever do!"

THE HOSPITAL

Mom wasn't at her office at Monkey Mountain. Kyle Reims, a young primatologist, was there instead. Kyle was still in college at the University of Texas, taking a semester off to do research on baboons; Mom was letting him use a spare desk in her office. He was tall and gangly, with hair that flopped down over his eyes. "Your mom's ankle was bothering her," he told me. "So she went to have Doc check it out."

Doc Deakin was FunJungle's head veterinarian. FunJungle had an actual doctor on staff—and a full medical clinic, given that the closest hospital was forty-five minutes away—but Mom and Dad both thought the doctor wasn't nearly as qualified as Doc. After all, Doc was one of the best vets in the world, while FunJungle's doctor had barely graduated from medical school.

"How long ago did she leave?" I asked.

Kyle checked his watch. "An hour at most. She's probably still there. Her ankle was looking pretty bad."

"Like how?"

"All purple and swollen. Hey, if you see Doc while you're there, could you tell him to call me? I think Bababoonie needs to see him."

Bababoonie was the alpha male gelada baboon. He was pretty scary as far as monkeys went. Baboons have serious fangs, and Bababoonie was always baring his at people, like he was a monkey vampire.

"Is that what Doc was here about last night?" I asked.

"No. He was here for one of the orangutans. Pancake, I think. He wasn't feeling good."

I glanced at Mom's desk. Her computer could access the security system, allowing Mom to bring up the feeds from any camera at Monkey Mountain. This meant she could watch any primate she wanted to without the animal knowing it was being watched. The feed for the backstage area of the orangutan exhibit was on her screen. I figured Mom must have been using it to check on Pancake before she decided to go see Doc.

Pancake was the only orangutan in the backstage area. It was easy to recognize him because he had a shock of orange hair that always stood up on top of his head, making him look like a perpetually frightened cartoon character. The rest of the orangs were on display in their exhibit. FunJungle went to a lot of effort to make sure this happened, because guests didn't like looking at empty exhibits. ("It's like paying for a museum and seeing only blank walls," J.J. had groused. "So make sure it doesn't happen.") All the exhibits at Monkey Mountain had been designed to be extremely comfortable and stimulating, with plenty of things to play on and the heat cranked up to tropical rain forest temperatures. The orangutan habitat had tons of plants, a waterfall, and a jungle gym of fake trees. The backstage area wasn't quite as nice to look at, but there was a great deal to stimulate the apes there, too: ropes to climb, cardboard boxes to shred, big plastic balls to throw around. Pancake wasn't playing with any of it, which was unusual. He was only eight years old and was normally a whirlwind of energy, bouncing off the walls. Today, however, he was merely lolling on a pile of burlap bags.

"What's wrong with him?" I asked.

Kyle shrugged. "I don't deal with orangs. I'm the baboon guy."

I got the impression that he wanted to do other things besides talk to me, so I said good-bye and headed across FunJungle to find my mother.

It was now nine thirty, only half an hour until FunJungle

opened for the day. There were lots of employees out now, making sure the park looked perfect.

I passed the wreckage of the Gorilla Grill. Pete Thwacker was there, watching a small bulldozer knock over the remaining walls.

"Getting ready to build the new restaurant?" I asked.

"No," Pete replied. "I'm only having this knocked down."

"Wait. You're making the mess *worse*?"

"We're enhancing the viewer experience," Pete corrected. "According to an exit survey we conducted yesterday, some of our guests were disappointed by the stampede scene. Apparently, there wasn't as much destruction as they'd hoped for."

"Half the restaurant was destroyed!"

"Yes. You'd think that a herd of elephants would have trampled the *whole* thing. But they didn't. It only looked damaged, rather than totaled. And if you don't meet the guests' expectations, that's a problem."

"So the elephant stampede wreckage didn't look enough like elephant stampede wreckage?"

"Exactly! Frankly, I would have preferred to do this more authentically. But J.J. is simply refusing to let me stampede the elephants again. In fact, he wouldn't even let them do their morning walk today. Apparently, he thinks it could be dangerous." Pete sighed and shook his head sadly.

"I would have thought you'd approve of that," I said.

"Well, I certainly don't want anyone getting hurt, but at the same time, you have to give the public what they want." Pete scratched his chin thoughtfully. "There must be some way to convince him to do this."

"Convince J.J. to let a herd of elephants destroy more of his park?"

"Well, not a lot more of it, of course. But some. He's never liked the Cajun restaurant here. Maybe I could convince him to let the elephants trample that. That'd be a win-win for everyone."

I shook my head. "If the elephants can't walk around the park in the morning, how are they supposed to get enough exercise?"

Pete's trademark grin spread across his face. "Hey, that's a great angle. The elephants' own health and well-being! I'll use that to get them out here again . . . and who knows? Maybe some more magic will happen."

I winced, afraid I'd just given Pete a good argument that would lead to more trouble.

"Hey," he said. "How's Lakeside Estates?"

"It's terrible."

Pete's smile faltered. "Oh, come now. It's much better than the last place you lived."

"It's exactly the same as the last place we lived. Only now

we have a big mud pit beside the house, no neighbors, and no running water."

"They haven't hooked up your water yet?"

"No."

"Well, I'm sure they will soon. In the meantime, it could be fun. You guys all lived in a tent when you were in Africa, right? You didn't have water then. So now it's kind of like a trip down memory lane."

"We had to poop in the bushes in Africa. You want us to start doing that here?"

Pete made a face of disgust. "Er . . . no. Come to think of it, scratch the whole memory lane thing. I'll make sure someone from plumbing gets out there today." There was a crash nearby as a wall collapsed. Pete turned to the bulldozer driver and desperately signaled him to stop. "Whoa! That's too much! I need this to look like elephants did it, not a wrecking crew!" He ran over to explain his artistic vision, and I continued on my way.

We hadn't really pooped in the bushes in Africa. We'd had a solar-powered composting pit toilet, but Pete didn't have to know that.

I stopped at Eleanor Elephant's Ice Cream Eatery next. Unlike the stampeded Gorilla Grill, this site had been cleaned up quickly. (I'd heard Carly Cougar's Candy Counter had been cleaned up too.) Either Pete Thwacker didn't know this was happening, or he'd decided that a smash-and-grab robbery site wasn't nearly as good for luring tourists as stampede wreckage. A crew of workmen was already fitting the windows with replacement glass. By the time the park opened, the shop would look good as new. It was ruined as a crime scene, however. All evidence had been swept away. FunJungle's sanitation crew was loading the last of the debris onto a flatbed truck; there were dozens of trash bags full of it. Two men were struggling to lift the trash can that had been thrown through the window on board.

I stared at them, struck by a thought. The trash can was even heavier than I'd realized. The sanitation guys were big and strong and they were having trouble moving it *together*. A new one had already been placed where the old one had been taken from. With the built-in solar compactor, it was a big, blocky object. I shoved against it and found I could barely budge the thing.

Suddenly, I had an idea who might have trashed the ice cream shop. And the candy store.

I ran the rest of the way to the veterinary hospital. Normally, I wouldn't have been allowed past the lobby, but the moment I entered, Roz, the receptionist, greeted me by saying, "Hi, Teddy. Here to see your mom?"

"I heard she's with Doc," I said.

"They're in operating room two. I'm sure she'd love to see

you." Roz pressed a buzzer under her desk, and the door to the hospital clicked open. I stepped in the tub of disinfectant to get any contaminants off my shoes and then passed through.

I couldn't help but peek through the windows in operating room one as I passed. Two vets and a nurse had an unconscious kangaroo on the operating table. I couldn't tell what they were doing, but I figured it wasn't an emergency, because if it had been, then Doc probably would have been in there with them.

Sure enough, Mom and Doc were in operating room two. The operating rooms looked very much like regular human operating rooms, only much bigger. Even the doors were enormous, so that something as big as a water buffalo could get through them. Mom sat on the operating table in the middle of the room, while Doc perched on a low stool, wrapping plaster around her ankle. Athmani was there as well, although it was evident his presence had nothing to do with Mom's ankle. He was talking to Doc.

Athmani and Doc were both facing away from me. I slipped inside so quietly, neither of them noticed me. Only Mom did. She grinned and gave me a wink as I came in.

"You won't even *consider* removing the horns?" Athmani was asking.

"No, I'll consider it," Doc grumbled. "But only as a last resort. And we're not there yet." Doc really cared about animals, but he wasn't so good with people. The only person he seemed to truly like was my mother. (He had a wife and a grown-up daughter, whom I assumed he was nice to as well, but I'd never met them.)

"Not there yet!" Athmani cried. He seemed extremely frustrated with this conversation. "Two attempts have already been made on Rhonda's life!"

"*One* attempt," Doc corrected. "As far as I know, that intruder didn't take a shot at her last night."

"He still had a rifle," Mom pointed out.

"That's right!" Athmani exclaimed. "If Charlene and Jack hadn't stopped him, we'd have a dead rhino on our hands right now."

"That's only speculation." Doc wrapped another strip of plaster around Mom's ankle. "The only thing we know that Charlene and Jack's actions did for sure was get Charlene's ankle busted." He turned his attention to Mom and said, for what probably wasn't the first time, "What were you even thinking, running around in that exhibit at night?"

"We *weren't* thinking," Mom replied, more to me than Doc. "We were worried about the animals."

"Exactly my point!" Athmani agreed. "We *all* should be worried about the animals."

Doc ignored him and stayed focused on Mom. "You really should have had this treated last night."

"I didn't realize how bad it was," Mom said.

Doc gave her a hard stare. "And you should have gone to a real doctor."

"You *are* a real doctor," Mom told him.

"I'm only seeing you because you let this go too long without attention as it was," Doc said. "You're lucky it wasn't worse."

Athmani interrupted, determined to get answers. "Exactly how bad do things have to get before you will admit we have an emergency on our hands here? Does a rhino actually have to die before you will act?"

Doc stiffened. Although his back was to me, I could tell he was angry. "I'm not making this decision lightly. Cutting off a rhino's horn isn't easy."

"I'm well aware of that . . . ," Athmani began.

"I'm not so sure you are," Doc snapped. "It takes quite a long time, which is complicated by the fact that the rhino doesn't want it done. Which means you have to sedate them. And sedation is always dicey. You put an animal to sleep, and there's always a chance it won't wake up again. I'm not about to do it for some unnecessary surgery. Especially not on a rhino that's pregnant."

"This surgery *isn't* unnecessary," Athmani protested.

"It very well could be," Doc shot back. "From what I understand, Chief Hornblower or whatever his name is has got men doing everything they can to find this hunter. If they can find him before he tries again—or scare him off for good—then we don't need to deface our rhinos."

"It's not defacement," Athmani argued. "The horn will grow back after a while."

"And you know as well as I do that removing the horn doesn't always—" Doc froze in midthought. He suddenly spun to face me, having sensed I was in the room somehow. "Teddy! What are you doing back here?"

"I came to see my mom."

"Go wait in the lobby. You can see her when I'm done."

"Doc!" Mom chided. "That's my son you're talking to!" She always seemed to think Doc was only pretending to be crotchety, like it was a joke. It wasn't, though. Doc was prick-lier than an angry porcupine.

Athmani was far more pleased to see me. He gave me a smile and a slight bow. "Good morning, Teddy. I hear you had quite an adventure last night."

"Yeah," I agreed. "What were you saying, Doc? About the dehorned rhinos?"

"It's none of your business," Doc growled.

Athmani answered me instead. "He was going to say that removing the horn doesn't always deter poachers."

"What do you mean?" I asked.

Doc said, "There have been cases in Africa where, even

after rhinos were dehorned, poachers killed them anyhow."

"*Rare* cases," Athmani pointed out.

"Still, it happened," Doc said.

"Why would someone kill the rhinos if they didn't have horns?" I asked.

Athmani shrugged. "Who knows why any human does anything so cruel? Some people think it's because you can't ever remove the whole horn, and so even the tiny bit that is left is worth killing for. But others think it's a statement by the poachers, that no matter what we try to do to stop them, it won't work."

"That's crazy," I said.

"Yes," Athmani agreed. "But they did it anyway." He turned back to Doc. "This is not Africa, though. Removing the horns here should deter any poacher."

"We have an entire security force whose job it is to deter poachers," Doc retorted. "You ought to be bugging them about this, not me."

"I *am* bugging them about this!" Athmani exclaimed. "I'm doing everything I can to protect these animals! I was hoping you'd care about them just as much!"

Doc grew angrier than I'd ever seen him—and I'd seen him plenty angry. He put the last bit of plaster on Mom's cast, then stood slowly, glaring bullets at Athmani. "Don't you ever accuse me of not caring for the animals at this park.

I spend sixteen hours a day, if not more, every day, looking after them. I care for them as much as any person here. And that is why I'm not going to do surgery on them without proper cause. Until there's concrete proof that dehorning the rhinos is going to save their lives, it's an unnecessary risk."

Athmani backed away, looking a bit ashamed of how he'd spoken to Doc. "And what if I *do* get concrete proof?"

"Then we can talk." Doc turned back to Mom. "It's going to take a few more minutes for that to set. You'll be able to get around on that leg, but you really ought to go over to the medical clinic and get some crutches. I don't have any here. My patients usually don't know how to use them."

Mom nodded. "Thanks, Doc."

"What's wrong with your ankle?" I asked.

"I fractured a bone," Mom replied. "It's no big deal."

"It's a very big deal," Doc corrected. "Injuries like this are nothing to take lightly. You need to be careful. Don't do anything stupid like chasing poachers through a herd of wild cattle from now on."

"Aye-aye." Mom saluted, then looked at me. "Was there a reason you were trying to find me, Teddy?"

"Marge came to the trailer this morning," I said.

Mom frowned. "What did she want now?"

"Remember the candy store robbery she thought I did? Well, last night, someone broke into the ice cream shop."

"And she accused you of that, too?" Mom asked.

Athmani had been preparing to leave, but now he stopped, intrigued. "When did this happen last night? At the same time as the poacher?"

"I think it happened later than that," I told him. "And I think one of the orangutans did it."

Athmani laughed, then caught himself. "You're serious?"

"Yes." I turned to my mother. "I'm pretty sure it was Pancake."

I couldn't quite read the expression on my mother's face. She looked a bit amused herself but also concerned. "Teddy, that's not possible. Pancake hasn't escaped."

"Well, what if he'd figured out how to get out of his cage and then got back in again?"

Mom pursed her lips, considering this. "I've never heard of that happening before. . . ."

"But it could, right?"

"Why are you so sure this was Pancake?"

"I saw the wreckage of the ice cream shop. Whoever broke in threw one of those big solar-compactor garbage cans through the window. But those things are so heavy, I don't think most grown-up men could even do that. Orangutans are a lot stronger than we are, though."

"That's true," Mom said. "But . . ."

I plowed on before she could contradict me. "Also, the

way the shop was all smashed up was weird. It didn't seem very human. Like, the thief punched through the freezer window instead of just opening it. No human would do that. But an ape might."

"Unless a human wanted us to *think* an ape had done it," Athmani suggested.

"Maybe," I admitted, then looked back to Mom. "But also, Pancake's not feeling well. Is it his stomach?"

Mom grew a bit intrigued. "That's right. Doc said he had indigestion yesterday."

"From eating too much candy?" I asked.

"I didn't determine the exact cause," Doc said sourly. "Pancake merely had an upset stomach. There are hundreds of things that could have caused that."

"He still looks sick this morning," I told him. "Maybe he ate too much ice cream last night! Is there any way we could figure that out for sure?"

"The best way would be to comb through his feces for any signs of undigested candy," Doc said. "You're welcome to do that if you'd like."

I shot him a sidelong glance. "Me? You're the doctor."

"And you're the junior detective. I'll make him feel better. You can look for clues." Doc checked his watch and started for the door. "Speaking of which, I have plenty of other sick animals to attend to today. I've wasted enough time on humans as it is. So, I need you all to clear out."

"Sure," Mom agreed, then looked to Athmani and me. "I could use a little help until I get my crutches, though."

"Of course." Athmani hurried to Mom's side even before I could and helped her hop off the table.

"Careful now, Charlene," Doc warned. "That cast doesn't give you free rein to do anything you want. Your ankle needs time to heal."

"I understand," Mom said. "Thanks."

Doc gave her the tiniest hint of a smile—which was the most smile I'd ever seen him give anyone—and then slipped out of the operating room.

I came to my mother's other side so she could put an arm around me, and we headed for the door. "So? Do you think I could be right about Pancake?"

"It's hard to believe," Mom said. "But if I had to bet on any animal being clever enough to get out of its cage and then get back in again, it'd be an orangutan."

"Why is that?" Athmani asked.

"They're incredible escape artists." Mom limped out of the operating room using Athmani and me as crutches, trying to keep any pressure off the foot in the cast. "Much more than the other apes."

"I thought chimpanzees were smarter than orangs," Athmani said.

"It's not an issue of intelligence," Mom explained. "It's about temperament. Suppose you accidentally leave screwdrivers in the cages of a chimp, a gorilla, and an orangutan. The chimp will probably try to use the screwdriver as a weapon. The gorilla will try to eat it. But the orang will hide it, watch you until it figures out how to use it, then wait for a quiet night when no one's paying attention and take its whole cage apart."

"Whoa," Athmani said, sounding impressed.

"There's an older orangutan here named Bung," I told him. "He used to get out all the time when the park first opened."

"Yes," Mom said. "Though all the security systems at Monkey Mountain weren't in place yet. And we devised some new ones after watching Bung. They all seem to have worked. We haven't had an escape in months."

"That you know of," I told her.

Mom said, "Why on earth would Pancake break out of his exhibit, attack the ice cream and candy stores, and then break back in again?"

"Because that's his home," I answered. "It's nice and warm in there, but it's freezing outside. Pancake isn't used to cold weather. He's from Indonesia."

"Also, his family is in there too," Athmani added. "Apes are very close to their families, yes?"

Mom looked at him, surprised. "You're on board with this idea too?"

"In the safari camps, you wouldn't believe what the monkeys get into," Athmani told her. "No matter how hard we try to lock things up, they always figure it out. We had a vervet monkey in Kruger who not only stole bottles of wine, but even learned how to use the corkscrew to open them. And he always stole the expensive bottles. Never the cheap stuff. That's only a monkey. If orangutans are as clever as you say, I'm sure they could cause a great deal of trouble."

He and I held open the doors to the lobby, and Mom hobbled through them.

Roz beamed from behind her desk. "Looks like Doc fixed you up nice and good, Charlene!"

Mom smiled. "He did."

Roz said, "I'll bet he appreciated working on something with only two legs for a change."

"I'm not so sure," Mom replied.

We continued out the front doors, into the cold.

"Can you check the security cameras at Monkey Mountain to see if Pancake got out last night?" I asked.

"I will," Mom agreed. "Although I think I have to ask security for help with that. They're the ones who control the recordings."

Athmani's phone beeped as a text message arrived. He paused to check it. "Speak of the devil. It's from Hoenekker." His eyes widened in excitement as he read on.

"Well?" Mom asked. "Has he found something?"

"Security footage of the hunter," Athmani replied excitedly. "We have a lead!"

12

SECURITY FOOTAGE

Once Athmani and I got Mom to the FunJungle medical clinic, Mom insisted we didn't have to sit around and wait to get her crutches with her. After she'd hobbled inside, Athmani surprised me by inviting me to come to his office to see the security footage Hoenekker had found.

"You're okay with that?" I asked.

"Why wouldn't I be? J.J. said you should be involved."

"Chief Hoenekker seems annoyed about the whole thing."

Athmani laughed. "He's annoyed that J.J. wants me involved as well. But we had a saying back in Africa: The more lions on the hunt, the better the chance that they eat."

Athmani's office was in the administration building, where most of the offices at FunJungle were. It looked like it had barely been used, which made sense because Athmani hadn't been working at FunJungle very long and he was usually out in the park. There was a desk, a computer, and plenty of office supplies that hadn't even been unpacked: boxes of pens and pencils, stacks of shrink-wrapped legal pads, a printer that was still in its original packaging.

"There's no chairs," I pointed out.

Athmani looked around, surprised. "It seems there aren't. I've never had anyone else in here."

"Don't *you* need one?"

"I'm rarely in here long enough to sit down. And besides, I prefer to stand. It's better for your health. It keeps the blood flowing." Athmani checked his watch. "I expected Hoenekker to be here by now. He sounded very pleased with himself."

The only personal items in the office were five small stone sculptures arrayed on the desk. They were all elephants, but they were abstract in form, full of delicate curves. One wasn't finished yet, still emerging from a chunk of rough-hewn gray rock. Athmani picked this one up along with a smaller white stone, which he rubbed against the unfinished rock.

"You make Shona sculpture?" I asked.

Athmani seemed surprised by my question at first and then pleased. "You know about Shona?"

"When we lived in the Congo, we got down to southern Africa a few times. I saw it there."

Athmani smiled. "My father is a sculptor in Zimbabwe. He taught me."

"It's very good."

"That is very nice of you to say. Though it's not nearly as good as my father's. I only do it to relax. It reminds me of home, of my family." Athmani stared at the sculpture in his hands as he spoke, rubbing it again and again with the white stone. With each stroke, tiny bits of the larger gray rock shaved off.

I noticed the carpet around the desk was covered with them, a field of flakes and curls.

"When do you get to go back home?" I asked.

"When I finish my work here, whenever that may be." Athmani sighed. "I thought I would be here only a few weeks, but as this rhino business shows us, there is a lot more to be done here than I expected."

"Like what?"

"Ideally, there ought to be a *wall* around this entire property, not a fence. The ease with which the poacher got onto the property last night was very disturbing. Plus, if anyone wanted to merely kill the animals for sport, they could easily shoot *through* the fence. You can't shoot through a wall. Sadly, J.J. is digging his heels in on this."

"Because walls are expensive?"

Athmani laughed. "I see you know how J.J. thinks. He's

balking at the price, even when his animals' lives are on the line. Although he claims it isn't only about the money. He says walls are ugly and make the animals look like they are in a prison. Fences blend in more. It looks like the animals are still in the wild. Or so he says."

"Is there any way to protect the animals without a wall?"

"There are certainly other ways to improve security. Although there are security cameras all over this park, there are barely any along the outer fence. Only one every fifty meters or so. And the fence ought to be electrified. Then no one would be able to simply climb over it with only a towel. It's as though it never occurred to anyone that somebody might want to harm the animals in this park."

I nodded agreement, although the truth was, I couldn't really blame J.J. It would never have occurred to *me* that someone would want to shoot the animals inside a zoo. The idea of it was so horrible, I still had trouble believing it was happening.

My phone buzzed in my pocket. I pulled it out to find yet another text from Summer. She was obviously getting annoyed that I hadn't been responding. This one was filled with extra exclamation marks to convey her annoyance: *Where R U?!!!!!!!!!!*

While Athmani worked on his sculpture, I stepped aside and wrote back: *Investigating.*

Summer responded: *U free @4 2day?*

I felt my heart rate spike, as it always did when Summer asked if I was free to see her. *Yes. Why?*

Got a lead.

What?

Tell U l8r.

Before I could press Summer for details, Chief Hoenekker walked into the office. He stopped in his tracks upon seeing me and frowned. "Shouldn't you be in school right now?"

"Since I was up so late with the poacher last night, my parents said I didn't have to go."

"Can't say I approve of that."

"Well, you're not my parents."

Athmani interrupted, trying to be diplomatic. "I invited Teddy to join us, Chief. I thought J.J. would have wanted him here."

Hoenekker's face quivered, like he was trying to keep himself from blowing his stack. Eventually, he muttered, "Fine," although he obviously didn't think this was fine at all.

Athmani waved to his computer. "So let's see what you have to show us."

Hoenekker took a flash drive from his pocket, plugged it into the computer, and uploaded some video files. "This is footage from our security cameras in the Asian Plains last night. I've had men combing through the camera feeds all night, and this is what they found. I shouldn't have to remind you, but this footage is extremely confidential and not to be discussed out of this room. Almost no one else has seen it. Now, this first bit is from the perimeter fence, right where the hunter came over last night."

A window opened on the computer screen, displaying the footage. The camera appeared to be posted atop the fence itself and was filming down the length of it, so the long stretch of barbed wire eight feet above the ground was pretty much all we could see. The video was color, but since it was nighttime, everything was in night-vision green. A time stamp at the bottom of the screen indicated the footage had been shot at 6:16 p.m.

Suddenly, a towel was unfurled over the barbed wire a few feet from the camera. It was a thick, plush towel, which lay heavily on the wire, covering the barbs. Then the poacher scrambled up over the fence, using the towel to protect himself from the wire, and dropped into the Asian Plains.

The entire break-in took less than ten seconds. The poacher was barely more than a blur.

Athmani whistled, like he was impressed. "He did that even faster than I expected. Is there any way to get an image of him?"

"My men have already done that." Hoenekker brought

up another image, this one only a still frame from the footage we'd just seen. "Here we go."

The image wasn't much help. The poacher was merely a dark, fuzzy shape. It was hard to even make out the arms and legs.

"Unfortunately, our target's rear end is facing the camera in this image," Hoenekker explained. "So we're basically looking at his butt. However, we can tell a few things. He's wearing camouflage, boots, and gloves. . . ."

"So, he basically looks like every other hunter in the state of Texas," Athmani said grumpily.

"Not exactly. We can also see the gun he's using." Hoenekker pointed to a long object strapped to the hunter's back. "Admittedly, this isn't a great image, but I can confirm this is most likely a .375 H&H Magnum rifle."

"As we suspected." Athmani sighed.

"Why's it so long?" I asked, pointing to the end of the barrel. It stretched well past the hunter's shoulder, going out of the frame.

"The H&H is a long rifle to begin with," Hoenekker informed me, "although it appears this one has been fitted with a silencer."

"Really?" I said. "'Cause he didn't use a silencer the first time."

Hoenekker and Athmani both turned to me.

"We *heard* the shot yesterday morning," I reminded them. "That's what spooked the elephants."

"Ah!" Athmani's eyes lit up. "Very good observation, Teddy! No wonder J.J. wanted you working on this."

Hoenekker scowled. "It probably doesn't mean anything."

"Why would the hunter not use a silencer in the morning, then bring one at night?" I asked.

"Because he probably realized not using a silencer was a mistake," Hoenekker said curtly. "After it made so much noise in the morning and alerted everyone, he chose to be quiet when he came back."

"You'd think he'd have *known* the gun was going to make a lot of noise," I pointed out.

Hoenekker ignored me, turning his attention back to the computer. "Now, if you'll look at this next shot taken from along the fence . . ."

"Is there any footage of the hunter from inside FunJungle?" Athmani asked.

"No," Hoenekker admitted. "Not that we've found so far. There aren't any cameras inside the SafariLand enclosures. They tried it once, but the animals knocked them all over."

"Are there cameras at the monorail station?" I asked.

"There are!" Athmani exclaimed. "Chief, have you looked

through the footage from when the shot was fired yesterday morning?"

Hoenekker looked as though this conversation were giving him indigestion. "Of course. It was the first thing we looked at. Only . . . there's no footage of the hunter at the monorail."

"Why not?" Athmani asked. "Was something wrong with the cameras?"

"Not as far as I can tell. But the hunter simply doesn't appear on them."

"How is that possible?" Athmani demanded. "This man isn't a ghost!"

"The most likely reason is that we misjudged where the shot was fired from," Hoenekker said. "The hunter isn't on the roof of the monorail station because he didn't fire from the roof of the monorail station."

"Then where did he fire from?" I asked.

"We don't know," Hoenekker admitted. "We are reviewing all other footage from yesterday morning, but so far we haven't found anything."

"So *this* is all you have?" Athmani pointed to the blurry image of the hunter on the fence. "After all your hours of searching through the footage? This is it?"

"No. As I was trying to say before I was interrupted . . ." Hoenekker gave me a pointed stare, as though I were the only one who had been asking questions. "We have another shot from the perimeter fence. In fact, it's from the same camera the last shot came from. The hunter went out the same way he came in."

Hoenekker ran the second piece of footage. The angle was the exact same as in the first piece. The towel still hung over the barbed wire, weighing it down. According to the time stamp, it was now 6:41 p.m., which was a few minutes after my family had spotted him. The hunter suddenly leaped into the frame, grabbing the towel and scrambling over the wires. Even though it happened as quickly as the first scaling of the fence, there was something different about this one. The first time the hunter had gone over, the movements had been smooth and graceful, perfectly planned. Now he was much clumsier, struggling to get over the top.

"He's hurrying this time," Athmani observed.

"Well, he was on the run," Hoenekker pointed out. "Teddy's father was chasing him. And in his haste, he made a mistake." He brought up another still frame from the footage.

This one was as blurry as the first had been, but there was a difference. Instead of aiming his rear end at the camera, the hunter was facing it. And yet there still wasn't a clear shot of the face. His head was angled downward, as he was focused on clambering over the barbed wire. And he was wearing a mask. A black knit ski cap was pulled down over his face.

"This is no better." Athmani sighed. "We can't tell anything from this!"

"That's not true," Hoenekker argued. "I have my men enhancing this image right now. They've already determined the type of ski mask it is, and we're canvassing all ski shops and sporting goods stores in the area to see if anyone purchased this kind anytime recently."

Athmani asked, "And if your hunter purchased it a year ago? Or longer? Or if they simply stole it? There must be thousands of ski masks like this in the world!"

"It's a start," Hoenekker said.

I stared at the image on the computer more closely. To my disappointment, I couldn't make out a single thing about the hunter. Between the mask, the clothing, and the gloves, there wasn't even a glimpse of skin. In a weird way, there seemed to be nothing human about the figure in the photo, as though a scarecrow were climbing over the fence.

"Wait." Athmani pointed at the screen. "What's that?"

Behind the hunter's head was a dark, twisted shape. It was black, or at least some dark color, so it blended into the night almost perfectly. If Athmani hadn't pointed it out, I might never have noticed it. I leaned in, squinting at it. Beside me, Hoenekker did the same.

The more I stared at the object, the more I could make

out. It snaked out from under the back of the hunter's ski mask, corkscrewing in the air behind his neck. It was even blurrier than the rest of the hunter, but then I realized this was because it wasn't one single object, but thousands, all bound together.

"It's *hair*," I said. "It's a ponytail."

"Whoa," Hoenekker said. "That's not a *he* after all."

"No," Athmani agreed. "It looks like our poacher is a woman."

PANCAKE

"As you can see, all the orangutans are present and accounted for," Kyle teased. "I've been keeping a careful eye on them today."

I sighed, realizing Mom must have told him about my theory. I was back at Monkey Mountain, standing in front of the orang exhibit. I'd stopped there on the way to Mom's office. Kyle had wandered up, a takeout bag from PastafaZoola in his hand. I hadn't actually expected any of the apes to be missing—although, in truth, I'd secretly *hoped* one might be, so it would prove my theory right.

The exhibit, like every other one at Monkey Mountain, was spectacular. It had been modeled after an actual place in the rainforest on Borneo, the orangutans' natural habitat. Although most of the trees were fake, they *looked* real enough, and they provided plenty of places for the orangs to climb and play. Unlike chimps and gorillas, orangutans spend most of their time above the ground, and this was certainly the case at FunJungle. The adults were nestled in crooks of trees, either eating or sleeping, while the younger ones were constantly on the move through the branches. At the moment, to the great delight of the tourists around me, they appeared to be playing a game of arboreal tag, chasing one another all around the forest.

"Where's Pancake?" I asked. "I don't see him."

"My goodness!" Kyle gasped, overdramatically. "You're right! He's busted out again!"

"Where is he really? Still sick?"

"I guess so. You heading to see your mom?"

"Yeah."

"Come on back."

Kyle led me to the closest door that accessed the employee area of Monkey Mountain, then entered that day's code on the security keypad. It clicked open and we slipped through quickly, trying not to draw much attention. A family still noticed us, though. I saw the kids staring after me jealously, wondering why I got to go behind the scenes and they didn't.

If the kids had been able to see the backstage area, they might not have been so jealous. The corridors were dull, unpainted cement, and the housing areas for the animals were much less beautiful than the parts tourists could see. Except for a window that looked out onto the gorilla exhibit, my mother's office looked pretty much like any other office in the world.

On the way through, Kyle paused by a window that went from the hall into the backstage area of the baboon exhibit. I joined him to see what he was looking at.

Bababoonie was curled up in the corner of his cage, which was unusual. As the dominant male, he was extremely proud and was usually parading in front of the tourists. "How's his tooth?" I asked.

"He definitely busted it," Kyle said. "I don't know how. Chewing on the bars or something. One of his big canines. Doc's going to replace it today."

"How?"

"The same way *you'd* get a tooth replaced if you cracked one. Doc will make a mold of the old one, use that to sculpt a new one, and then screw it into Bababoonie's jaw. Primate teeth are almost exactly the same as ours."

He led the way onward to the office.

Dad was waiting there with Mom. Both of them were eating lunch. Homemade tuna-fish sandwiches and carrot sticks. Mom had the camera feed from the orangutan backstage area up on her computer monitor. Pancake was still lounging listlessly. Dad was sitting at Kyle's desk.

"Hey," I said, pleased to see him. "I didn't know you were gonna be here."

Dad tossed me a sandwich wrapped in tinfoil. "If my son's going to play hooky from school, I figure I might as well eat lunch with him."

"That's my desk," Kyle told him.

"Sorry." Dad grabbed his sandwich, hopped out of the chair, and waved graciously to it. "It's all yours," he said, then perched on top of a large black case marked FRAGILE.

"What's that?" I asked, taking a bite of my tuna salad.

"Camera equipment," Dad told me. "To record the orangutans."

"There's already cameras to record the orangutans," Kyle said. He sat at his desk and unloaded his takeout bag from PastafaZoola. He'd gotten the lasagna, which I considered a mistake. It was always frozen and then reheated, and sometimes they didn't cook it all the way through. Kyle was still pretty new at FunJungle, though; he hadn't learned which foods to avoid yet.

"Yes, there are cameras," Mom agreed. "But I can't get what I want off of them at the moment." She turned to me. "I did what you suggested when I got back from Doc's. I called security to see if they could dig up any footage of Pancake getting out of his exhibit. . . ."

Kyle laughed. "You really think that could have happened?"

"I thought it'd be best to examine the evidence before completely dismissing the theory," Mom told him. "Unfortunately, security can't give me the evidence right now. Both techs are too busy scanning all the park footage for any trace of the rhino hunter."

"Oh," I said. While this was disappointing, it was also reassuring to know that security was working so diligently to find the shooter.

Dad patted the black camera case. "So I'm going to install our own camera. Then we'll have access to the footage without needing to go through security. It'll record all night, and we can check it in the morning to see if we really have an escapee or not."

"Looks like not to me." Kyle pointed to the camera feed from the orangutans. "Seeing as Pancake is still there."

"But he's still not feeling well," I countered.

"Animals get sick," Kyle said. "They don't usually break out of their exhibits, rob ice cream stores, and then break back in again."

"Most animals aren't as clever as Pancake is," Mom told him.

Kyle rolled his eyes, like he couldn't believe any of us were taking this seriously, but he didn't say anything else.

"Can we go see Pancake?" I asked.

"After you finish your lunch," Mom said.

I crammed as much of my tuna-fish sandwich into my mouth as I could, then spoke with my cheeks stuffed like a chipmunk's. "Okay. Now?"

Dad laughed while Mom shook her head and sighed. "For heaven's sake, chew your food," she warned. "Or you'll choke to death."

"I'm kind of interested to get in there myself," Dad said, balling his used tinfoil and tossing it into the recycling bin.

Mom knew there was no point in trying to dissuade both of us any longer. "Oh, all right." She grabbed her new crutches and got to her feet.

Dad hoisted the camera case onto his shoulder and started for the door.

I followed him and Mom dropped in behind us.

Kyle waved good-bye from his desk. "Have fun." He jammed a forkful of lasagna in his mouth, then gagged. "Ugh! This is half frozen!"

While he was spitting it into the trash, we slipped out of the office.

"What did Athmani want with you today?" Mom asked as we headed through the corridors of Monkey Mountain.

I was still trying to chew up all the sandwich I had in my mouth. "What do you mean?"

"You went off with him after you left me at the medical clinic." Mom wasn't having any trouble adapting to her crutches at all. In fact, she was flying along on them like she'd been using them her whole life.

I hadn't realized Mom had been watching me with Athmani. I pretended to be busy chewing to give myself time to work out an answer. "He just had some questions about what happened in SafariLand last night."

"Like what?" Mom sounded as though she didn't quite believe me.

"Whether I'd had a good look at the hunter. Did I think he was going after Rhonda again. Stuff like that." I hated lying to my parents. Absolutely hated it. But I knew that if I told them the truth, that J.J. had railroaded me into helping, they'd go right to him to complain, and then J.J. would be upset with me for betraying his confidence and things would probably get worse from there.

"Does security have any leads?" Dad asked.

"Athmani said they had footage of the hunter going over the fence on one of the security cameras, but they couldn't tell anything about him from it." I purposefully omitted the part about the hunter being a woman, because Hoenekker had warned me not to share anything I'd learned after our meeting. Even with my parents.

"They don't have anything?" Mom sighed. "Guess that's why they're monopolizing all the security footage."

"I suppose," I said, although talking about the cameras

made me think of something. I tried to pick my words carefully, not wanting to let on how much I knew. "Dad, you followed the hunter over the fence last night, right?"

"Well, I didn't exactly follow him," Dad corrected. "I lost him in the exhibit. But then I found where he'd gone over and used that route myself."

"Athmani said it was close to where one of the security cameras was posted."

Dad thought about that for a moment. "Was it? I didn't notice. Or maybe I couldn't see it. It was awfully dark out there."

We reached the door to the orangutan area. Inside the employee areas, the doors didn't require coded keypad entries, but there was still security to protect the animals. Mom's official FunJungle ID had an electronic sensor built into it. She waved this in front of a sensor built in the wall—which wasn't so easy to do on crutches—and then the door unlocked automatically. "What are you thinking?" she asked me.

"Well, there aren't very many cameras out on that fence," I said, holding the door open for Mom. "They're pretty spaced out. So why did the hunter go over so close to one?"

"He was in a hurry," Dad said.

"On the way *out*. Not on the way in. If you were going to sneak into the park to commit a crime, you'd probably take your time doing it, right? So wouldn't you scope out the fence and pick the spot *farthest* from a camera?"

Inside the orangutan care room, Mom and Dad both turned to me, impressed. Dad said, "I didn't even think of that. I wonder if Hoenekker has."

I lowered my eyes, even more frustrated that I couldn't reveal I was actually helping investigate.

"Maybe the hunter didn't see the camera," Mom suggested. "Your father didn't see it in the dark."

"But I wasn't looking for it." Dad set the camera case down and popped the latches on it. "If I were planning on sneaking into the zoo—or anyplace—I'd certainly be on the lookout for security cameras."

In a way, Dad was an authority on sneaking into places. On occasion, he had been assigned to take photos of animals in countries that were closed to tourists and journalists. At times like that, he had to find other ways over the border. (For example, he'd once had to infiltrate Somalia to get photos of herola, one of the most endangered antelope in the world.) It was dangerous—Mom had made him promise to stop taking those assignments—but he'd been very good at it. After all, he'd never been caught.

The backstage area for the orangutans was a mess—but there was a good reason for that. Orangutans, like all primates, are very smart and need plenty of mental stimulation. So the keepers gave them lots of stuff to play with—the orangs were very fond of cardboard boxes and burlap bags—as well as mental challenges to work out. These usually involved food; the keepers would hide treats inside wads of newspaper or freeze them inside giant cubes of ice, and the apes would have to figure out how to get it. None of these things were allowed on exhibit because they made a mess and looked inauthentic in the rain forest (as if an Indonesian rain forest inside a fake mountain in Texas was in any way authentic in the first place), but the orangutans loved them, so their backstage area was often full of garbage.

Pancake was the champion cardboard box shredder of the orangs. He could turn a good-size box into scraps within minutes. But today he had ignored the three that had been given to him. In fact, he hadn't moved from his nest of burlap sacks.

However, he perked up as we entered, excited to have company—and intrigued by Dad's big camera case. When Dad opened it, he hauled himself up and approached the bars of his enclosure, grunting eagerly, wondering what could possibly be hidden inside the mysterious black object.

"Hiya, Pancake," Dad said. "You look like you're feeling a little better."

"He does," Mom agreed. "He was pretty miserable when I first saw him this morning."

Pancake knew my whole family and seemed to especially like Dad. Now he grinned at him, revealing a set of teeth that, except for their size, looked surprisingly human.

Although I normally would have been thrilled to be so close to one of the orangutans—it wasn't something I got to do often and it was always a treat—I was distracted by several things at once. I was still thinking about the hunter and how she'd climbed over the fence. It was hard to believe she hadn't seen the security cameras, even at night. If anything, the cameras were *designed* to be seen. That way they'd act as a deterrent; someone was much less likely to climb the fence if they thought they'd be recorded doing it.

Meanwhile, the blurry images of the hunter still stuck in my mind. Although I'd been surprised that the hunter was a woman at first, it sadly didn't narrow the field of suspects down that much. Women might not have hunted as much as men did, but there were still plenty who did it. And lots of them probably had dark hair long enough to make a ponytail out of.

Then there was the gun to consider. The fact that the hunter had been using a silencer at night—but not the previous morning—still nagged at me. Something seemed important about that fact, but I couldn't figure out what it was.

And if all that wasn't enough to distract me, I was finally

in the orangutan habitat, site of the potential jailbreak. As adorable as Pancake was, I found myself drawn to his habitat itself, looking for evidence that there'd been an escape. Unfortunately, I couldn't see any. I realized, to my own annoyance, that I'd been hoping for something obvious, like a poorly hidden tub of melted ice cream or misshapen metal bars that had been twisted open and shut again. Instead, the habitat looked exactly like it always did.

Pancake was sticking his arm through the bars now, palm open, gesturing for Dad to give him what was inside the case. Orangutan arms are startlingly long when fully extended, almost twice the length of the ape's legs.

Dad laughed. "Sorry, buddy. This is way too expensive to let you have it."

Pancake now made an overblown sad face, like a little kid who hadn't gotten what he wanted and was trying to make his parents feel bad about it. And it kind of worked. I immediately started to feel sad for him, even though I knew he was probably only acting.

"Pancake," Mom said, "you know you can't have that. But how about this instead?" She took one of the carrot sticks she'd brought for lunch out of her pocket.

Pancake's frown immediately melted away. His open palm shifted in Mom's direction.

Mom set the carrot in Pancake's hand, and within a

second, it was inside Pancake's mouth. The orangutan happily munched away.

"Doesn't look like your stomach's bothering you anymore," Mom said.

"That doesn't mean he didn't eat the ice cream though, right?" I asked.

"Of course not," Mom replied. "Stomach aches don't last forever."

I asked, "Did anyone ever check his poop for signs of candy?"

Dad wrinkled his nose in disgust. "Eww. Gross."

"I told the orangutan's keepers to keep an eye out," Mom said. "But I didn't hear anything from them."

"Do you think they even did it?" Dad inquired. "I wouldn't sift through orangutan poop if I didn't have to."

Mom shrugged. "It'd probably be a wild-goose chase anyhow. The candy's probably already out—and the chocolate ice cream would have already looked kind of like poop on the way in."

"Please." Dad grimaced. "I just ate."

"Get over it," Mom teased. "You want to work at a zoo, there's going be poop talk."

Pancake finished eating the carrot, then extended his hand for another treat.

Mom turned her pockets inside out to show that they

were empty. "Sorry, Pancake. That's all I had."

Pancake pasted his comic frown back on and immediately aimed his open palm at Dad again.

"Forget it," he told him. "You're not getting this." He took the video camera out of the case.

"Why's that so big?" I asked.

"Because unlike the camera on your phone, this one can record all night. There's sixteen hours of storage in it." Dad looked up at the corners of the room that faced the exhibit. "Guess this should go right up there next to the official security camera."

Sure enough, there was a security camera already mounted in the corner, aimed right at the orangutan exhibit. This was the one Mom had been accessing the feed from in her office. The one security hadn't reviewed the footage from yet.

I looked back to the cage. There was only one gate built into it, a gate that worked like a sliding door rather than hinging open, like a normal door. Instead of a key-based lock, however, it had an electronic one.

"How's that lock work?" I asked.

"The same way the lock on the door to get in here does," Mom said. "With *this*." She pulled out her ID with the electronic sensor, then pointed to a sensor pad on the wall six feet away from the orangutan cage. "If you wave it by that pad, the cage unlocks."

At the sight of the ID card, Pancake forgot all about trying to get the camera from Dad and turned his attention to Mom again.

"Sorry, boy." Mom tucked the card away again. "I was only displaying it. You're not getting out right now."

The frown creased Pancake's face a third time.

"He knows the card opens the gate?" I asked.

"Of course," Mom said. "Pancake doesn't miss a trick."

Dad looked at the gate again, intrigued. "Wasn't there a lock that needed a key here before?"

"Yes," Mom replied. "Back before the park opened. But you might recall that didn't work so well. Bung swiped a key off one of the keepers within the first few days, hid it away, and kept letting himself out at night. So we switched to this new system. Even if the orangutans steal an ID card, they won't be able to work the sensor. It's too far for them to reach—even with those enormous arms."

I looked from Pancake, whose arm was still outstretched, to the sensor on the wall on my side of the bars. Mom was right. The orang was three feet short of being able to trigger the gate to unlock. "But suppose Pancake *did* figure out how to escape the cage? There's nothing that would keep him locked in this room, right?"

"True," Mom agreed.

"So he could go right through the halls and get out into the park?" I asked.

"Yes," Mom said. "It wouldn't be that hard. But getting back *in* would be impossible. At night, Monkey Mountain is locked down tight. You can't enter the building without knowing the entry code—and there's no way an orangutan would know that."

"He could guess it," I suggested.

"Two nights in a row?" Mom asked skeptically. "It changes daily. The odds against guessing the right code *once* must be astronomical, let alone twice. Assuming Pancake even knew how the key-code entry worked in the first place. And then, once he got past that, he'd have to get the code right *again* to access the behind-the-scenes areas—and then he'd *still* need the electronic ID card to get back into this room. Orangutans are smart, but I can't imagine one of them could figure out how to do all that."

"What if he propped all the doors open after he went through them?" I asked. "Then he wouldn't need the codes to get back in."

"Good point," Mom said. "Only, at night, the alarms will trigger if any door is left open for more than five minutes. So that wouldn't work. And if there's any other way in or out of here, I don't have the slightest idea what it could be."

Dad held up the camera he'd brought. "Well, that's what this is for." He looked up to where the other security camera was mounted, high above the floor. "I'll need a ladder to get this up there."

"I think there's one in the maintenance closet," Mom said. "I'll show you where it is."

Dad asked, "Mind if Teddy sticks around and helps me set things up? I could use an extra hand."

I looked to Mom expectantly. "Can I?"

"I suppose," she replied. "Though you two better keep a good eye on your tools. Don't leave them anywhere near Pancake here. If you drop your guard for a moment, he'll swipe something—and the next thing you know, this whole cage will be in pieces. Then we'll be up to our armpits in escaped orangutans."

"We'll be careful," I told her. "I swear."

Dad moved his tools to the wall right beside the door, several feet out of Pancake's reach. Then we headed out to get the ladder.

As we did, Pancake starting hooting sadly. We all turned back to him.

He was frowning again, smushing his face between the bars, making himself look as pitiful as possible.

"He doesn't want us to leave," I said.

"He doesn't really care if we leave or not," Mom said.

"He's only trying to manipulate us. Pancake's as smart as they come. If any orang *could* figure out how to get out of here and back in again, I'd bet on him."

We left the room. Pancake hooted even more sadly, but after the door closed, I glanced back through the window at him. The frown instantly left his face, and he quickly turned his attention to shredding one of the cardboard boxes.

"I'll be darned," Dad said. "That ape could win an Oscar."

My phone buzzed in my pocket. I pulled it out to see that Summer was calling. "Mind if I take this?" I asked. "It's important."

"Who is it?" Mom inquired.

"Summer," I said.

Dad and Mom instantly shared a knowing smile, then turned away hoping I wouldn't see it.

I sighed, stepped away from them, and answered. "Aren't you supposed to be in class right now?"

"You should talk," Summer shot back. "You aren't even in *school*. We still on for four o'clock today?"

"Sure. Where are we going?"

"To Violet Grace's aunt and uncle's ranch."

My parents were trying to act like they weren't eavesdropping on my conversation, but they were. Dad whispered something to Mom that made her giggle, and then she punched him in the arm lightly. I figured it all had to do with me and Summer.

"Why?" I asked.

"Remember those exotic game ranches we were talking about yesterday? The ones where people pay to kill animals from all over the world? Well, they own the biggest one in this whole area."

I lowered my voice so my parents wouldn't hear me as I asked, "And you think they might have something to do with Rhonda?"

"Probably not," Summer said. "But they know pretty much every big-game hunter for a couple hundred miles in any direction. Which means they might have a very good idea who our poacher is."

THE GAME

Summer's driver, Tran, picked me up at FunJungle and brought me to school. Only, we couldn't simply grab Summer and Violet and head out to the ranch, because there was a basketball game, and as head cheerleader, Violet had to be there.

The game was just starting the third quarter when I arrived. We were already down by twenty-six points to Eisenhower Middle School—though, sadly, that was actually pretty good for us. Our basketball team was pathetic. Two weeks before, we'd lost to a team that had only four players. There was almost no one in the stands except for the team's families. Despite this, Violet and the other cheerleaders were still prancing on the sidelines, doing their best to keep the small crowd revved up.

"We're awesome!" they chanted, even though this obviously wasn't the case. "Oh yeah, we're awesome. A-W-E-S-O-M-E. That's right, we're awesome!"

Behind them, one of our forwards took a shot and missed the hoop by ten feet.

It wasn't hard to spot Summer in the sparsely filled stands. She was wearing her usual pink, and Hondo was looming close by. She waved to me, then pointed to the seat she'd saved for me, as if there weren't a few hundred free seats available around her.

I circled around the court to join them, trying my best to be inconspicuous. After all, I'd skipped school that day and now there I was at the game. It was hard to be inconspicuous around Summer, though. The few kids who were actually in the stands ignored the game to stare at me.

Eisenhower's team blew through our defense like it was made out of tissue paper and scored an easy layup.

"That's all right. That's okay," Violet and the cheerleaders chanted supportively. "We're gonna come back anyway!"

I was almost to the stands when someone grabbed me from behind.

It was Xavier Gonzalez. "What are you doing here?" he asked. "Summer said you stayed home today to investigate this rhino thing."

"I did," I told him. "But Summer has a lead."

"Hey, so do I!"

"Really? What?"

"TimJim!"

"TimJim?" I asked, trying my best not to sound too dismissive.

"Yeah. I've been keeping an eye on them since yesterday, and they're definitely up to no good. Come see." Xavier grabbed my arm and pulled me toward the exit.

I looked back toward Summer, who gave me a "What's going on?" look. I replied with a shrug and mouthed, "I'll be back."

Our team actually stole the ball and attempted a fast break. One player passed to another, but the throw was off by several feet. It sailed into the stands, where it clocked one of the team moms in the head hard enough to knock her out of her seat.

Violet and the other cheerleaders grimaced at this. They seemed to be running out of ways to put a positive spin on things.

The referee blew his whistle, calling a time-out while everyone went to check on the mom.

I followed Xavier outside. He quickly yanked me behind a bush, then whispered, "TimJim's over by the cafeteria. I was watching them right before you showed up, and they're plotting something."

"And you think it has to do with the rhino?" I peered through the leaves. TimJim were hunkered down by the garbage bins at the back of the cafeteria. I couldn't see what they were doing, but they certainly seemed to be plotting. The garbage bins always smelled like a week's worth of rotten food. The only reason anyone ever hung out near them was when they were trying not to get noticed; that was where the kids who smoked snuck cigarettes. Plus, TimJim kept looking up now and then to case the area.

"I overheard them talking before school this morning," Xavier said. "Know what they did last night? Went poaching."

"They actually said that?"

"Yes! Because they're idiots. They were talking about how they'd snuck onto someone else's property to try to shoot something. And what happened at FunJungle last night? Someone snuck onto the property and tried to shoot something."

"True," I admitted. "But TimJim's two people—and only one person snuck into FunJungle last night. Plus, it was a woman."

Xavier looked a bit shocked to hear this. "How do you know that?"

"They have video footage of her from one of the cameras."

Xavier suddenly lit up with excitement as he thought of something. "Maybe it's TimJim's mom! She's even worse than they are!"

"She is?"

"Oh yeah. How do you think TimJim got to be such jerks? Both their parents are bad news—and always have been. They used to pick on *my* dad when he went to school here."

Through the bushes, either Tim or Jim—I couldn't be sure which—looked around furtively, then pulled something in a brown bag out from under his jacket. His brother peeked into it and laughed.

I told Xavier, "Just because their parents are jerks doesn't mean they tried to kill Rhonda."

"They're poachers," Xavier told me. "They've been busted, like, a hundred times for hunting on other people's land. And not small stuff, either. They walked right onto Paul Dague's ranch a couple years back and shot one of his cows. Then they tried to drag it off. If Paul's dad hadn't caught them, they'd have made off with a couple hundred pounds of meat."

"There's a big difference between shooting a neighbor's cow and shooting a rhinoceros."

Xavier frowned at me, like he was annoyed I wasn't

getting on board with his theory. "Yeah, a rhino's worth a lot more than some stupid cow. If their mom was willing to sneak onto someone's property for only a hundred bucks' worth of steak, you don't think she'd be willing to do it for a horn worth half a million dollars?"

That actually made sense. "I guess. But how would their mom have gotten the horn? Rhonda was locked up in her house."

"Maybe she didn't realize the house was locked. It doesn't matter whether she had a good plan to steal the horn. What matters is whether she was dumb enough to *try* to steal it. And TimJim's mom isn't any smarter than they are. The Barksdales aren't exactly a family of rocket scientists."

I considered that. I'd been thinking all along that the hunter must have had a plan, but the idea that she was merely bumbling along idiotically actually explained some things. Like why she hadn't used a silencer the first time. Or why she'd climbed the back fence so close to the camera. "So you think what? That their mom heard the horn was worth a lot and decided to try to get one?"

"Exactly. Or maybe it's not about the horn at all. Maybe she only wants to kill a rhino because she's a horrible person."

"I don't know about that."

"Sometimes people do things just to be jerks," Xavier told me. "Back before I was born, there used to be this tourist attraction near here called Balanced Rock. It was this huge boulder that was perfectly balanced up on the top of Bear Mountain. It took millions of years to form and was really amazing. And then one day some vandals blew it off with dynamite. They ruined the whole thing forever for no good reason. Sometimes stupid people just want to make a mark on the world."

I sighed, saddened by this, because I knew Xavier was right. "And you think TimJim's mom is like that?"

"Absolutely. If there were only one rhino left in the world, she'd probably shoot it. And she'd probably be proud that she'd made a species go extinct. Maybe I heard TimJim wrong today. Maybe they weren't saying that *they'd* gone poaching. Maybe they were talking about their mom. Or who knows? Maybe the whole family went, but their mom was the one who decided to go over the fence while the others stood guard or something. Hey! They're going!"

I turned back to peek through the bush. Sure enough, TimJim were now slinking off with their brown paper bag, heading around the back of the gym.

"C'mon!" Xavier said. "Let's go see what they're up to."

"Summer's saving me a seat," I pointed out. "I told her I'd be right back."

Xavier huffed, annoyed. "They're up to no good right now."

"Then we should tell the principal about it."

"Mr. Dillnut won't do anything and you know it. What if this has something to do with the rhino?"

"Like what?" I asked skeptically.

"I don't know. Maybe they're meeting with their mom to plot another attempt."

While Xavier had convinced me that Mrs. Barksdale might have been the hunter, I was quite sure TimJim weren't sneaking off to plot with her right then. Plus, I was getting cold, and I really didn't want to be tiptoeing around after TimJim when I could have been hanging out with Summer inside. "I'm going back in," I said.

"Well, I'm not," Xavier told me defiantly. "I'm gonna find out what their scheme is." Before I could protest again, he slunk off after them. He was a little too excited by his own mission; I could hear him humming the James Bond theme as he slipped around the gym in pursuit of them.

I headed back into the gym. It wasn't well heated, but it still felt nice after being outside. The game was back under way. The mom who'd been beaned now had an ice pack clutched to her head but seemed to be all right otherwise. The team was still playing terribly, though. The cheerleaders appeared to have given up on saying how good we were. Instead, they were now pleading with the team to try harder.

"A tisket, a tasket, we want a basket!" they yelled.

Up in the stands, Summer had stopped watching the game entirely and was doing her homework. She didn't even notice as I came back in.

Violet saw me, though. "Hey, Teddy!" she said, waving a pom-pom.

"Hey," I said back.

"Where were you today?"

"Dealing with the rhino."

"Oh. Cool." Our team started bringing the ball down the court, and the other cheerleaders looked to Violet expectantly. She sighed, like she wasn't thrilled she had to get back to rooting on the team. "Well, I'll see you after the game!"

"I'll be right up there." I pointed up to Summer in the stands.

Violet smiled, then got the girls cheering again. "Let's go, Wildcats. Let's go!"

Hondo nodded to me as I climbed up the stands. "You're missing a great game here," he said sarcastically.

Summer looked up, saw me, and returned her attention to finishing an algebra problem. "What was all that about with Xavier?"

"TimJim's up to something. And Xavier thinks their mom might be the hunter."

I'd expected Summer to not take this seriously. Instead, she cocked an eyebrow, intrigued. "Why?"

"She has a history of poaching. And apparently, she's dumb enough to go after the rhino just to do it."

Summer nodded. "Yeah. Daddy went to school here with her. He says she and TimJim's dad were about the two dumbest people he ever met. Everyone always knew they were going to end up together because each of them had only half a brain."

"Think she's worth looking into?"

"Any lead is worth looking into. I'll text my father and have him tell Hoenekker." Summer finished the problem she was working on, then picked up her phone.

I sat beside her. By this point, it was obvious that the only way our team was going to win the game was if our opponents all came down with food poisoning and had to forfeit. Even our coach wasn't watching anymore—although he might have only been averting his eyes from the tragedy.

Violet and the other cheerleaders were still doing their best to put on a good show. Our team actually made a basket, and the girls went wild, whooping and hollering as if we'd won the state championship. Violet ran down the sidelines and did an impressive handspring flip at center court.

The fans cheered more loudly for her than they had for the team all game.

I realized Summer was no longer texting. She was watching Violet intensely, with a look I'd never seen before. I couldn't quite read it, but it looked like she might have been jealous.

"Have you ever thought about going out for the squad?" I asked her.

Summer looked at me, then laughed like this was ridiculous. "Never."

"I'm sure you'd make it. Everyone here likes you."

"Maybe, but . . . There's no way. I could never do that stuff."

"Well, Violet's really the only one who does flips and things. The rest of them only cheer."

"That's not what I meant. I could never be a cheerleader, period. Or anything public like that." There was an unusual tone to Summer's voice. Normally, she was the most confident, positive person I knew. Now she sounded kind of sad.

I turned to her, intrigued. "Why not?"

Down by the court, one of the other cheerleaders—Shannon Butler—attempted the same handspring Violet had done. She didn't stick the landing quite as well, though.

Her feet went out from under her, and she tumbled backward onto her rear end. Violet and the other cheerleaders still clapped for her, though, and Shannon got back to her feet quickly and resumed cheering.

"That's why," Summer told me. "Shannon does something like that and it's no big deal. Maybe it's a little embarrassing, and maybe some kids joke about it, but most likely it's forgotten about in a few minutes. That's not the way things work with me, though. The whole world knows who I am. If I were a cheerleader and wiped out like that, someone would record it on their phone and stick it on YouTube with a title like 'Summer McCracken's Epic Fail,' and the next thing you know, there'd be a million hits and I'd be the laughingstock of the country."

"That wouldn't happen," I said supportively, though I actually wondered if it might.

"It would," Summer said flatly. "Sooner or later. There's a lot of people out there who don't like me simply because I'm me. They're angry that I'm rich and they're not, and they assume I must be some kind of spoiled brat and can't wait for a chance to bring me down. So I have to be careful not to give them any ammunition. If someone in a crowd insults me, I can't flip out or insult them back like a normal person. I just have to suck it up. If I go shopping, I can't say anything bad about any of the clothes I try on. If I eat out, I can't diss the food, even if it stinks. I can't ride a skateboard or a bike or anything in public, because I might wipe out. And I can't show up at a public pool in a bathing suit, because every magazine on earth will say I look fat. I can't have a normal life, because my life isn't normal."

I stared at her for a moment, not sure what to say. I'd always assumed that Summer's life was nonstop awesomeness—and I knew everyone at school thought so too. And despite the issues she'd just laid out, I knew her life was still better than most people's. She never went to bed hungry and cold and wondering where her next meal was coming from. But she still had a right to be upset about what she was missing out on. I found myself feeling sorry for her.

It occurred to me that maybe this was why Summer was so determined to push her boundaries when the public wasn't around, why she snuck away from her bodyguards when she could—and why she'd been so eager to show me how to swim in the hippo exhibit right after she'd met me. If I needed to be so cautious in public all the time, I'd probably want to blow off steam in private too.

I was trying to figure out something supportive to say when the fireworks went off.

They detonated right under the stands at center court.

They weren't big, fancy fireworks, merely little packs of gunpowder that went off one after the other, startling everyone in the gym. Violet and the other cheerleaders shrieked in fear. So did several of the basketball players. The mom who'd been clocked in the head earlier toppled out of her seat and whacked herself in the other temple.

After all my time tracking down the hunter, I had guns on the brain and thought someone was shooting. I grabbed Summer and yanked her down, using the seats of the stands as cover. Hondo had the same fear, except he went the other way, snapping to his feet with surprising speed, his hand dipping below his sports jacket to the gun he kept holstered there.

"It was TimJim!" Xavier yelled, racing into the gym. "They set the fireworks off! I saw them!"

"Where are they?" Coach Redmond demanded.

Xavier pointed to a door behind the stands. "They went that way!"

Coach ran out the door, determined to catch TimJim—and probably thankful for an excuse to leave the game. The whole basketball team did the same thing.

I sat up next to Summer, feeling embarrassed for overreacting. "Sorry."

"Why?" she asked. "You were only looking out for me."

"I guess that's what TimJim was plotting," I said.

Hondo came over to us, extending a hand to help Summer up. "You all right?"

"I'm fine," she said, then cased the gym. "Thank God this game is finally over. Let's get Violet and get the heck out of here."

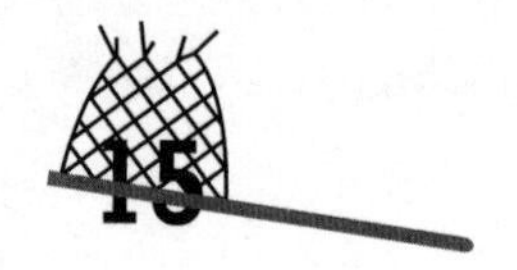

TAXIDERMY

"My aunt and uncle aren't jerks," Violet said.

She was sitting with Summer and me in the back of the McCrackens' SUV as we headed out to the ranch. I was in the middle, between the girls, while Hondo was up in the front seat with Tran. Violet had changed from her cheerleading uniform into jeans and a sweater. She was obviously thrilled to be in the car with Summer, though she seemed a bit nervous about it too.

It was strange to see Violet acting self-conscious. Until Summer had transferred to our school, Violet had been the queen there, the girl everyone wanted to be friends with. But despite Summer's complaints earlier, she was still rich and famous, and now everyone wanted to be friends with *her*. Including Violet.

“Why would we think they’re jerks?” Summer asked.

“A lot of the time people just assume they are—without even meeting them,” Violet replied. “Especially people who don’t like hunting. They hear what my aunt and uncle do and figure they must be horrible people. But they’re not. They’re really nice.”

“Sure,” I said, although the truth was, I *had* assumed Violet’s relatives were jerks. I couldn’t imagine how anyone nice could possibly run an exotic game ranch for a living. But now I felt like a bit of a jerk myself for making big assumptions.

Now that she’d cleared the air, Violet seemed relieved and gave us all the background on the ranch. We didn’t even have to question her about it; Violet could talk a mile a minute when she got excited about something. Her family had been raising cattle in the Texas Hill Country since before the Civil War, but that wasn’t as profitable as it used to be. So when her uncle saw that lots of other ranches in Texas were converting from traditional ranching to raising exotic species for hunting, he’d decided to do it too. They still had cattle, but now much of the property was given over to exotics. Violet thought they had at least twenty different species there and more than a thousand different animals. “It’s not quite as many animals as your dad has,” she told Summer. “But we’re getting there! In fact, my family even sold him some antelope for SafariLand.”

"I didn't know that," Summer said. "That's really cool."

Violet beamed at the praise.

It had never occurred to me to ask where J.J. McCracken had gotten all his animals. I'd simply assumed they had mostly come from zoos. But now I realized that was probably wrong. After all, J.J. had acquired thousands of animals in a very short time, which was a lot for zoos to provide. J.J. wouldn't have been able to capture that many endangered species in the wild, either. It made much more sense that he'd bought them from exotic animal breeders. Which meant Violet's claim that these places could help with conservation wasn't a bunch of hot air.

We arrived at the entrance to the ranch. It wasn't very dramatic, merely an iron gate set between two stone pillars along a two-lane back road. It looked like a hundred other ranch entrances we'd passed on the way. The fence along the road was only barbed wire strung between ancient wooden posts.

"This is it?" I asked. "There's no sign or anything."

"My family doesn't like to advertise that it's here," Violet explained. "If we did, we'd have animal rights protesters camped out here all the time."

Tran gave our name at the call box, and the gate swung open, revealing a rutted dirt road beyond. We bumped along it slowly for the next few miles, passing through hundreds of acres of scrubby oak and cedar forest. I kept my eyes on the windows, expecting to see exotic animals gamboling past, but instead, all I saw were longhorn cattle.

After ten minutes I asked, "Where's all the exotics?"

"On the back half of the property," Violet replied.

"We're not even halfway across yet?" I asked. "How big is this ranch?"

"Forty thousand acres."

For once, even Summer seemed surprised. "That's more than sixty square miles!"

Violet shrugged. "Yeah, it's pretty big. I don't think even my daddy has seen all of it. But my uncle says he knows the whole thing like the back of his hand."

I turned back to the window again. The scrub forest outside looked similar to many parts of southern Africa, with shorter trees and thick underbrush in which even large animals could easily camouflage themselves. I thought I caught a glimpse of a large brown antelope with long, curved horns bounding away from us.

"Was that a sable?" I asked.

Violet shrugged. "I don't know the animals here that well."

We eventually emerged from the woods and found ourselves before a small hunting lodge. It looked a lot like some of the safari lodges in Africa. It was one story tall, with only four rooms flanking the road. There was no one around it, though.

"That's not very big," Summer pointed out.

"No," Violet said. "We have only eight guests here at a time, max."

"Is anyone staying here now?" I asked.

"Oh yeah," Violet replied. "We're always full up. There's a waiting list to stay here that's, like, a year long. Everyone's just out on the hunt."

"Now?" Summer asked. "It's getting dark."

"The animals are more active at dusk," Violet explained. "Now and dawn are the best times to hunt."

A little past the lodge, we came to the main house. This was a sprawling one-story building that sat at the top of a hill, with several mud-splattered four-wheel-drive vehicles parked in front. A middle-aged couple stood at the edge of the drive, eagerly awaiting our arrival.

"That's my aunt and uncle," Violet said.

They didn't look anything like I'd expected—but then, I realized that I'd rather stupidly been expecting them to look like cartoon hunters. I'd pictured them clad in camouflage gear, with ammunition belts and combat boots, which was as silly as assuming that Doc would wear surgical scrubs all the time. Instead, Violet's aunt and uncle had dressed up to meet us. She wore a floral-print dress and had her hair done nicely.

He was wearing a suit with a button-down shirt and a bolo tie. They both might as well have been at a country club.

The moment the SUV stopped, Violet sprang out and gave both of them big hugs. "Uncle Adam and Auntie June, these are my friends Teddy Fitzroy and Summer McCracken."

The smile on Uncle Adam's face faltered as we emerged from the rover. He turned to Violet and spoke quietly, as though hoping we wouldn't hear. "Vi, I thought you said *J.J.* McCracken wanted to visit our ranch."

Violet shook her head. "No, I didn't. I said Summer. That's J.J.'s daughter. She's my friend." She pointed to me. "And this is Teddy. He's the one who dealt with that bully who was causing so much trouble for me."

Uncle Adam's eyes lit up with understanding. "You're the boy who found the koala!"

"That's right," I said.

Adam broke into a big, friendly smile. "It's a pleasure to meet both of you. Welcome to the Flying J Ranch." He extended a hand to me and I shook it.

"Come on in," Auntie June said sweetly. "We just brewed some iced tea, if you'd like any."

They ushered us through the front doors. Hondo followed us, though Tran stayed in the rover.

Inside, the house was rather modest; it would have been completely ordinary if not for all the animals. There were six hunting dogs—all alive—and dozens of other creatures—all dead. The dead were stuffed and mounted in various poses around the regular furniture. It was quite jarring, as if the animals had started migrating through the house and then time had stopped while they were in midstride.

There was a stuffed grizzly bear by the front door, standing on its hind legs. It was twelve feet tall, and its mouth was open in what was probably supposed to be a frightening snarl, although whoever had done the taxidermy had messed up and the bear looked sick, rather than imposing. Like it was about to barf on us. In addition, it also held a small serving tray upon which the iced tea sat. This once-majestic animal had been turned into a stuffed, nauseated butler.

Hondo eyed it uneasily, as though worried it wasn't actually dead. The whole room seemed to be giving him the willies.

Auntie June waved to the iced tea. "Please, help yourselves."

We each took a glass.

"Do you raise bears on this ranch?" I asked.

"No. I shot Jeeves here up in the Brooks Range in Alaska," Adam told me. "I'd love to be able to breed grizzlies for hunt down here, but there's simply no way to control a carnivore of this size. It'd eat all my other stock. So we only raise herbivores."

"Uncle Adam didn't just shoot him," Violet said proudly. "He also did the taxidermy."

"Really?" I asked, trying to sound impressed. "It's very good."

"That's kind of you to say." Adam waved an arm to all the other animals. "I did all these, too. The way I figured it, the local taxidermist was charging so much, I was gonna go broke having all the animals I shot mounted. So I built my own shop here and started doing the taxidermy myself."

He led us into the living room, where we could see his work up close. It was immediately evident that Adam was much better at shooting things than he was at mounting them. He'd done a decent job with the poses, but he couldn't seem to get the faces right. A lion by the sofa was supposed to look regal, but it was comically cross-eyed instead. A bighorn sheep looked constipated, rather than imposing, while a kudu seemed to be having terrible indigestion.

"These are really nice," I said, trying my best to be a good guest.

"There's plenty more, if you'd like to see them," Auntie June said.

"Oh yes," Summer said politely. "I'd love to."

"Right this way!" Adam said, leading us onward.

Summer came up beside me and whispered, "Is it just me, or is all this freaking you out?"

Before I could respond, Violet slipped between us. She was beaming, pleased that everything seemed to be going so well. "Pretty cool, huh?" she asked.

"Yeah," I agreed. "Pretty cool."

"Here we go!" Adam announced. "The pièce de résistance!" With that, he led us through a doorway into his trophy room.

As soon as I entered, I froze in my tracks. The room was enormous, twice as tall as the other rooms and ten times the size of my family's entire trailer. It was filled with dead animals. There were dozens lined up on both sides of a wide center aisle, while the walls were lined with disembodied heads. There must have been more than a hundred and fifty. And Uncle Adam had botched the mounting of almost every single one of them. They all had the same nauseated look, as though each had died in the act of smelling something terrible.

"Oh my," Summer said. I couldn't tell if she was stunned by the sheer amount of dead animals or amused by the looks on their faces.

"Thanks," Adam said proudly, mistakenly thinking she was impressed. "It wasn't easy to bag all these animals—or to mount them."

Hondo didn't even enter the room. He stayed right outside, looking like being around so many animals—even dead ones—was giving him hives.

“How many of these are from your ranch?” Summer asked.

“Only about a fourth,” Adam said. “Truth be told, I don’t do too much hunting for exotics on this property myself. They’re for the paying customers. But every now and then, there’s one like this bad boy here that I simply can’t resist.” He patted the hide of a disturbed-looking sable antelope. “The rest of them, I’ve traveled far and wide to find. Fifty-five countries on six different continents.”

Violet led me into the middle of the room. To my surprise, there were lots of smaller stuffed animals—mostly squirrels—interspersed with all the bigger ones. Only, rather than being posed majestically, these had been dressed in doll clothes and given tiny props. I realized they were supposed to be famous people. There was a squirrel Ben Franklin in bifocal glasses flying a little kite; a prairie dog Abraham Lincoln with a top hat, a beard, and a teensy Gettysburg Address; and a weasel Franklin Delano Roosevelt with a cigarette holder and a wheelchair.

“These are Auntie June’s handiwork,” Violet told me. “Aren’t they adorable?”

“They really are,” I said, trying to sound like I meant it.

“Well, thank you,” Auntie June said sweetly. “I don’t hunt myself, but once Adam started doing taxidermy, I thought it looked like fun, so I took it up myself. Here’s one you might like, Teddy. I understand you’re named after him." She pointed me to a squirrel Teddy Roosevelt, dressed in safari gear with a tiny rifle, its foot propped on a badger it had "killed."

"Wow," I said. I was well aware that Teddy Roosevelt, while a great conservationist, had also been an avid big-game hunter; in fact, he'd shot many of the animals on display at the American Museum of Natural History in New York City. But seeing a rodent version of him killing another animal was disturbing.

On the wall behind it, the head of an African white rhino was mounted. It looked like it had died in the middle of a belch. It had an exceptionally long horn, almost two feet tall, tapering to a perfect point.

"You don't raise rhinos here, do you?" I asked.

"No, though I've thought about it," Adam replied. "It's legal, but I'd still catch way too much flak. No one seems to care that I've got a thousand antelope out there. If I brought in a rhino, though, I can guarantee you the anti-hunting folks would be clamoring to shut me down within days. Which is a darn shame, because rhino hunting's practically the only way to save those animals."

"Wait," Summer said. "How do you *save* an animal by hunting it?"

"It's all a question of money," Adam explained. "Big-game hunting brings in far more money than safari tourism does—and most of that goes right to conservation efforts. Hunters don't want these animals to go extinct any more than the animal rights activists do."

"Because if they do, there won't be anything left to kill," Summer muttered under her breath.

Adam didn't hear her. "In fact," he went on, "there are plenty of wild animals that have been *saved* from extinction by places like this ranch. I have quite a few endangered species on my property, and I know other ranchers who do too. We don't hunt all those. Instead, we've sponsored reintroduction of these species back into the wild. I'd love to try to do the same thing with rhinos, help them build back up their populations."

"Wouldn't you be worried about poachers?" I asked pointedly.

"Oh, I think any rhinos I had here would be equally as safe as the ones at FunJungle," Adam replied. If he knew anyone was going after our rhinos, he did an amazing job of hiding it. "I've never had an issue with poachers before."

"But rhinos are different," Summer pointed out. "A poacher's not going to come onto your property and make off with a whole antelope. But with the rhino, they'd only want the horn, which would be a lot easier to get."

Adam sighed sadly. "True. Poaching's a big problem for rhinos. But there's a lot of evidence that legalized hunting cuts down on that too. See, when you make killing something illegal, that doesn't stop folks from killing it. In fact, you make the value of it go up so high that killing it becomes impossible to resist. A poacher in South Africa can make more money selling one rhino horn than he can working an honest job for three years. But if you legalize the harvesting of horns and regulate it—maybe even grow horns for sale—then the bottom would drop out of that market and there'd be far less incentive to kill those poor animals."

"Except for sport," Summer pointed out.

"Right," Adam said.

I noticed another rhino head on the opposite side of the room. Adam had actually done a decent job of mounting this one, for once. It might have looked majestic if it hadn't been directly above thirteen stuffed squirrels reenacting George Washington crossing the Delaware. They were all rowing a toy boat surrounded by Lego icebergs, while squirrel Washington stood ramrod straight in a tiny powdered wig.

"Is there anyone in Texas who lets people hunt rhinos?" I asked.

Adam and June looked at each other, then shook their heads. "I doubt it," June said. "If there were, we'd know. Exotic ranching is a small community."

"Do you know of anyone looking to hunt one here anyhow?" Summer asked.

Adam and June regarded Summer with stunned silence. "What do you mean, exactly?" Adam asked.

Summer turned to Violet. "You didn't tell them why we were coming here?"

"I thought you wanted me to keep it a secret," Violet said.

"What's this all about?" June asked.

Summer returned her attention to the adults. "We're having some trouble at FunJungle, and we thought you could help with it."

"Well, we'd be happy to," Adam told her.

"Great," Summer said. "But the thing is, this is top secret. No one's supposed to know. In fact, my dad would probably have a cow if he knew I was talking to you about this."

"Wait," Adam said. "J.J. doesn't even know you're here?"

"Yesterday morning someone took a shot at one of our rhinos," Summer said.

June gasped in alarm. Adam took a step back. Their surprise seemed genuine to me.

"How so?" Adam asked. "Like some dumb kid taking a potshot with an air rifle?"

"No," I told them. "It was a real hunter. Using a .375 H&H Magnum."

Adam sighed heavily. "That'd take down a rhino, all right."

Summer said, "So we were wondering: Do you know any

hunters who want to kill a rhino so badly that they'd come to a zoo to do it? Maybe someone who couldn't afford a trip to Africa? I mean, that can't be cheap, can it?"

"No," Adam admitted. "Hunting a rhino legally can run up to a hundred thousand dollars. But I can't imagine any real hunter going after one in a zoo. A rhino in captivity is a sitting duck. That goes against everything hunters believe in."

"But real hunters come *here*, don't they?" Summer pressed. "And your animals are in captivity."

"It's different." Adam led us to the end of the room, where a large window looked out over the property. Since we were up on a hill, we could see miles of woods spread out below us in the setting sun. "Yeah, our animals are fenced in, but they still have thousands of acres to roam. If you want to hunt something here, you have to go find it. Then you have to stalk it. And only after all that can you kill it—if the stars all align. I've hunted an awful lot of animals in the wild, and I can guarantee you the hunts we run here are virtually the same experience. A real hunter doesn't want me to make it easy for them. Hunting's a sport."

"A sport one team doesn't know it's playing," Summer whispered to me.

"The point of hunting isn't killing simply to kill," Aunt June added. "It's pitting yourself against the animal.

I can't imagine any self-respecting hunter shooting something in a zoo. Certainly, none of our clients are like that."

I nodded, aware their argument made sense. "What if we're not talking about someone hunting the rhino for sport? Do you know anyone who'd want to kill it only for the horn?"

Adam bristled, a bit annoyed. "I don't associate with poachers."

"But you must know most of the big-game hunters around here," I pressed. "And whoever did this was really good with a rifle. They shot through a small window from at least a hundred yards away and came awfully close to hitting Rhonda."

June whistled, impressed. "Your shooter knows what they're doing, all right."

"And they used a .375 H&H," Summer added. "That's not cheap, is it?"

"No," June admitted. "They're several thousand dollars. And the ammunition is pricey too."

"Could you use that gun on anything local, like deer or turkeys?" I asked.

"Of course not," Adam said. "You'd blow them to pieces."

"Then the only people who'd have rifles like that would be big-game hunters," I concluded. "The kind of people who might hunt at your ranch."

Adam's eyes flicked to meet his wife's. Then he sagged a bit and nodded. "I suppose you've got a point."

Summer asked, "So do you know anyone with a gun like that who might need the kind of money that a rhino horn would bring in?"

Adam said, "Look, there's thousands of big-game hunters in Texas. I don't know them all. . . ."

"There's a good chance that it's a woman," I said.

Everyone looked to me, surprised—including Summer.

"You didn't know?" I asked her, then explained. "Security found footage of the hunter going over the fence last night. It looks like it's a woman, if that helps narrow things down."

Adam thought about this for a bit, then started to shake his head.

Then June said, "Lydia Trask."

Adam spun on her, angry. "Lydia wouldn't do any such thing."

"She might," June said firmly. "She's a good shot, and she's fallen on hard times. Her family needs money, and you know it."

"Who's Lydia Trask?" Summer asked.

"One of our clients," June said quickly, before Adam could speak. "Or at least, she used to be. Her husband had a big construction company, but it went bankrupt. Now they're deep in debt."

"That doesn't mean she'd kill a rhino," Adam snapped. "And besides, they're in the hole to the tune of millions. The money a rhino horn would bring in would barely be a drop in the bucket."

"But it'd still be a drop," Summer pointed out.

Adam swung back to face her. "I wouldn't put my money on Lydia Trask. But you know who I *would* look at? Abby Duntz."

I stiffened at the last name. "Is she related to Hank Duntz?"

"His sister," Adam replied.

"Who's Hank Duntz?" Violet asked.

"Most people call him 'Hank the Tank,'" Summer informed her. "He was a professional criminal who worked for a rival of my father's. He tried to sabotage one of our exhibits last year, but Teddy caught him and he went to jail."

Violet turned to me, intrigued. "You caught another bad guy besides Vance Jessup?"

"And he caught both the same day," Summer said.

"Wow," Violet said, impressed. "How?"

"I didn't really catch him," I told her, not feeling like telling the whole story. "Security did. I only figured out he was the one who'd caused all the trouble."

"Well, whatever the case, he's in jail because of Fun-Jungle," Adam told us. "So it stands to reason that his sister might have a grudge against that place. Now, we don't know her. She lives way out by Houston. But she's a crack shot and she's won some state rifle tournaments in the women's division."

Summer asked, "So you think she might be shooting at the rhino just to get even with my dad?"

Adam shrugged. "That rhino's pretty valuable. And someone interested in revenge wouldn't need to get the horn from the rhino. They'd simply want the rhino dead."

"But why would she only go after the rhino?" Violet asked. "If someone was really angry at J.J., why not go after any of the other animals?"

"Maybe she still will." Adam turned to Summer. "I'm not saying Abby's behind this, but if she is, then *all* your animals could be in danger."

I leaned against the window and looked back at the room full of poorly mounted animals, feeling as nauseated as all of them appeared to be. Hank Duntz had been a nasty, dangerous man. If he had a sister with a grudge, that could be very bad news indeed.

SUSPECTS

"There's another basketball game this Friday after school," Violet told me. "Are you coming?"

Summer's SUV was idling in front of Violet's house. We'd stopped at the Dairy Queen for takeout on the way back, and now the rear seat was littered with wrappers and used napkins.

"I don't know," I said. "I hadn't planned on it."

"Me neither," Summer said.

"You should come!" Violet told us. "It'll be fun. Even though the team stinks. Dash and Ethan are coming. Everyone's gonna go out for pizza afterward."

That *did* sound fun. "Maybe," I said. "If I can get a ride."

"If you can't, let me know," Violet said. "Maybe we can

figure something out." She batted her eyes, slipped out the door, and hurried up the walk to her house.

Tran started driving us toward FunJungle.

"Oooh," Summer teased. "She *likes* you."

I could feel my cheeks warming as I blushed. "She does not. She was asking both of us to come."

"She was asking *you*." Summer did an amped-up imitation of Violet, batting her eyes at me. "You should come. It'll be sooooo much fun. And afterward, maybe we can go smooch somewhere."

Now it felt like my whole face was red. Thankfully, the glass partition was closed between us and the front seat, so Hondo and Tran couldn't hear anything. "I'm only in seventh grade. Why would she like me?"

"Because you punched out the school bully. And solved the case of the stolen koala. And you're more interesting than anyone else at school. Face it—she likes you. The *head cheerleader* likes you. You should be thrilled. That's every guy's dream come true, isn't it?"

It was definitely the dream of lots of guys at my school. Xavier Gonzalez, for one. He'd had a crush on Violet since kindergarten. But I wasn't into Violet, and I really didn't feel like telling Summer *why*. So instead I asked, "Do you think Violet's uncle was telling the truth?"

"Don't try to change the subject."

"We're supposed to be trying to figure out who killed Rhonda."

Summer sighed dramatically, letting me know I was being a bore. "The truth about what?"

"Big-game hunters. When he said none of them would shoot a rhino in the zoo. That it wouldn't be enough of a challenge."

Summer stared out the window thoughtfully as we cruised through Violet's neighborhood. "I suppose he made sense," she said. "And he knows more about how hunters think than we do. So yeah, I guess I believe him. Besides, he gave us a good lead with Abby Duntz."

Summer had texted her father about Abby the moment we'd gotten into the car. She'd also used her phone to find a photo of Abby online. It was from when she'd won a sharp-shooting competition the year before. She looked almost exactly like her brother Hank—short and stout, with the kind of face that would give small children nightmares.

"I don't know," I said.

"You don't think Abby Duntz is a good lead?"

"He brought her up really quickly once his wife mentioned Lydia Trask. Like *he* wanted to change the subject."

Summer considered that, then nodded. "You're right. He did." She pulled out her phone and ran a quick search. "Trask Construction went bankrupt last year, but their website's still up. They list FunJungle as a client. Claim they built some of the exhibits."

"Which ones?"

"They don't say."

"That'd give Lydia some inside knowledge of the park," I said.

"I guess. But . . ."

"But what?"

Summer turned her phone around so I could see it. She'd found some photos of Lydia Trask on the web, mostly of her with her family. She had three kids, all of whom were older than us. "She's a mom."

"Moms can commit crimes."

"Yeah, but think about this. Like Violet's uncle said, the rhino horn still isn't worth enough to get the Trasks out of debt. Plus, there are laws to help people who've gone bankrupt. So would a regular mom really commit a serious crime like poaching to only partly erase her debts? Especially when there's still the issue of getting the horn off the dead rhino? The Abby Duntz story makes much more sense."

"Maybe," I said. "But a lead's a lead. Hoenekker ought to investigate everything he can."

"I guess. Okay, I'll share Lydia Trask with Daddy, too."

While Summer typed another text to her father, I stared out the window. We were now past what few suburbs there were in town, heading out the long, lonely road toward FunJungle.

Summer asked, "Any other leads you've come up with, as long as I'm sending them to Daddy?"

"Besides TimJim's mom?"

"I already sent that one earlier."

I shook my head sadly, feeling frustrated. "No. No other leads. Only a bunch of things that don't add up."

"Like what?"

"Why didn't the hunter use a silencer the first time she went after Rhonda? She had to know it was going to make a lot of noise and alert everyone, right? And if she was trying to poach the horn, the last thing she'd want to do would be to draw attention."

Summer chewed her lip. "Maybe she *wanted* the attention. If it was Abby Duntz, trying to get revenge, maybe she was trying to send a message."

"If that's the case, why didn't she do the same thing the next time? Last night she brought a silencer and snuck all the way across SafariLand toward the rhino house. It was a completely different style of attack."

Summer's eyes went wide. "Maybe there are two different people trying to kill the rhino!"

I stiffened in my seat. "Two poachers? At the same time?"

"Yes. Working together. Suppose it's the Trasks. They

both need money bad and decide to go after the horn. They helped build the park and know how to sneak in and out. Maybe they even know a way to get into the rhino house. So the husband tries first, but he royally screws up his attempt. He doesn't bring a silencer; he starts an elephant stampede—and he misses the rhino. So now Lydia tries. And she knows her husband's way was idiotic, so she changes the whole way of doing things, top to bottom."

"So now you think it *could* be Lydia Trask?"

"And her husband, yeah."

I mulled that over. Summer's theory certainly answered some of my questions, though not all of them. "Why'd they go after Rhonda, then? There were other rhinos that were easier to get to."

"Maybe they knew how to get into Rhonda's house but not the others."

"The other rhinos were right out in the open yesterday morning."

"They might not have noticed that. And besides, Rhonda's got a pretty big horn. Those things sell by the pound. If you need money, you might as well go for the biggest one you can get your hands on."

"Good point," I admitted.

"And who says she was only going after Rhonda?" Summer added. "Maybe the plan was to go after all the rhinos, but she didn't get the chance."

"I hadn't thought of that," I said. It hadn't been that late when my parents and I came along and spotted the hunter. If she'd had all night, she easily could have wiped out all five rhinos in the Asian Plains.

Summer's phone buzzed with an incoming text. She read it, then reported, "Daddy says thanks. He's gonna pass these leads on to Hoenekker right away."

"Make sure he doesn't tell Hoenekker they're from us."

"Why not?"

"Because Hoenekker's not happy your dad asked us to help out. He might not be very keen to follow up on any of our leads."

"If Daddy tells him to investigate something, he'll investigate it. It's his job," Summer said, then paused to think about this. "Unless he's a lousy detective. Do you know if he's any good?"

I shrugged. "Your dad seems to think so. He gave him the job."

"He also gave Large Marge the job. And look how well that worked out."

"True, but Hoenekker does have his men working hard on this, though. They're combing through all the footage from all the cameras to see if they can find another shot of the hunter."

"That's it? He ought to be doing more than that, don't you think? Why are *we* the ones finding out about TimJim's mom and the Trasks and Abby Duntz? Why isn't Hoenekker doing that?"

"Maybe he did and he simply didn't tell *us*. Maybe he's got plenty of leads we don't know about."

"And maybe he doesn't. Maybe he doesn't have any leads at all." Summer sat forward, excited. "Maybe he's tanking the entire investigation because he's in cahoots with the bad guy!"

"Cahoots?" I repeated.

"Yeah, cahoots! Like, maybe he knows the Trasks and they promised him a cut."

"But Hoenekker's the one who found the footage of a woman going over the fence."

"Big whoop. We've got ten million cameras around the zoo and he found one grainy shot? Maybe there were plenty of other shots—good ones—and he trashed them all to show you the worst one. To make it look like he was doing his job. I mean, do we really know if he's got his guys combing through all this footage? Have we seen them doing it?"

"No," I admitted.

"Then maybe they're not. If they were, they should have

found something else by now, right? But we haven't heard a thing."

I started to argue that, even if Hoenekker *had* found anything important, he probably wouldn't have shared it with us, when something occurred to me. "He said there wasn't any footage of the hunter from the roof of the monorail station."

Summer looked to me, confused. "What do you mean?"

"Hoenekker originally figured that the hunter must have fired at Rhonda yesterday morning from the roof of the monorail station, but when they looked at the footage from there, there wasn't anybody in it."

"That doesn't make any sense. See? Maybe he's lying to protect the bad guy!"

"Or maybe the hunter didn't fire from above the monorail."

"Oh," Summer said. "Yeah, I guess that's possible too."

"That was Hoenekker's idea," I told her. "He said he was going to try to figure out where else the hunter could have fired from—"

"That's easy," Summer interrupted. "World of Reptiles." There wasn't a trace of doubt in her voice.

"Really?" I asked. "How can you be so sure?"

"Because I know FunJungle better than anyone. Except you, maybe. The place was my idea, remember? I've spent half my life looking at blueprints for it. World of Reptiles is close to SafariLand, and it's the tallest building around. If the shooter didn't fire from the monorail station, the dome of World of Reptiles would be the next best place."

I realized Summer was right. World of Reptiles had a direct shot at the rhino house too. The previous night, when I'd been at the rhino house, I'd seen the monorail station silhouetted against the dome of that building. "It'd be an awfully long shot, though."

"Yeah, but a good hunter with a good rifle could still do it."

I frowned. "It seems like Hoenekker should have figured that out."

"Yeah, it does," Summer said suspiciously, then grinned with excitement. "I guess that means we need to check it out."

"We?" I repeated. "How?"

Summer glanced toward Hondo. He was chatting in the front seat with Tran, unaware of anything we were saying, thanks to the glass partition between us. "We go up on the roof of World of Reptiles and see if we can find any evidence up there."

"You mean like bullet casings?"

"What are those?"

"When someone fires a gun, the casing gets ejected," I explained. "And each gun leaves different marks on the casing, like a fingerprint. So if the shooter left a casing behind, we might be able to use it to figure out who they are."

"Really?" Summer asked, growing even more excited. "Yeah, we should definitely look for those. And who knows? Maybe we'll find something else important up there. It doesn't sound like security's checked it out yet."

"It won't be easy to get up there."

"Sure it is. I've been up there plenty of times."

"When?"

"When they were building it. And even a few times since. It's really cool up there. And don't worry. It's totally safe."

"Maybe we should tell Hoenekker."

"I don't trust Hoenekker. C'mon. You aren't chicken, are you?"

The truth was, I *was* a little scared. It wasn't that I didn't trust Summer about the roof being safe. It was that I had a bad track record with ending up in danger at FunJungle. Lots of times, things that should have been safe turned out to be not so safe when I was there. I'd even had a bad experience in World of Reptiles once before, with an escaped black mamba. A mamba that had never been found again.

But I didn't want to admit I was scared. Not in front of

the girl who I liked a hundred times more than I liked Violet Grace.

So I tried to figure some other way out. “There’s no way Hondo will let us go up on World of Reptiles.”

“I know that,” Summer said, smiling mischievously. “That’s why we’re going to ditch him.”

THE DOME

Once Summer got an idea in her head, there was no talking her out of it. She didn't even bother trying to convince me. She simply acted like I'd already agreed. As the SUV pulled up in front of FunJungle, she told me, "Meet you at the World in fifteen minutes." Then she banged on the glass partition by the front seat and said, "Hondo, I have to make a bathroom stop."

Hondo groaned and slid the partition open. "You can't wait to get back home?"

"No!" Summer exclaimed. "I drank a ton of iced tea at Dairy Queen and I'm gonna burst. I'm lucky I made it this far! I'll be right back!" She hopped out of the car with me.

"Wait!" Hondo yelled, then cursed under his breath

when she didn't. He ordered Tran to park in a red zone and then ran after her.

The park was closed for the night, so we all headed for the employee entrance.

Summer didn't try to outrun Hondo. If she had, he would have alerted park security before she could get very far. Her plan was almost as simple, though. Once we were inside the park, she went into one of the public bathrooms and then climbed out the window while Hondo waited. Summer had pulled this stunt on her bodyguards before, but she saved it for occasions when she really needed to use it and hadn't sprung it on Hondo yet.

Therefore, she caught Hondo with his pants down. Literally. It turned out, he'd also drunk plenty of iced tea and had a full bladder. So when Summer went into the women's room, Hondo ducked into the men's room and missed her escape. By the time Hondo realized Summer had given him the slip, she was well on her way to World of Reptiles.

I took my time heading there, trying to appear inconspicuous, while Summer ran flat out, trying to leave Hondo way behind—so by the time I arrived, she was already there, panting from exhaustion. She tried to hide it, though, straightening up and declaring, "You're late."

"I'm actually early," I pointed out. "You said fifteen minutes. It's only been twelve."

Summer waved this aside, as though it didn't make sense. "Whatever. Let's go." She quickly typed her father's entry code into the security keypad, and the door to World of Reptiles clicked open.

The building was constructed to look like a giant turtle, with a wide glass dome at the top of the shell. Beneath the dome was an enormous indoor rainforest, which housed a few hundred reptiles—as well as plenty of non-reptiles, because frankly, reptiles are rarely very exciting to watch. Since they're cold-blooded, they tend to stay very still for hours, if not days. So the other animals had been brought in to spice things up. There were lots of brightly colored birds, small-clawed otters, capuchin monkeys, and some sloths. In truth, the sloths moved even less than a lot of the reptiles, but they were kind of cute and the tourists loved searching for them.

The rest of the exhibits at World of Reptiles weren't quite as impressive. Most were simply aquariums built into the walls with lizards, snakes, and turtles in them. While many of these animals were fascinating, they were often small, lethargic, and well camouflaged, so tourists tended to ignore them. Summer and I did the exact same thing, blowing past terrapins and skinks and puff adders in our hurry to get to the rain forest.

The lights were still on inside and the fake waterfalls were still gushing, but there weren't any other people there.

Without the crowds, it really did feel like we were off in the Amazon together. It was nice and warm—the heat was always set to the mideighties to keep the reptiles healthy—far more comfortable than the raw, chilly weather outside. I would have loved to just hang out there with Summer, watching the animals where it was safe and cozy, but she didn't slow for a moment in her rush to get to the roof.

A series of staircases, platforms, and rope bridges headed upward into the rainforest. The official reason for these was to let guests see some of the tree-dwelling creatures up close, but they were really there to make the exhibit more exciting to explore. Summer quickly led me up a staircase that spiraled around an enormous fake fig tree, then started across the longest bridge in the forest.

The bridge was the most visited place in the atrium, as it extended past the saltwater crocodile exhibit. It didn't go *directly* over the salties, but it angled close enough to give the impression that you were over them, allowing you to see them in all their glory down below. Even though the crocs didn't move much, they were among the most popular animals in World of Reptiles, because they were big—and they were dangerous.

Crocodiles are among the most deadly large animals in the world—if not the deadliest. It's estimated that they kill around three hundred people a year in Africa alone, although that number might be higher, because they don't leave much evidence of the kill. They either wolf the entire victim down in a few gulps or drag their remains down to the bottom of lakes and rivers to store in holes there. Which was why the bridge didn't go directly over their exhibit. The last thing J.J. McCracken needed was some idiot climbing over the safety rail, falling into the crocodile pit, and getting munched in front of the other tourists.

Saltwater crocodiles are from the rain forests of Australia, and while they don't kill quite as many people annually as their African relatives, they still take out a good number. (Of course, as Mom would point out, the number of people killed every year by crocodiles is only a tiny fraction of the number of people killed every year by *people*.) Saltwater crocs can be enormous, too. FunJungle had seven on display, each at least seventeen feet long and a thousand pounds—although the biggest, Didgeridoo, was twenty-three feet long and weighed more than a ton. They were so impressive that, even though Summer was in a hurry, she paused on the bridge to check them out.

"Is this the only way up to the roof?" I asked.

"It's the only way *I* know," Summer replied. "A little farther up, there's an access to a secure staircase that goes up to the dome."

"Sounds pretty complicated. There's no direct staircase?"

"I don't think they wanted to make it *easy* to get onto the roof. Why?"

"If the hunter really did shoot from up here, it's far more difficult to get to than the roof of the monorail. Anyone who wanted to get onto the monorail station could easily climb up there. But to get to the roof here, you'd need to know the route—*and* have an access code. Which means the hunter would have to work for FunJungle."

"Not necessarily," Summer said. "There could be a way up without going through the building."

"You mean like climbing the outside?"

"The walls aren't that steep. In fact, they kind of curve inward to make the building look all turtle-y. A good rock-climber could probably do it. If people can climb El Capitan in Yosemite, they could climb this."

"So in addition to being a great shot, the hunter would also have to be a great rock-climber."

"Maybe." Summer took one last look at Didgeridoo, then crossed the rest of the bridge and headed up another arboreal flight of stairs. "Or maybe it's someone who knows how to get around the security system. Maybe the Trasks built *this* building and installed some kind of loophole."

"Just in case they someday went bankrupt and needed to poach a rhino horn and wanted to come to the roof of this building to do it?"

"I don't know," Summer said curtly, annoyed at me for poking holes in her theory. "If it's so hard to believe the hunter shot from up here, why don't *you* come up with another solution?"

We reached the top of the stairs, arriving at the highest viewing platform in the rain forest; it was four stories up, so close to the dome that we could see the rivets in the steel girders that supported the glass. A rope bridge extended from our platform to a matching one on the far side of the room. A lot of birds were nesting in the treetops close by, where they'd be safe from most predators in the wild. To my surprise, one of the sloths was moving along a branch right above the bridge.

I'd seen the sloths hundreds of times, but this was the first time I'd ever seen one moving. It was hanging from the branch by its claws, poking along at a speed that made turtles look fast. Sloths are the slowest of all mammals; like koalas, they survive on leaves, which provide very little nutrition, and moving slowly conserves precious energy. (So does not going to the bathroom; most sloths only poop once a week.) In fact, sloths are so lethargic, they are their own ecosystems. There are species of moth and algae that live only in sloth fur; the sloths can't even expend the energy to groom them away.

This one seemed startled to see Summer and me, as if

it knew humans normally didn't come here at this time. It actually tried to swat at us in self-defense, but even this was done in slow motion. I could have waited five minutes and still had time to get out of the way. Instead, I backed off, raising my hands to show the sloth that I meant no harm.

"I'm not saying you're *wrong* that the hunter shot from up here," I told Summer. "In fact, you're probably right. I'm only trying to make sense of everything."

Summer turned away, still seeming annoyed at me. "You want to make sense of everything? How's this? Hoenekker knows how to get around security. And I'll bet you he knows how to get up here. So he could easily be our hunter."

I thought about pointing out that Hoenekker didn't seem to have a motive but figured it would probably aggravate Summer even more.

The wooden platform butted up against the wall not far below the dome. There was a door in the wall, though it was so well camouflaged—there was actually moss and other plants growing on it—that I'd never even noticed it before. A security keypad was hidden among the greenery. Summer tapped in her code and we slipped through the door.

It led to a small cement room lit by bare bulbs. A steel ladder was bolted into the wall. The room was so cold and industrial compared to the rainforest that it felt as though we'd entered another dimension rather than merely passed through a door. There was no heat here. The rungs of the ladder felt like solid ice.

Summer quickly scaled the ladder to a metal hatch in the ceiling. Then she flipped the hatch open and clambered outside.

I followed her out onto the roof. The part we emerged onto was cement and surrounded the glass dome covering the rain forest—but it still tilted more than I'd expected, slanting downward at a dangerous angle. Thankfully, there was a low wall built around the edge of the roof, so that if one of us fell, we wouldn't tumble right off and splatter on the ground, but I watched my step anyhow. Two metal catwalks ringed the dome, one down by the wall below us and one higher up, circling the glass portion, so that maintenance workers could get around. We headed for the higher one, which was closer and better lit; the lights from inside the rain forest shone so brightly through the glass, the dome seemed to glow.

I'd never realized it before, but except for the administration building, World of Reptiles was the highest structure in the park. So we had a great view of not just all of FunJungle, but of a great swath of the hill country as well. As big as the park was, it looked like a small bubble of light surrounded by a great dark sea of forest. In the distance, I could see the lights of town, and far to the south, San Antonio glimmered on the horizon.

The building was also tall enough to catch a lot more wind than the rest of the park. It knifed through my clothes, chilling me quickly, and blew loud enough that it was hard for Summer and me to hear each other.

The hatch we'd come through was located on the opposite side of the dome from SafariLand. "The hunter probably shot from the other side," Summer said, leaning in close so she wouldn't have to shout. I got a strong whiff of her shampoo, which smelled like flowers. "If there's any evidence, it'd be over there."

"Probably by the wall," I added. "If she dropped a bullet casing, it'd roll down there, right?"

"Good thinking." Summer flashed a smile. Her face was only a few inches from mine, and for a few moments, I no longer felt cold at all.

Then she turned away and started along the upper catwalk.

The glass portion of the dome was only about fifteen feet tall at the highest point, but it was as big around as a baseball diamond. We circled clockwise around it, keeping the glass to our right. Now, close up, I could see there was a grid of curved steel beams that provided a frame for the glass, as well as a narrow catwalk on the inside of the dome that looped around its base. Every few feet, we passed a sliding panel in the glass to access the inner catwalk from outside.

"What do you think these panels are for?" I asked Summer.

"Maintenance, I guess," she replied. "They have to clean the windows every few days."

SafariLand came into view. Since it was unlit, it blended into the dark forest that bordered the park, but I knew Fun-Jungle well enough to know exactly where it was. Summer was right. From where we stood, there was a direct shot straight down over the monorail station to the house where Rhonda lived. I could make out the light in her window. It was about a quarter mile away, a long shot, but probably not too difficult for a crack shot with a good rifle. After all, a rhino was a big target. In fact, any rhino out on the Asian Plains would have been a relatively easy target as well.

I shifted my attention to the edge of the dome below us. It wasn't nearly as well lit as where we stood, full of shadows. "It's not going to be easy to find anything down there," I said.

"Then we'd better start looking," Summer told me. She stepped off the upper catwalk and started edging down the slanted roof toward the wall.

I was about to follow when something made me stop. I wasn't sure what, exactly. Maybe a sound so low that it was almost swallowed by the wind, or a vibration in the roof, or just a feeling. But whatever it was, I turned around and looked up, toward the very top of the glass dome.

Something was up there. For a moment I thought it was actually *inside* the dome, like one of the bigger birds flapping up against the glass. But then I realized that it was outside, on top of the building, and that it was far too big to be a bird.

It was the hunter. She was sheathed in dark clothing so she melted into the night, but she was there, lying prone on the top of the dome. She hadn't noticed us yet, because she was focused on her rifle. She was peering through the scope with her finger around the trigger, aiming toward SafariLand.

CROCODILES

I yelled at the top of my lungs.

I didn't think about it. There was no time to think. The hunter was about to pull the trigger, and all I knew was I had to do *something*.

"No!" I yelled, as loud as I could, trying to be heard over the wind. "Stop!"

The hunter looked toward me. I couldn't see her face in the darkness, but the way her body moved, I could tell she was startled. She certainly hadn't expected anyone to catch her in the act up there, let alone a couple of kids. She snapped to her feet, holding the rifle.

Summer raced past me, grabbing my hand. "Come on!" she shouted, dragging me along the catwalk. "Let's get out of here!"

"No!" I shouted back. "We have to stop her!"

"We *have* stopped her! For now! She's not gonna shoot the rhino as long as we're around to call security on her! But if she gets rid of us . . ."

Summer didn't get to finish the thought. The hunter suddenly dropped onto the catwalk ahead of us. Rather than circling around the glass dome as we had, she'd raced across the top and now stood between us and the hatch that led down from the roof. Her face was hidden beneath a ski mask, but I could clearly see the rifle cradled in her hands.

Summer and I pivoted on our heels at once, racing back the way we had come.

"That's the only way out!" I yelled. "She's got us trapped!"

"No, she doesn't." Summer slid open one of the glass panels in the dome. Warm, humid air blasted out of it. Summer dropped to her knees and crawled through onto the inner catwalk.

I scrambled through after her, sliding the panel shut behind me. The sudden warmth inside was a welcome change from the cold and the wind, but our new position seemed worse in every other way. The catwalk was surprisingly narrow, with no safety rail. Instead, there was a bar around the dome so maintenance workers wearing safety harnesses could clip onto it, but Summer and I didn't have anything like that. We were essentially on a narrow ledge hanging over a five-story drop. And to make matters worse, we were directly above the saltwater crocodile tank. Far beneath us, I could see Didgeridoo lolling in the water. The big croc looked deceptively sluggish, but I knew that, should one of us happen to fall into the tank, we'd be attacked instantly. Escape would be impossible.

If Summer was worried about the crocodiles below, however, she didn't show it. Instead, she was far more concerned about the hunter. She pointed to a tree a few feet from the catwalk. It was the tallest in the atrium, rising so high its leaves brushed the glass. "There!" she exclaimed. "We can climb down that!"

I considered the tree uneasily. The branches this high didn't look very strong. And it still seemed disturbingly far away, given that falling short of it would result in a plummet into the croc tank. "I don't know . . ."

"There's no choice!" Summer told me. "The hunter's coming for us!"

I glanced at the dome, looking for the hunter, but the glass was too fogged with moisture to see through it. I couldn't tell if the hunter was following us or not, but if she was, Summer was probably right to expect trouble.

I turned back to Summer just in time to see her jump. She leaped though the air high above the crocodile tank and slammed into the tree, wrapping her arms around the trunk. The sudden jolt shook the whole tree, startling dozens of birds that had been roosting in the canopy and sending them screeching into the air. One nearly flew right into me, forcing me to rear back so quickly I nearly pitched off the catwalk. If I hadn't snagged the safety bar at the last second, I would have been crocodile chow.

In the tree, Summer was also having a bit of trouble. Her feet were slipping around on the smooth bark while she struggled to find a decent foothold. But then she located a small branch that could support her, and after that, she seemed perfectly fine. She turned to me, looking hugely relieved, and yelled, "It's not too hard! Come on!"

"You need to get out of the way!" I told her. "Start climbing down!"

Summer had realized the same thing and was already moving. She scrambled down through the branches quickly, clearing a spot for me to jump to. The last few birds flapped past, clearing the air between me and the tree.

I took a final second to gather my nerve. If I'd been on solid ground, I wouldn't have thought twice about making the jump. But the penalty for failure here was death by crocodile, so I didn't want to make any mistakes.

There was a thump outside the glass of the dome. It could have been a dozen things: a strong wind blowing something into the glass, some of the machinery on the roof turning on, or a local bird landing outside. But at the moment, I assumed it was the hunter trying to slide the glass panel open to get me.

I jumped.

I was in the air less than a second, but it seemed a lot longer. Somewhere along the way, I felt a pang of fear that I hadn't leaped far enough and was going to tumble down into the croc tank. And then, suddenly, I was at the tree. I smashed into the trunk far harder than I'd expected, so hard that I almost bounded right back off again. I started to drop down through the branches and lashed out, scrabbling for a handhold. A branch caught me under the right arm, and I clung on for dear life. The branch bowed, but it held, and I heaved a massive sigh of relief that I was safe. For the moment, at least.

Unfortunately, my sudden impact had shaken the tree again. Summer, climbing down below me, wasn't ready for it. She lost her balance and ended up with far too much of her weight on one spindly branch, which snapped beneath her. The crack echoed like a gunshot, followed by a scream from Summer. She pitched forward, arms pinwheeling madly, and would have tumbled out of the tree if her right hand hadn't somehow found another branch. She seized on it as she fell. It splintered, but held, leaving Summer dangling by one arm high above the crocs.

One of her pink shoes slipped off her feet, cartwheeled down through the air, and plopped into the crocodile tank.

Didgeridoo's attack instincts triggered instantly. One

moment, he was still as a statue; the next, he was an explosion of energy. He whipped around, sensing prey, roiling the water as though a depth charge had gone off. His massive jaws snapped shut, and the shoe was gone. Didgeridoo gulped it down easily, then remained on the alert—as did the other six crocs, who'd been roused by his actions. Two slithered off the bank into the water and began to circle ominously below us.

The branch Summer hung from splintered some more.

"Teddy!" she cried. "Help me!"

I was already on my way, climbing down as quickly as I could, taking care not to put any more weight on the branch she was dangling from. Soon I was even with her, but to my dismay, she was hanging four feet away from the trunk, as far as I could reach. I propped one foot on the jagged stump of the branch that had broken beneath her, hoping it would hold, then extended my hand toward her. "Grab my arm! I'll pull you back!"

"I can't!" Summer looked to me. Her breath was coming in quick, ragged spurts. I could tell she was terrified but fighting to remain calm. "If I fall, both of us will go."

I hadn't thought of that. And now that I did, I realized she was probably right. I quickly looked around for any other way I could help her but saw nothing. We weren't far from the highest rope bridge now. I could have shimmied along a branch over it and dropped to safety, but that wouldn't help

Summer. I could have phoned my parents for help, but they were certainly at least five minutes away, if not more, and Summer didn't have that kind of time. The branch she hung from was splintering more every moment. And there was still the hunter to consider. Hanging out in the open over the crocodile pit, Summer was an easy target.

There was no other choice. I wrapped my left arm as tightly as I could around the tree, then held out my right arm again. "Summer! Grab on! We won't fall! I promise!"

The branch Summer clung to cracked a bit more and bent lower. Summer gave a yelp of fear and reached for me.

Far below, Didgeridoo had spotted us. He opened his massive mouth wide like a bear trap, waiting for us to fall.

Summer's fingers grazed mine. I fought the urge to simply grab her hand, knowing that I'd never be able to keep hold of her that way. I'd learned this from my father, who'd been in more than his share of tough spots. Our hands were slick with sweat; hers would slip right out of mine. The trick was to grasp each other's wrists, which would be far more secure.

Only, Summer's wrist was too far away. And her arm was waving wildly as the branch she hung from jostled and cracked.

"Summer, keep still," I ordered.

"I'm trying!" she yelled, panic starting to kick in now. "It's not easy!"

"Just try!"

Summer did her best to steady herself, stretching her free arm toward me as far as she could, desperation in her eyes.

She was too far to reach with my left arm locked around the tree trunk. I found a branch to grab instead, which gave me another few inches but left me in a far more precarious position, and extended out as far as I could.

There was now nothing between me and Didgeridoo but air.

Summer swung toward me and desperately lashed out her arm. We clenched our hands around each other's wrists.

Right as the branch in her other hand snapped off.

There wasn't even time for Summer to scream. It happened so fast, neither of us was fully aware of what was going on. All I knew was that suddenly I felt as though both of my arms were going to rip from their sockets. I'd braced myself well, though, and held on tight, as did Summer. Instead of tumbling down through the branches into Didgeridoo's mouth, I stayed put, while Summer swung like Tarzan into the tree below me. Within a second, she had found hand and footholds and was clinging on tightly, safe and sound.

The broken branch dropped downward and landed right in Didgeridoo's mouth. His bear trap jaws snapped shut so hard that the branch shattered into toothpicks. The other crocs, sensing prey, pounced on top of him, and the water boiled as they thrashed about.

Summer was now right by the branch that extended over the rope bridge. Without a moment's hesitation, she scurried along it and dropped down to safety. I followed only a second behind her. The rope bridge jounced as we hit it and shook wildly, and we tumbled onto its wooden slats, tangled up together.

Somehow, our faces ended up only inches from each other. I was looking right into Summer's eyes and saw her panic fading and relief flooding in. "You saved my life!" she exclaimed.

And then, before either of us even realized what was happening, she kissed me.

It was the opposite experience of jumping over the crocodile pit. Neither event took very long, but while the jump had felt like it lasted forever, the kiss seemed to barely exist in time at all. It seemed to be over before it had even started: not a big, smoochy movie kiss, but a quick, thankful peck on the lips. And yet it was the first time I'd ever been kissed by a girl—a girl who I actually *liked*, no less—and as brief as it was, it still rocked my world. All the scares and near-death experiences of the past few minutes seemed completely worthwhile in exchange for it.

I was so startled by it, I didn't even notice the hunter had arrived.

19

THE SLOTH

Summer noticed the hunter first. She suddenly pulled away from me and leaped to her feet, staring fearfully toward the end of the rope bridge.

The hunter was standing on the wooden platform. Rather than following us through the window and down the tree, she had taken the much safer route, through the hatch in the roof—the same way Summer and I had gone up. The moss-covered door hung open behind her. The hunter was in the shadow of the big tree there, the ski mask still pulled down over her face, the rifle in her hands.

There was another staircase behind us, at the opposite end of the bridge, but it was too far away; we didn't have time to run to it. So Summer did the only thing she could think of. She grabbed the closest large object and threw it at the hunter. It turned out, the closest large object to us was the sloth.

It was the same sloth we had startled earlier. The entire time we'd been up on the roof and dangling above the crocodile, it had gone a whole two feet along the branch and was now hanging right over the railing beside us. It went a lot faster once Summer threw it. Her aim was dead-on. The sloth hurtled straight for the hunter's chest.

The hunter instinctively dropped her rifle and caught the sloth. The sloth—even more startled now that it had flown for the first time in its life—instantly sank its claws into the hunter's arms. Meanwhile, the hundreds of moths that had been roosting in its fur took to the air, creating a living cloud. The hunter staggered backward, either from the pain of being clawed or the shock of suddenly finding a smelly, moth-infested mammal clinging to her, and slipped on her rifle. She crashed to the ground, and the sloth landed right on her face. The sloth gave a surprised bleat, the only sound I'd ever heard a sloth make in my life. The rifle skittered across the wooden platform, flew over the edge, and tumbled down into the rainforest. It caromed off a branch, spun through the air—and plopped right into the crocodile tank, where Didgeridoo, desperate to eat *something* besides a shoe and a tree branch, immediately pounced on it. Several of the other crocs lunged at it too, churning the water into froth as they battled for it.

Now unarmed, the hunter shoved the sloth off her face and scrambled down the stairs from the platform, spitting out sloth hair as she went. By the time Summer and I made it off the wobbling rope bridge to the platform ourselves, the hunter was already two flights down and moving fast. She darted across the long bridge below us, cutting past where the crocs were fighting for her rifle, and disappeared under the cover of the trees.

I started down the stairs after her, but Summer blocked my path. "No," she said firmly. "We've faced enough danger today."

"She's getting away!" I argued.

"Or she's preparing to ambush us. For all we know, she has another weapon. A knife or something." Summer whipped out her phone and told it, "Call security."

She had a good point. Besides, I was wiped from our experience in the tree. Now that the adrenaline rush was over, I felt weak in the knees. I sagged against the railing of the platform while we waited for the phone to ring.

"You threw a *sloth* at her," I said.

"It was self-defense," Summer informed me. "I grabbed the closest thing I could find. I didn't even realize it was a sloth until I'd already thrown it. I thought it was a big old fruit or something."

A dispatcher answered the phone. "Security."

"This is Summer McCracken," Summer said. "I'm in World of Reptiles and I've just been attacked by the hunter who's been trying to kill the rhino here. She's still in the building, but she's on the run. I need all available security here now!"

"Is this a joke?" the security officer asked.

"No!" Summer snapped. "It's really me! Check the caller ID if you need proof! And then get everyone out here right now! If the poacher gets away, I'll make sure my father knows it was your fault!"

"Yes, ma'am!" the security dispatcher said, cowed by Summer's threat. "I'm sending out all available officers right now."

"Tell them to hurry," Summer said.

"Can you stay on the line?" the dispatcher asked. "In case we need more information?"

"Sure," Summer told her.

The sloth was still lying on the platform near us. It appeared to be exhausted after its ordeal, having worked very hard for a sloth. Something dark was wadded up in one of its front claws.

I knelt down to inspect it closer. It was part of the hunter's ski mask, a clump of cotton that must have torn off when the hunter had yanked the sloth off her face. I reached down to take it.

The sloth, already on edge, attacked me. However, since it was a sloth, the attack wasn't very fast. Its arm swung at me in slow motion, claws extended. I probably had a minute to get out of the way, but I stepped aside quickly anyhow.

The sloth bleated at me angrily. It wasn't very frightening. Instead, it looked like a perturbed teddy bear.

The dispatcher came back on the line. "Security is en route. Can you describe the perpetrator?" he asked.

"Sure," Summer replied. "She's wearing camouflage gear, a hunting jacket, gloves, a ski mask—"

"A *torn* ski mask," I corrected.

"A torn ski mask and boots," Summer said. "She had a rifle, but it kind of got eaten."

"I'm sorry," the dispatcher said. "Did you say *eaten*?"

"Yes," Summer told her. "By a crocodile."

"A crocodile?" the dispatcher repeated.

"A big one," Summer said.

"Right." The dispatcher seemed to be taking a moment to make sense of this. "Can you describe the perpetrator herself—not merely what she's wearing? Height, weight, hair color, eyes, distinguishing birthmarks . . ."

"Um . . . hold on." Summer looked to me blankly. "What did she look like? I didn't get a good look at her."

I realized I hadn't either. I'd only seen the hunter in the dark, or the shadows, or with a sloth over her face. And she'd been wearing heavy clothes and a ski mask. I didn't even know the color of her skin. "She's medium height, I think. And kind of skinny."

"Medium height and skinny," Summer reported.

"That's all you've got?" the dispatcher asked, sounding somewhat annoyed.

"She might have some claw marks on her from an angry sloth," Summer suggested helpfully.

"What's a sloth?" the dispatcher asked.

The sloth in question was coming at me again. Slowly. It was crawling across the platform at about two miles an hour. I wasn't really worried about it, but I signaled Summer we should head down the stairs anyhow. The sloth had experienced enough excitement that night.

Summer followed me down. "A *sloth*," she repeated to the dispatcher. "It's a medium-sized tree-dwelling mammal. Lives in the rain forest. Hangs upside down its whole life."

"Are you making all this up?" the dispatcher asked.

"No!" Summer said. "It's a real animal! You've never heard of one? You work at a zoo, for Pete's sake!"

"Can you add anything else to the description of the hunter?" the dispatcher asked. "Like ethnicity?"

Summer looked to me. I shook my head. "Er . . . no," Summer said.

The dispatcher sighed. "That's not very helpful."

"It's a woman dressed in hunting gear with claw marks on her arm, running away from World of Reptiles!" Summer said angrily. "How many of those could there be? You know what'd be helpful? If your people got out here faster and caught the criminal!"

"I told you there were agents en route," the dispatcher replied curtly. "They will do their best, but it'd be useful to have a more accurate description. Clothes can be changed. Skin color can't."

Summer and I reached the long bridge that veered closest to the crocodile tank. The huge reptiles were no longer battling for the rifle. Either they had realized it wasn't prey—or one of them had swallowed it anyhow.

"Freeze!" someone yelled.

Summer and I did, reflexively putting our hands in the air.

A security guard had entered the rain forest. It was Kevin, the exceptionally young guard we'd met at the entry booth the day before. He looked very nervous and unsure of himself. His gun was pointed at us. "Security!" he announced. "Get your hands up!"

"They *are* up," Summer said.

"Oh," said Kevin.

"We're not the bad guys!" I told him. "We're the ones who called for you! The hunter was running *out* of the building."

"Oh," Kevin said again. He lowered his gun sheepishly. "I didn't see anyone out there."

Another guard suddenly entered the other side of the room, having come in through the exit. She looked slightly older and seemed more competent. But then, the sloth seemed more competent than Kevin. "Any sign of her?" she asked.

"No," Kevin said. "You?"

"Would I be asking you if you'd seen her if I'd seen her?" the second guard asked.

"Oh," Kevin said once more. Then he looked at Summer and me. "Sorry, guys. Looks like she got away."

"Great," I muttered, staring down at the crocodile tank. "The hunter's gone, we nearly died, and all our evidence got eaten."

"We chased her off and got her gun," Summer pointed out. "So maybe she won't come back again."

"You really think so?" I asked.

Summer considered it, then frowned. "No."

"Me neither," I said.

DAMAGE CONTROL

Within the next half hour, dozens of adults descended upon World of Reptiles. Some had still been at the park when the alert had gone out, but many had raced there from their homes.

Chief Hoenekker was there, along with every security guard he could round up. Some of them took statements from Summer and me about what had happened. Others went up on the roof to search for clues. Large Marge simply lurked in the rain forest, pretending to be busy while giving me the stink eye.

Then there were the keepers. Vicky Benbow, the shy rhino keeper, had come from Rhonda's quarters. According to her, Rhonda and all the other rhinos were unharmed; Summer and I had stopped the hunter before she'd had a chance to shoot.

All available herpetologists were making sure that none of the reptiles had been hurt, while the crocodile specialist was helping security fish what little remained of the rifle out of the exhibit. And a biologist had examined the sloth; she reported that it was exhausted, but otherwise fine.

J.J. McCracken was there too. Once he'd made sure that Summer was all right he had chewed out Hondo for letting her ditch him, and then ordered him to take her home. Then he'd shifted into business mode, trying to determine what had happened and what could be done about it. Pete Thwacker and Kristi Sullivan were close by. So was Athmani, who was now pressing J.J. to consider removing the rhino horns once and for all.

And my parents were there. They'd come directly to World of Reptiles after I'd called them to let them know what had happened. (It had taken them a little longer to get there than it usually might have since Mom was on crutches.) Both were relieved I was all right but upset at me for putting myself in danger once again. Mom was particularly angry.

All of of us were gathered in the atrium. The animals had finally calmed down after all the excitement. The crocodiles had gone back to being practically motionless. The birds had returned to their roosts. The sloth had climbed back up into a tree and was contentedly eating leaves.

"Why on earth did you and Summer decide to investigate

this yourselves?" Mom demanded. "Especially after what's happened to you in the past?"

I glanced toward J.J., feeling more annoyed than ever that I couldn't tell the truth about what was going on. Especially now that I was in trouble for helping investigate. "We didn't think we were going to find the hunter," I explained. "We were only trying to see if the shot might have been fired from up there."

"That's no excuse," Mom said angrily. "Going out on that roof would be dangerous whether the hunter was there or not. That's why it's off-limits. If you thought there was a lead up there, you should have called security."

"Summer didn't trust Chief Hoenekker." I spoke as quietly as I could, since Hoenekker wasn't far away.

"Why not?" Dad asked.

"He just hasn't been that good at investigating stuff," I replied.

"So you don't have any concrete evidence against him?" Dad inquired.

"No," I admitted.

"Teddy shouldn't have any concrete evidence against anyone," Mom pointed out; then she shifted her attention to me. "You shouldn't be investigating this case, period. We have a security division to handle things like this. This is their job, not yours."

"You're letting me help investigate Pancake's escape," I countered.

"There's a big difference between helping put a camera in the orangutan exhibit and going up onto the roof at night without permission. Especially when there's a killer running around this zoo."

"She's trying to kill animals, not humans," I argued.

"You have no idea what she'd do!" Mom snapped. "She was armed and dangerous, and you put yourselves right in her way! What were you thinking?"

I looked toward J.J. again. He didn't seem to be aware of what was going on with my parents and me, as he was surrounded by a dozen people who all wanted his attention at once. Even though most of them were taller than he was, he still seemed bigger than them somehow. He radiated a sense of power. I really didn't want to get him angry at me.

"Teddy," Dad said, not pleased that I hadn't answered the question, "Your mother and I have given you a lot of freedom lately. You're almost thirteen and we thought you deserved it. But behavior like this makes us think you might need more restrictions. . . ."

"That's not fair," I said, before he could go on.

"Well, we obviously can't trust you to not take risks like this," Mom said.

"I didn't want to go up there!" I exclaimed, before I could control myself. "I was forced to!"

"By Summer?" Mom asked. "If that's the case, then maybe you shouldn't be allowed to see her anymore."

"No!" I yelled, louder than I'd meant to. Having more restrictions placed on me would have been bad enough, but not being allowed to see Summer was the worst punishment I could imagine. "Summer didn't force me to do anything."

Mom leaned forward on her crutches. "Then who did?"

I looked J.J.'s way one more time. Which was one time too many. Mom and Dad both realized what was going on.

"J.J.?" Dad asked, sounding stunned. "He forced you to go up there?"

I thought about denying it, but I was tired of lying to my parents. Plus, I was pretty sure they'd know I was lying. "Well, he didn't force me onto the roof, exactly. . . ."

"What did he do?" Mom pressed.

I lowered my voice as much as I could. "He asked me to help investigate."

"Why didn't you tell us?" Dad asked.

"He told me not to. He didn't think you'd let me."

"And you didn't tell us anyhow?" Mom asked angrily.

"He . . . uh . . . ," I stammered. "He kind of . . . threatened me not to tell you."

Rage flashed in Mom's eyes. She spun on her crutches and started hobbling toward J.J.

Dad blocked her path. "Whoa, Charlene. Where are you going?"

"To punch J.J. McCracken's face in," Mom replied, then tried to go around him.

Dad blocked her again. "Let's not do anything we're going to regret."

"Oh, I won't regret this at all," Mom said. "In fact, I'm going to enjoy it. Anyone who coerces a kid into doing his dirty work deserves a punch in the face." She slipped away from Dad with amazing agility, given her crutches, then bore down on J.J.

Dad and I ran after her. Chief Hoenekker seemed to recognize Mom's intent, because he placed himself in her way. "What's going on, Charlene?"

"I'll tell you what." Mom aimed a crutch toward J.J. and yelled, "That little weasel forced my son into investigating this case!"

J.J. and the entire crowd around him turned to face her. J.J. gave Mom a puzzled stare and lied to her face. "I don't know what you're talking about, Charlene."

"Don't give me that garbage!" Mom shouted. "You know exactly what I'm talking about."

J.J. kept up the confused act. "Did Teddy *tell* you I forced him into this?"

Before Mom could answer, Marge popped out from behind a planter, where she'd apparently been eavesdropping on us. "He sure did!" she crowed. "Instead of taking the blame for his actions, he blamed everything on you!"

Mom wheeled on her. "Marjorie, if you don't stop sticking your nose in our business, so help me, I will rip it off your face and feed it to the crocodiles!"

Marge recoiled from Mom in surprise, stumbled over the edge of the planter, and toppled into it.

Mom turned back to J.J. "Teddy didn't tell me anything. He tried to keep your secret, exactly like you told him to do. But I'm not as dumb as you think I am."

"Now, now, Charlene," J.J. said calmly. "I think there's been a misunderstanding here. I *did* ask Teddy for his thoughts on the case. But I certainly didn't encourage him to help investigate. I would never do anything that would put his life in danger. However, it seems that he and my daughter got a bit overzealous."

He spun the lie so well that I almost believed it myself. And my mother seemed to buy it too. J.J. had chosen his words well; sadly, I *had* been overzealous before. I looked to Chief Hoenekker, hoping he'd back me up and tell Mom the truth—after all, he'd been annoyed by the whole thing—but to my surprise, he avoided my gaze and kept quiet.

Instead, it was Athmani who spoke up. "Charlene, your son is being honest. J.J. requested that he help us with the investigation."

J.J. glared at Athmani, angry at being betrayed—but his anger was nothing compared to Mom's. Before J.J. could say a word, she cut him off. "You deceitful little rat! It's not enough that you strong-arm a twelve-year-old boy into risking his life? Then you have the gall to lie about it?"

Athmani raced to Mom's side, signaling her to calm down. "Please!" he cried. "I understand you are angry. And J.J. certainly has much to answer for. But for the moment, we have a very serious issue at hand that must be dealt with immediately. Our rhinos are in grave danger, so I beg of you all, let us put these other issues aside and figure out what to do."

Everyone nodded agreement and turned to Mom expectantly.

Mom looked to all of them, then took a deep breath, forcing herself to calm down. She was obviously still livid, but she seemed to realize Athmani was right. "All right," she said. "But this isn't over, J.J."

J.J. didn't reply to her. For once, it appeared that he didn't know what to say.

Athmani turned back to him. "It must be obvious to you by now that the situation is critical. The hunter can get inside the park, she is relentless, and we have no clue who she is."

"That's not exactly true," J.J. told him. "We have a few leads. Hoenekker, have you followed up on the names I gave you this evening?"

I figured he meant the names Summer and I had found. If he'd admitted they'd come from us, Mom probably would have flipped out again.

"I was starting to," Hoenekker replied. "But I didn't have much time before this came up."

"It doesn't matter if we have leads or not," Athmani said. "This hunter knows we're looking for her, and she has continued to infiltrate the park. What's to say that she will not do so again?"

"Is anything left of the rifle?" Dad suggested. "Something we could get a fingerprint off of?"

Hoenekker shouted across the room to where Deirdre Garcia, a female security guard, was perched on some rocks on the edge of the crocodile tank with Jon Mattingly, FunJungle's crocodile specialist. "Garcia, what's the situation with the gun?"

"Not good," Garcia reported back. "The crocs ate most of it—and what's left is trashed. The barrel's too mangled to do a ballistics test, the stock is too messed up to get a fingerprint, and the plate with the registration number for the weapon seems to be, er . . . inside one of the crocs."

"Any chance it'll get pooped out anytime soon?" Hoenekker asked.

Garcia looked to Mattingly, unsure.

"Could be a few days," Mattingly said. "If it comes out at all. And chances are, it won't be much use. Our crocs all use gizzard stones."

"What are those?" Hoenekker demanded.

"They're rocks," Mattingly replied. "The crocs swallow them to help with their digestion. They stay in the stomach and help pulverize anything that comes in there. It's quite common. Ostriches use them. So do chickens."

"I don't need a biology lecture right now," Hoenekker said curtly. "I need evidence. What's the final analysis here?"

Mattingly said, "Anything those crocs consume, even inorganic matter, is going to take a real beating inside their digestive tract."

Hoenekker grimaced, then ordered, "Well, do what you can to get that tank swept anyhow. Maybe there's something we can use down in the drain somewhere."

"We're working on it, sir!" Garcia saluted, then returned her attention to the tank.

"No gun, no evidence," Athmani told J.J. "We're not any closer to catching this hunter than we were two days ago."

Hoenekker bristled at this, as though it were an attack on his competence. "That's not true. We've already caught the hunter on camera once. I have my men combing through the security footage from this building as we speak. The hunter might show up on one of the cameras."

"*Might*," J.J. repeated, sounding doubtful. "Or they might not, either. Your men have spent the whole day going over last night's security footage and they've found one grainy still. That ain't much."

Athmani added, "I don't think we have time to sort through all the footage from this building. That could take hours—and even if you do find the hunter again, she had a mask on. Meanwhile, she could still be on the property right now. For all we know, while we're all sitting here, she could be going after the rhinos."

I found this idea disturbing, and I could see that many other people—including my parents and J.J.—did too.

"She lost her gun," Hoenekker said weakly.

"She could have another," Athmani replied. "In my experience, poachers usually bring more than one weapon." He turned to me. "Did she have only the one rifle with her when you saw her, Teddy? Might she have had another slung across her back?"

I thought back to my confrontation with the poacher. Sadly, even though it had taken place only a short while before, everything about it seemed as hazy as though it had been years earlier. I'd never had more than a quick glimpse of the hunter, and she had always been in darkness or shadow. Plus, there had been so much else going on—dangling over the crocodiles, dealing with the sloth, getting kissed by Summer—that I hadn't focused on the hunter as much as I should have. "I don't know," I said sadly. "She might have."

"Is there anything else you can tell us about her?" J.J. asked.

"No," I replied. "Everything happened so fast."

J.J. pursed his lips, looking displeased. "Do you have any other thoughts on who this woman might be? As long as the cat's out of the bag that you're helping on this, you might as well put your two cents in."

Everyone looked toward me expectantly. Even Mom and Dad, despite their anger at J.J. for pressing me into investigating, seemed hopeful that I'd figured everything out.

But I hadn't. To my frustration, I wasn't even close. Instead, everything I'd learned had muddied the picture even more. Nothing made sense. Why had the poacher shot from the top of World of Reptiles one morning, then tried to cross SafariLand at night, then returned to World of Reptiles for the third attempt? Why had she not used the silencer the first time, then brought it afterward? Was she really trying to get the rhino's horns, and if so, how did she plan on getting them out of the park? And if she didn't want the horns, why was she trying to kill Rhonda, rather than any of the other rhinos? Why had she gone through so much trouble to figure out how to break into SafariLand, but then climbed over the fence so close to one of the few security cameras? All those questions seemed linked somehow, like the explanation for any one of them would explain all the rest as well, but for the life of me, I couldn't imagine what it was. My head felt empty inside, and having everyone staring at me, hoping I'd figure it all out, only made the situation worse.

I lowered my eyes and shook my head. "No," I said again. "I'm sorry."

Everyone looked very disappointed. Especially J.J. "Great," he muttered under his breath. "That's just great."

Dad slipped an arm around my shoulders, trying to comfort me. "There's nothing to be sorry about," he said.

Mom kneeled beside me. She tried her best to be sympathetic, although it was obvious she was still angry at J.J. "You're only a boy," she told me. "This isn't your job. It's theirs." She pointed toward where J.J. and all the others were clustered together.

I nodded understanding, but I still felt terrible. Maybe J.J. had sought my help in the wrong way, but it was still a show of faith—and I'd failed him. I'd failed the rhinos, too. In fact, I'd failed everyone.

"We have to take action," Athmani was telling J.J. "This poacher is running circles around us. If we don't act soon, we are going to have a dead rhino on our hands. Or possibly several dead rhinos."

J.J. shook his head, looking defeated, then glanced around the rain forest. "Where the heck is Doc?" he demanded.

"I'm here," Doc replied, entering the room behind us. He was dressed in surgical scrubs, though he'd pulled a winter coat on over them.

"I called you more than half an hour ago," J.J. said pointedly.

"First of all, I'm not your butler," Doc growled. "I don't have to come running the moment you decide you need me. Second, I was in surgery, taking care of one of your baboons, which I figured you wouldn't want me running out in the middle of."

J.J. looked annoyed—he wasn't used to people speaking to him the way Doc did—but he let it slide.

"How is Bababoonie's tooth?" Mom asked as Doc passed us.

"As good as new." Doc gave Mom one of his rare smiles. "The surgery went well. Give him a day to sleep it off and we'll get him back on exhibit." He continued on to join J.J. and the others. "What's the story here?"

"The poacher made another attempt and got away again," J.J. informed him. "I want you to take the horns off the rhinos. Tonight."

A stunned silence filled the room. It seemed as though even the birds stopped making noise for a moment.

"You know how I feel about doing that," Doc said.

"I do," J.J. replied. "I wouldn't ask you to do it if there were any other option. But at this moment, it doesn't appear there is."

"Of course there is," Doc snapped. "Find the dang poacher!"

"I'm trying my best," Hoenekker said defensively. "My men are working around the clock on this."

"Doc," Athmani said pleadingly, "the rhinos are in grave danger. The poacher knows how to get in and out of Fun-Jungle at will. She made another attempt tonight—and might have been successful if not for Teddy and Summer. She could easily strike again. I know there is some risk in sedating the rhinos while we remove the horns, but not doing anything will be even riskier. You are the very best at what you do. The rhinos will be fine under your care."

"I'm not any happier about it than you are," J.J. told Doc. "I don't want a whole mess of hornless rhinos. But at least it ain't permanent. Once we *do* catch this poacher and put her behind bars, those horns will grow back." He looked to Pete Thwacker. "You can soft sell this to the public, right?"

"Sure," Pete said. "We'll issue a press release saying we're doing it to make a statement about rhino poaching in the wild. We're asking the public if they're ready for a world where every wild rhino looks like this."

We could call it 'Rhinoplasty for Rhino Awareness,'" Kristi suggested.

"That's good!" J.J. exclaimed. "I like it."

Doc ignored them and spoke to Athmani. "You really think it has to be done *tonight*?"

"The sooner, the better," Athmani said. "For all we know, the poacher is still inside the park." He turned to Hoenekker. "For the time being, each rhino we have here ought to be given armed protection."

Hoenekker nodded, looking embarrassed about his failure to catch the hunter. "I'll bring in people right away." He stepped aside to make some calls.

"That's the *other* reason J.J. wants this done tonight," Mom whispered to me. "He doesn't want the public seeing armed guards surrounding his rhinos and asking what they're there for."

Doc was still mulling things over. "I really don't want to do this," he told J.J.

"I really wish you didn't have to," J.J. replied. "But we're at a red alert here."

Doc sighed heavily, then gave in. "These horns will need to be protected," he told J.J. "Once they're off, they'll still be extremely valuable. They need to be delivered to the Convention on the International Trade of Endangered Species."

"Of course," J.J. agreed. "I know the drill. And in the meantime, there's a safe in my office that's more secure than Fort Knox. We can keep the horns there for the short term."

"This isn't going to be easy," Doc told the billionaire. "It'll take most of the night to get every rhino done. I'm going to need a lot of help, and they'll all want double overtime."

"I won't," Vicky Benbow said.

We all turned to her, surprised. Vicky was so meek and quiet, everyone seemed to have forgotten she was there, even though she'd been standing right near all of us.

Vicky shrank back, embarrassed by the sudden attention. When she spoke again, it was barely above a whisper. "I'll work for free tonight if it means saving the rhinos. And I'm sure a lot of the other keepers would too."

All around the room, people chimed agreement with this.

"I'm happy to volunteer as well," Athmani told J.J.

"Me too," Dad put in.

"And me," I said.

Athmani turned to me and smiled. "You have done more than enough for the rhinos tonight, Teddy. What you need to do now is go home and get some sleep." He looked to

Dad. "We'll be okay, Jack. Go spend your precious time with your boy."

"Teddy and I will be all right on our own," Mom said, tousling my hair.

"Looks like I'm in," Dad told Doc.

"Thanks," Doc replied. "Glad to have you aboard."

Dad knelt before me and gave me a tight hug. "No more adventures tonight, okay?"

"I've had enough," I told him. "I promise."

"I'm proud of you," Dad whispered, then stood and gave Mom a kiss good-bye.

Mom and I headed out of the rainforest. We passed the saltwater crocodile tank, where Jon Mattingly was using a net on a long pole to gingerly scoop remnants of the gun off the bottom. There wasn't much left of it except splinters of wood.

"I should have stopped the gun from falling in," I said. "I didn't think about it until it was too late."

"Don't blame yourself for *anything* that's happened," Mom told me. "As angry as I am with J.J. for putting you up to this, if you and Summer hadn't come up here, we might have a dead rhino right now. Or more. You *saved* them. You're a hero."

I glanced back toward the group of people planning how to dehorn the rhinos. Even if Mom was right, I didn't feel good at all. Instead, I felt frustration for not being able to figure out who the hunter was and for not doing more to try to catch her. The rhinos were still in danger, and it was partly my fault. I'd stared right at the hunter, but I still didn't have the slightest idea who she was.

I didn't feel like a hero.

Instead, I felt like the biggest failure in the world.

THE ESCAPE

"Teddy, wake up."

I pried my eyes open to find my father sitting on the edge of my bed. My immediate thought was that something terrible had happened. I bolted upright, kicking the sheets off. "What is it? The rhinos?"

"The rhinos are fine," Dad said comfortingly. "Doc took great care of them. We wrapped things up about half an hour ago."

I glanced at my alarm clock. It was a few minutes after six a.m. Dad was still wearing the same clothes he'd been in the night before. He smelled like rhinos. "What's wrong, then?"

"Pancake escaped."

I scrambled out of bed and started grabbing clothes out of my bureau. "When?"

"Sometime last night. We're not sure. Kyle just called from Monkey Mountain and said he wasn't there."

"But the other orangs are?"

"Yes. The cage door is locked."

I paused in the midst of trying to find a matching pair of socks. "Then how'd Pancake get out?"

"We don't know. But the video should have recorded everything. Want to come check it with us?"

"Definitely."

"Okay." Dad stepped out of the room to give me privacy but spoke through the door. "Your mother thought you should sleep in, but I figured you'd never forgive us if we didn't give you the chance to come along."

"I said you needed your rest," Mom corrected from the kitchen. "You had a lot of excitement last night."

"Well, I'm up now," I told her, yanking my jeans on. "And there's no way I'm getting back to sleep." I grabbed the rest of my clothes and exited my room.

Mom leaned on her crutches in the kitchen, already in her work clothes, cutting a slice of homemade banana bread for me. "I assumed that'd be the case," she said.

I got the rest of my clothes on as quickly as I could, then ate the banana bread as I hurried to FunJungle with my parents. A second trailer had been moved to Lakeside Estates the day before, bringing the grand total up to two. It didn't look like the fancy community Pete had promised so much as a dumping ground for crummy mobile homes.

It was cold and blustery outside. It had rained at some point in the night, and the ground was now icy, which made it trickier than usual for Mom on her crutches.

As we made our way to Monkey Mountain, Dad brought us up to speed on what had happened with the rhinos. J.J. had mobilized his security force, bringing in everyone necessary to work through the night. Some guards had provided protection for all the rhinos while others swept the zoo for any sign of the poacher. They hadn't found her—but she hadn't made any more attempts on the rhinos, either.

Much of the veterinary staff had returned to work for the night as well. Since the operation was relatively simple, everything had been done in the field, rather than going through the trouble of bringing the rhinos into the animal hospital. Each rhino had been led into a house like Rhonda's, away from the other animals, and then sedated. Doc had removed each horn himself. It wasn't that he didn't trust anyone else to do it, Dad said, so much as that he didn't want to make anyone on his staff do such a distasteful thing. The sedation was the most dangerous part of the surgery. Doc had used a special saw to cut the horns off, and he'd taken great care to get as much of each horn as possible.

"So all the rhinos are safe now?" I asked.

"Assuming the hunter was actually going for their horns and not merely looking to kill them for sport," Mom said.

"Right," I agreed, hoping that wasn't the case. It was still hard for me to imagine anyone killing a rhino merely to kill it—especially after talking to Violet's aunt and uncle—but you never knew what humans might sink to.

"And there's still Rhonda," Dad said.

"What's wrong with Rhonda?" I asked.

"Doc thought it was too risky to sedate her during her pregnancy," Dad replied. "She's close to due, and he doesn't want any complications with the baby. So J.J. assigned teams of armed guards to protect her twenty-four hours a day. She's going to stay locked up and under protection until her baby is born."

"How long will that be?" I asked.

Dad shrugged. "Even Doc can't tell for sure. He thinks it's only a few more days, but it could be another week or two."

"J.J. really approved that much protection for that long?" Mom asked skeptically. "He didn't gripe about how expensive it would be?"

"He says he's willing to pay whatever it takes to protect his rhinos," Dad told us.

"You can't believe anything that snake says," Mom grumbled. Her anger at J.J. didn't seem to have lessened overnight. "The man's as two-faced as they come."

"Maybe so," Dad admitted, "but I do think his concern for the rhinos is real."

Mom gave Dad a hard look, annoyed at him for taking J.J.'s side. "The man can't be trusted. He moved our entire house simply because he felt like doing it. He promised he wouldn't build roller coasters here, and now he's building them. He forced our son to investigate a crime and lied to him about why. . . ."

"He didn't lie to me," I said defensively. "He thought I could help find the hunter."

Mom winced, looking upset with herself. Like she'd said something she hadn't meant to.

"You don't think that's the reason?" I asked.

"I'm sure it's part of the reason," Mom hedged. "But with J.J. McCracken, there's always an ulterior motive. You have a history of investigating things without permission here. Sticking your nose where it doesn't belong. Well, if J.J. makes you part of his team, he can keep a better eye on you. He can make sure you report everything you find directly to him. And he can exert control over what you investigate and what you don't."

I didn't really want to believe all that. I wanted to think that J.J. had come to me only because he respected my crime-solving abilities. But I realized Mom was probably right. Which immediately made me question everything J.J.

had said and done over the past few days. I found myself wondering if he even might be involved in trying to get the rhino horns somehow. After all, he had admitted FunJungle was losing money—and rhino horns were worth a lot. He obviously wasn't the hunter—he wasn't a woman, and he was a good few inches shorter than the person I'd encountered at World of Reptiles—but he could have hired someone to get the horns for him.

We arrived at Monkey Mountain. Mom entered her code on the security keypad and led us inside.

"Are the rhino horns in J.J.'s safe?" I asked.

"Yes," Dad told me. "After we finished the dehorning, Athmani took them to J.J.'s office."

"You didn't go with him?" Mom asked.

"I came home to see *you*," Dad replied. "But I know they got there. J.J.'s the only one with the combination, and he stayed here all night so that he could put them in the safe himself. Athmani sent me a photo of them inside as proof." He dug out his phone and brought up the picture.

I examined it as we walked through the halls. The safe was surprisingly large, the size of a small closet. There were several shelves, one of which looked like it held stacks of cash. The horns were piled on the bottom shelf. There were eight in all, four from our Asian rhinos, four from the African ones. Cut loose from the rhinos, they didn't look like anything special, merely lopsided whitish pyramids. "How much do you think they're worth?" I asked.

"They're each a few pounds," Dad said. "At current prices, that's around four million dollars' worth of horns. Maybe even more."

I shook my head in disbelief. It was hard to believe anything could be worth so much money. Or worth killing a living thing for.

And now J.J. McCracken controlled all the access to them. I really hoped that this time he could be trusted.

Mom led us into the backstage area of the orangutan exhibit. Kyle was waiting for us there.

The exhibit looked almost exactly the same as it had the day before. The cage door was closed and locked. The orangutans were inside, behaving like it was a completely normal day. But Pancake was gone.

On our side of the steel bars, six feet above the ground, the metal cover for the air-conditioning vent had been removed. The air-conditioning shaft was visible beyond. It was big enough for a young orangutan to get through.

"That's obviously how he's been getting out of the building," Kyle said. "Clever guy. Look how careful he was. Instead of ripping it off, he actually unscrewed it so he could put it back on again."

The vent cover was lying on the floor. Sure enough, the

four screws that had held it in place were all lying beside it.

"But how'd he get out of the cage in the first place?" I asked.

"Let's check the footage," Dad said. "Teddy, let me boost you up."

Dad had mounted his camera up by the ceiling of the room. Now he knelt beneath it and laced his fingers together, making a step with his hands. I put my foot in it, and he stood, hoisting me up to his shoulders. From there, I was able to reach the camera easily.

"The memory pack is attached to the back of it," Dad told me. "Unclip it and leave the camera there for now."

The camera was still running, having been recording all night. I flipped it off and unclipped the memory pack, which was a black box the size of a deck of cards. "Got it."

"Good work." Dad gently lowered me to the ground.

We all then went to Mom's office, where Dad plugged the memory pack into Mom's computer and accessed the footage he'd shot the night before. It had a time stamp at the bottom, beginning at five p.m. The orangutans were eating dinner, big platters of fruits and vegetables.

Dad started fast-forwarding.

The orangutans on the screen began to move at super-speed, polishing off their food and preparing for bed. Orangutans in the wild often make large nests out of leaves and branches. The ones at FunJungle did the same thing with burlap bags. At seven p.m. a keeper came in to check on them, and by seven thirty the apes were all asleep.

They stayed that way until five a.m.

"Look!" Mom said.

Dad slowed the footage down to normal speed.

While all the other orangutans were still asleep, Pancake was on the move. He emerged from his burlap nest and looked around furtively, like a kid who was planning to raid the cookie jar. Then he shimmied up the bars to the top of the exhibit.

"Can you zoom closer on him?" Mom asked.

"Give me a sec." Dad shifted the mouse around and zoomed in on Pancake. The lights were dim in the room, but not completely dark, simulating a moonlit night in Borneo. We could barely make out what Pancake was doing.

Close to the ceiling of the exhibit, the orangutan had hidden some objects atop one of the horizontal bars. He carefully picked them up and slid back down.

"My goodness," Mom said. "He really is a smart one. The keepers probably only search the floor of the exhibit for things that shouldn't be in there."

"They never look higher?" Dad asked.

"Would *you* have thought to look up there?" Mom replied.

Dad considered that a moment, then admitted, “No. I guess not.”

“What’s he have there?” Kyle asked.

“Looks like a stick,” Mom said.

Sure enough, Pancake had a thin stick, about three feet long. It had most likely come from one of the trees in his exhibit, but he’d obviously taken great care to select it. It was about as straight and thin as a stick could be. Pancake was examining one end of it. There was a small glob stuck there. Pancake prodded it with a finger, then yanked it off, placed it in his mouth, and chewed on it for a bit.

“What’s that?” I asked. “Gum?”

“I hope not,” Mom said. “The keepers certainly wouldn’t let him have any. But it’s always possible that some tourist let a piece fall into the exhibit. Or maybe they threw it in, thinking it would be funny if the orangs got it.”

“Or maybe it’s tree sap,” Dad said.

“Could be,” Mom agreed.

Pancake took the stuff he was chewing from his mouth and tested it again. Whatever it was, it certainly appeared to be sticky. Pancake seemed pleased with its adhesiveness and put it back on the end of his stick once more.

“Look at him,” Mom said, impressed. “He’s making a tool. For the longest time, humans thought we were the only animals intelligent enough to do something like this.

It wasn't until women like Jane Goodall, Dian Fossey, and Birute Galdikas began observing great apes in the wild that anyone realized they could be as smart as we are."

Pancake held up one more object that had been hidden at the top of the exhibit. It was about the size and shape of a playing card.

"That looks like a FunJungle ID card," I said.

Mom peered closer at the screen. "It certainly does. How on earth did he get one of those?"

"Oh no," Kyle said quietly.

We all turned to him. He seemed startled that he'd even spoken out loud and now grew embarrassed.

"Is that *yours*?" Mom demanded.

"Maybe," Kyle said, so softly we could barely hear him. "I lost my ID card a few days ago. I figured I'd dropped it somewhere, but I *was* in with the orangutans right before it disappeared, so maybe Pancake swiped it from me."

"I'll bet that's the case," Mom said. "He's quite the little thief."

On the screen, Pancake affixed the ID card to end of the stick with the gum. Then he held it out through the bars of the cage. With his arm fully extended, holding the stick straight, he could get the ID card in front of the electronic pad, six feet away.

The gate to the exhibit clicked open.

Pancake quickly snapped the ID card off the end of his stick, as he'd need it to get back into the cage, then took the stick back up to the top of the cage and hid it again. After that, he slipped out of the cage, shut the gate behind him, and tucked the ID card into his mouth.

"He's storing the card in his *mouth*?" I asked, surprised.

"Orangutans don't have pockets," Mom replied. "The best thing they have is their mouths. Look how big his lips are. He could store a couple whole oranges in there."

None of the other orangutans had woken as Pancake exited the exhibit. Now Pancake climbed the outside of the cage to get to the air-conditioning vent and went to work on the screws.

Dad zoomed in to watch him there. "Holy cow," he said. "He's using his fingernail to unscrew them."

"Doesn't that hurt?" I asked.

"I doubt it," Mom said. "His fingernails are much thicker and tougher than ours are."

"That is one smart ape," Kyle stated.

"Okay," Mom said. "We know how he got out. Now we have to find him." She grabbed her crutches and started for the door.

The rest of us followed her. Kyle's coat was slung over the back of his desk chair. As he grabbed it, he knocked something off his desk. It tumbled to the floor with a crack. "Aw, nuts," he muttered. "I am not having a good day."

I came around the desk to see what the object was. It looked like an abstract sculpture about the size of a coffee mug. I couldn't tell what it was supposed to be, except that it was lime green and had now broken in half, leaving a lot of green dust on the floor.

Kyle bent to clean it up, but Mom said, "We can deal with that later. Right now, let's find Pancake."

Kyle sadly stuck the two pieces of the green thing in his jacket pocket and followed us out the door.

"Pancake raided stores selling desserts before," Mom said as we raced through the halls of Monkey Mountain. "So he's probably doing it again. I think the candy store and the ice cream shop are still closed for repairs. What's left?"

"There are two other ice cream shops," Dad said. "One out by SafariLand and one by the Polar Pavilion."

"There's another candy store near Carnivore Canyon," I recalled. "And a bakery, too."

"We'll cover a lot more ground if we split up," Mom suggested. "I'll do the Polar Pavilion; Jack, take SafariLand. Kyle and Teddy, head toward Carnivore Canyon. If you find Pancake, do not try to capture him yourself. He's a wild animal. Call security and then call me."

"Okay," I agreed. We exited Monkey Mountain, and Mom and Dad veered off in different directions.

Kyle and I stayed together as we headed toward Carnivore

Canyon. Although I was supposed to be thinking about Pancake, I couldn't get the object that had been on Kyle's desk out of my mind.

Something about it struck me as important, although I couldn't figure out what.

"What was that green thing you just broke?" I asked.

"The mold for Bababoonie's teeth." Kyle pulled the pieces out of his pocket and showed them to me. "Doc made it last night before the operation."

I examined it as we hurried through the park. The green mold looked somewhat like a small brick, nice and square on one side, while the other side showed the indentations of the baboon's teeth and even the ridges in the palate at the top of its mouth, as though the big monkey had bit into it. "What's it for?"

"To make the fake tooth for the one Doc had to replace. The tooth had to be sculpted out of porcelain—and it had to be exactly the size of the old tooth so it fit into Bababoonie's mouth. So Doc did exactly what a dentist for humans would do to make a new tooth. First he made this mold of Bababoonie's teeth." Kyle pointed to the indentation of the baboon's canine tooth. It was much bigger than the others, indicating that the tooth was a spike nearly two inches long. "Then he heated the porcelain until it was liquid and poured it in here. When the porcelain hardened again, it looked exactly like the original tooth."

"What's the mold made of?" I asked. "Clay?"

"It's actually something called dental alginate. It's some kind of plaster that hardens really quickly. This set in about five minutes, so Doc didn't have to wait too long to make the tooth. Pretty cool, huh?"

"I guess."

"Doc didn't need it anymore, so he said I could keep it." We arrived at Carnivore Canyon. The candy store was one way, the bakery the other. Kyle split off from me. "Let me know if you find Pancake!"

"Wait!" I called, holding up the mold. "Don't you want this?"

"Not anymore!" Kyle called back. "It's broken! Just chuck it!" He disappeared around a clump of landscaping.

I continued on toward the bakery, though my attention was riveted on the broken mold in my hands. The outside of it was smooth, but on the inside, where it had broken, it was rough and flaky. I used my thumbnail to scratch off a bit.

The feeling reminded me of something. . . .

There was a loud clatter ahead of me. It sounded like a dozen pots and pans being dropped on a hard floor. I looked up to find I was almost at the bakery.

And I wasn't alone there.

Exactly like at the candy store and the ice cream parlor,

the front window had been smashed in. A large trash can lay on the floor inside.

With the window gone, it was easy to step right into the bakery. All the glass cases that had held cakes and other pastries had been broken into. Sometimes the glass had been punched out. Sometimes the doors had been ripped off. Pancake had gone to town on the baked goods. He'd apparently tried to taste everything. Cakes had craters bitten into them. Pies had handfuls scooped out of the middle. The floor was littered with half-eaten doughnuts, beheaded cupcakes, and gutted éclairs.

Behind the main counter, a swinging door led to the kitchen, from which the sounds of pots and pans being banged around continued. Pancake was still there.

I pulled out my phone, intending to call my mother.

Then I noticed something else on the floor. A chocolate cupcake with neon pink sprinkles. I picked it up.

The pink color triggered a memory. Suddenly, I realized what the mold of Bababoonie's teeth had reminded me of. I remembered feeling something like it before.

Instead of calling my mother, I ran a search on my phone for "pink dental alginate."

A lot of information about it came up—along with hundreds of images. Not only did dental alginate come in pink, but that was apparently the most popular color. A bright bubblegum pink.

It was exactly the same color of the little bit of mud I'd found in Rhonda's paddock two days before. Only now I realized it wasn't mud at all.

Understanding descended on me. All the questions that had stumped me over the last few days now had answers. Everything suddenly made sense.

I knew who had been shooting at Rhonda.

Pancake was no longer a priority. There was plenty of cake left, so he probably wasn't going anywhere soon.

But I was going to have to move fast to stop the poacher.

I started to dial my phone.

A hand clamped on my arm.

Large Marge spun me around to face her. She had a knowing grin on her face and dangled a pair of handcuffs from her finger. "Looks like I caught you red-handed this time, Teddy," she said. "You're under arrest."

THE POACHER

"I didn't do this," I told Marge.

"Sure you didn't," she sneered. "You're just sitting here at the scene of the crime, surrounded by half-eaten food, with a piece of red-hot evidence in your hand." She snatched the pink-sprinkled chocolate cupcake from me and held it in front of my nose. "This time I've got you and you're not getting away."

"Marge," I said. "I know who the rhino poacher is, but we're running out of time. If you let me go—"

"Shut your trap," Marge interrupted. "I'm not falling for that hooey. I'm not as big an idiot as you think." She clapped one of the handcuffs around my wrist.

"Marge, look around you!" I argued. "Do you really think I ate all this food by myself?"

"Maybe."

Obviously, using logic wasn't going to work. So I went with plan B.

I stomped on Marge's toe as hard as I could.

I'd hoped that the sudden pain would make her release my arm. Instead, it only made her scream like a banshee right in my ear. And then she got mad.

"You little toad!" she snarled. "You're in for it now!" She tried to grab my other wrist and cuff it while I did my best to get away.

Unfortunately, Marge was much bigger and stronger than I was. She quickly overpowered me, slamming me chest-first onto a table and wrenching my arms behind my back.

She was so busy cuffing me, she didn't notice that Pancake had emerged from the kitchen.

The orangutan was watching us from behind the counter. He knew me, but he didn't know Marge—and he didn't like what Marge was doing to me.

Marge clicked the handcuffs around my other wrist.

"Marge," I said. "You better let me go right now."

"Or what?" she said snidely.

"Or you're going to be attacked by an orangutan."

Rather than back off, Marge got even rougher with me. She flipped me onto my back and thumped a meaty finger into my chest. "I told you to shut your trap, Teddy. So help me, if you say one more word, I'll smack your fibbing mouth right off your face." With that, she raised a hand, as though she was thinking of striking me anyhow.

Pancake sprang over the counter, landing on the floor beside us, and grabbed Marge's arm.

Marge reared back in surprise. From the blank, uncomprehending look on her face, I could tell she didn't understand what was going on. Instead of realizing that the very orangutan whom I'd explained had caused all the trouble was right there at the scene of the crime, she seemed to be under the impression that it had appeared out of nowhere and interfered with my arrest. Anyone who knew anything about orangutans—or any animals at all—would have known not to antagonize it. Marge did exactly the opposite.

"Let me go, you stupid monkey!" she shouted. "Or I'll arrest you for assaulting an officer."

Pancake's lips curled back in a snarl, revealing a set of sharp teeth that put Bababoonie's to shame.

The color drained from Marge's face so quickly, it looked as though she'd been bleached. *Now* it occurred to her that Pancake might be dangerous.

Marge got lucky. If Pancake had wanted to, he probably could have torn Marge's arms out of their sockets. Or crushed the bones of her wrist with one squeeze. Instead, he simply picked up a banana cream pie and smashed it right into Marge's face.

Given that he was an orangutan, though, he did it quite hard. Marge sailed backward, smashing into a cake display, which promptly collapsed on her. A dozen cakes tumbled out, each splatting all over her. A triple-decker chocolate cake plopped right onto her head.

Marge screamed and staggered back to her feet, blinded by icing, spluttering banana cream. I spotted the key to the handcuffs dangling from her belt.

"Pancake," I said. "Get the keys."

As I'd guessed, an orangutan who spent so much time trying to get out of his cage knew exactly what keys were. Pancake grinned and pounced.

"Keep your mitts off me!" Marge yelled. She tried to run but slipped in a slick of icing and went down again, this time face-planting into a doughnut rack. Dozens of the pastries exploded on impact, splattering the walls with raspberry jam and Bavarian cream. Pancake hooted happily, as though he found the entire thing hilarious. While Marge writhed on the floor, the orangutan deftly plucked the key off her belt.

I turned around, showing the cuffs on my wrists to Pancake. "Now unlock these!"

Pancake looked at the handcuffs curiously, then the key. Then he turned his attention to the doughnuts and started cramming them in his mouth.

It had been expecting a bit too much for him to unlock

me. He was only an orangutan, after all. "Okay, just give me the key!" I said, thrusting my hands toward him with the palms open.

Pancake happily plunked the key into my hands, then squirted the raspberry filling from a doughnut down his throat.

With my hands behind my back, I couldn't unlock my cuffs—or phone anyone—so I simply ran from the bakery, looking for help.

Marge lurched into my path in a desperate last-ditch attempt to stop me. She had so much icing in her face, she couldn't even see me. Her hair was shellacked with chocolate. Two frosted doughnuts were stuck where her eyes normally would have been, giving the impression that she was wearing oversized glasses. "Stop!" she ordered. "You're under arrest!"

Pancake barreled into her, knocking her down once more. This time, Marge landed on her rear in a pile of cherry pies, which made a sickening squelch beneath her bottom. Marge roared in disgust and frustration.

I raced into the park.

Pancake stuffed a few more pastries into his mouth and followed me. He had a chocolate éclair dangling from his lips like a cigar.

Marge howled after me. "This isn't over between us, Teddy! I'll get you one of these days!"

Bizarrely, this was the second time I'd run through Fun-Jungle with my hands cuffed behind my back. The first time had happened while investigating the disappearance of Kazoo the Koala. So I already knew that it wasn't easy. As I raced through the park, I looked around for someone who could uncuff me.

A low rumble echoed, so deep I could feel it in my bones.

I froze, recognizing the sound. It was the purr of a happy elephant. Though most people think that elephants usually vocalize by trumpeting, they actually use lower tones much more often—including ultrasound, which is so low that humans can't even hear it. These tones can carry great distances, allowing elephants miles apart to communicate with one another. Their happy purring sounded a lot like a cat's—if the cat weighed four tons.

I hopped onto a nearby bench, looking for the elephants. Pancake sat next to me and noisily slurped the cream filling out of his éclair.

I spotted the backs of the elephants above some landscaping near Shark Odyssey. Apparently, Pete Thwacker had been successful in getting them to resume their morning walks. They were heading toward us, just beginning their loop of the park.

I ran after them and Pancake joined in the chase. "Bonnie!" I yelled, figuring the head keeper would be out with them. "Help!"

"Teddy?" I heard her respond.

I cut around behind the landscaping to find Bonnie at the front of the herd. I'm not sure which startled her more, the fact that I was handcuffed or that I was accompanied by a chocolate-smeared orangutan.

"What happened to you?" she asked.

I tried to explain as quickly as possible. "Pancake escaped and broke into the bakery, but Marge thought I did it and tried to arrest me. We escaped and I know who shot at the rhino, so I need my hands free."

Bonnie didn't question any of this. At FunJungle, bizarre events were starting to become commonplace. "Do you have the key?"

"In my hand."

Bonnie quickly took it from me and unlocked one of the cuffs, freeing my arms. Time was so precious, I couldn't even wait for her to unlock the other. I simply took the key back from her and started running again. "Thanks!" I cried.

"Need me to do anything else?" Bonnie yelled after me.

"Call Chief Hoenekker!" I shouted back. "Tell him to meet me at Athmani's office!"

Pancake sprang off the bench and bounded along beside me, enjoying our romp through the park.

I fished my phone out of my pocket, speed-dialed my father, and told him to call Mom and meet me at Athmani's office as well. He had lots of questions, but there wasn't time to answer them and I needed to save my breath. "It's urgent," I told him. "Just meet me there."

"Will do," Dad said.

I hauled through the rest of the park as fast as I could. I tried to unlock the remaining handcuff en route, but I couldn't do it while running, so I crammed the key in my pocket instead. The administration building was on the opposite side of FunJungle from where I'd started, so it was a long run. I was nearly exhausted by the time I got there. Pancake seemed to be, too, although maybe he was nauseated from exercising so much on a stomach full of pastries.

"Teddy!" Mom yelled. She was at the door of the administration building, waiting for me. "You found Pancake, too?"

"Yeah," I panted. "He was in the bakery."

"Pancake," Mom chided. "You've been a bad boy."

Pancake grinned in response, revealing plenty of chocolate frosting jammed in the gaps between his teeth. He followed us right into the main lobby of the administration building.

The guard posted at the desk snapped to his feet in astonishment. "You can't bring a monkey in here!"

"It's an *ape*," Mom corrected. "And he escaped his exhibit. Call Monkey Mountain and have a keeper come over to get him right away. And keep a close eye on him in the meantime. J.J. McCracken doesn't want him getting away again."

While we passed through the metal detector, Pancake vaulted over the security desk and plopped into the guard's chair. There was a bowl of candy on the desk and, despite the fact that he'd recently eaten several pounds of cake, he went to work on this as well.

"Hey!" the guard snapped. "That's for humans!"

Before he could protest that we were leaving him with an orangutan, we ducked into the elevator. Normally, we would have run up the stairs, but Mom couldn't handle them so well on her crutches.

"Where's Dad?" I asked.

"Already here," Mom said. "And Hoenekker is too."

"Great." We emerged onto the third floor and raced down to Athmani's office. His door was open. As Mom had said, Dad and Chief Hoenekker were waiting, along with Athmani.

Dad gave me a hug as I arrived. Hoenekker gave me a scowl. "This better be good," he said. "We've been here all night. I was about to go home and finally get some sleep."

"You know who tried to shoot the rhinos?" Athmani asked curiously.

"Yes," I said. "*You* did."

All the adults reacted with astonishment, as though I'd

done something terribly offensive, like made a rude noise in church. Even Athmani. "Me?! Is this a joke?" He did such a good job of acting confused that for a moment I actually doubted myself.

But then I looked down at the floor of his office. As I'd remembered, the carpet was still covered with tiny shavings from his sculptures. Little flakes and curls. The moment I saw them, I knew I was right.

"He wasn't trying to kill the rhinos," I explained to the others. "He was only trying to make us *think* someone was trying to kill them so that we'd cut the horns off."

Athmani laughed as though this was ridiculous. "Oh, goodness me, Teddy. I thought you were going to be serious. We all know the hunter was a woman. . . ."

"No," I said. "The hunter was *you*. You wore a wig to throw us off your trail. Along with doing a whole lot of other things."

Athmani started to protest again, but Hoenekker held up a hand, silencing him. "Let the kid talk."

"Oh, come now!" Athmani cried. "You can't possibly believe this nonsense!"

"I'm at least going to listen to it," Hoenekker told him. "McCracken's forcing me to work with Teddy, so let's hear what he has to say. If it's crazy, you've got nothing to worry about, right?"

"I suppose." Athmani rolled his eyes in annoyance and sullenly leaned against his desk.

Hoenekker turned back to me. "For your sake, this better not be a big waste of our time."

"It won't be," I said, and then launched into my explanation. "There were a bunch of things that kept bothering me about the hunter's behavior through all this. Why did the hunter not use a silencer the first time? Why did the hunter climb over the back fence so close to the camera? Why did the hunter go after a rhino inside a building instead of a rhino out in the open? No real hunter would do things like that. A real hunter would try to make sure we didn't know he was here. But what if the hunter *wanted* us to think he was going after the rhino? Then all those things made sense. The morning of the elephant stampede, the reason we heard a rifle without a silencer was because Athmani wanted us to hear it."

"How could I have fired the rifle?" Athmani asked. "I was with you and the elephants when it went off!"

Hoenekker spun toward me, annoyed that I'd overlooked this. Even Mom and Dad looked concerned by the flaw in my logic.

"He triggered it remotely," I told them. "So that he'd have an alibi. Dad, the other day you said you could set up a remote system to do almost anything. Could you make one fire a rifle?"

"I suppose," Dad said thoughtfully. "Setting up a wireless control system is quite easy. You could even control it with a smartphone. But rigging a machine to depress the trigger on a rifle would be a little more difficult."

"It could be done, though," Hoenekker said. "I've seen setups before. They use hydraulics to pull the trigger."

"Well, Athmani did something like that," I said. "He set the rifle up close to FunJungle—probably in the woods—then made it go off when he was with all of us to give himself the alibi. And to frighten us all into thinking there was a *real* hunter around."

"But the bullet went through the window of the rhino house!" Athmani exclaimed. "Are you honestly saying that I set up a rifle to make that difficult a shot remotely?"

"No," I replied. "You'd already taken the shot at Rhonda much earlier. Only, you used a silencer then so no one would hear. You missed her on purpose, but made sure there was plenty of evidence of an attack. Then, at Rhonda's house later, you pointed out the bullet in the wall to us—and we all simply *assumed* it had been fired from the gun we'd heard. That's why you shot at Rhonda, rather than a rhino that was outside. Because a bullet in the wall would be easy to see and would make it obvious that someone was specifically going after the rhinos.

"But that didn't convince everyone to cut the horns off yet. So you tried again. This time you climbed over the back fence. And even though there were plenty of places where there were no cameras, you came over right by one to make sure it filmed you. To throw us off the scent, though, you wore a wig to make it look like a woman was the hunter."

"And I suppose you're going to say that I purposefully allowed you all to see me out in SafariLand as well?" Athmani chided.

"No," I said. "That was an accident. I think you were going to take another shot at Rhonda, this time from close range, to worry us even more. That's why you brought a silencer that time. Because you didn't want the shot to alert security while you were on the property. Only we happened to see you. But that actually worked out for you, because it was even more proof there was a hunter on the loose.

"However, Doc still refused to cut the horns off, so you made one more attempt to convince us all the rhinos were in serious danger. Since security was now amped up in the park, you had to shoot from World of Reptiles. I'll bet that this time, you actually planned to hit Rhonda. Not to kill her or anything, but to wound her so we'd know you meant business. But then Summer and I stumbled across you. You didn't end up shooting at the rhino, but it didn't matter. You had finally created enough evidence to convince J.J. the rhinos should all be dehorned."

"And what would be the point of all this?" Athmani asked. "I didn't steal the horns. They're locked in J.J. McCracken's safe!"

"No, they're not," I said. "The ones in the safe are fakes."

Mom, Dad, and Hoenekker gasped in surprise at this.

Athmani didn't. He flinched. But then he quickly did his best to pretend that he hadn't. "What are you talking about?"

"The pink stuff I found in the rhino house that you said was clay wasn't clay. It was dental alginate. Dentists use it to make molds of teeth and stuff, but according to the Internet, sculptors use it too. You're a sculptor. If you took a mold of a rhino horn, I'll bet you could make a copy of it that looked exactly like the real one."

"I sculpt *stone*," Athmani said, pointing to the Shona sculptures in his office. "A rhino horn made out of stone would weigh forty pounds and wouldn't look a bit like the real thing."

"You didn't make the fakes out of stone." I bent and picked one of the curled bits off the carpet. As I'd suspected, it wasn't stone at all. It was plastic. "You made it out of *this*.

Right here in this office. Stone doesn't curl. But plastic does. And the right kind of plastic probably looks and feels exactly like rhino horn. Or at least close enough to allow you time to get away with the real ones."

Hoenekker took the curl of plastic from my hands and examined it closely. Then he looked at Athmani suspiciously.

"Oh, come on, now!" Athmani cried. "This is even crazier than I suspected! Remote-controlled rifles and fake rhino horns! These are the inventions of a boy with an overactive imagination!"

"You were the one who delivered the horns to McCracken's safe," Hoenekker said suspiciously. "In fact, you volunteered to do it. No one was with you during that time. You could easily have stopped by here on the way, swapped the real ones for the fakes and then delivered those to McCracken's office."

"I could have, but I didn't," Athmani said flatly. "I have done nothing but try to protect those rhinos!"

"You've been arguing for dehorning them harder than anyone else," Hoenekker replied.

"To protect them!" Athmani argued back. "From a poacher who is still out there while you entertain ridiculous stories from a meddlesome boy!"

"It wouldn't be hard to check out Teddy's story," Mom said. "All we'd have to do is have J.J. open the safe and examine the horns left inside."

Hoenekker nodded, then turned to Athmani. "I think that'd make sense. Though you'll be staying right here until we get to the bottom of this."

"I'm afraid that won't be happening," someone said.

Hondo stood in the doorway, his gun aimed at us. "Get the horns," he told Athmani. "Looks like it's time for us to go."

CAPTURED

All of us put our hands up.

Among the many unpacked boxes in Athmani's office was one marked LAW ENFORCEMENT SUPPLIES. Hondo found several sets of handcuffs in it and tossed them onto the desk beside Athmani. "Lock them up and let's get out of here."

"I didn't do anything," Athmani told us weakly.

"Oh, for crying out loud." Hondo groaned. "Drop the innocent act already. There's no point anymore. The kid figured everything out, and we have to go."

Athmani sagged. Up to that point, he'd done an impressive job of feigning innocence and pretending to be offended by my accusations. But now he showed his true self. He picked the handcuffs up, looking embarrassed about how everything had turned out.

Hondo took Hoenekker's gun from him, then ordered us, "Get down on the floor."

We did as he said.

"I'm sorry," Athmani told us as he cuffed Mom to the leg of his desk. "I didn't mean for this to happen."

"We trusted you to protect those rhinos," Mom said angrily.

"And I *did*." Athmani turned his attention to cuffing Dad. "Hondo wanted to simply kill them and take their horns. I came up with a way that let them stay alive. If Teddy hadn't caught on, we wouldn't have to do this."

"And you would have gotten away," Mom spat.

"We *are* getting away," Hondo reminded her. "Hand over your phones."

We did. Hondo pocketed them.

Athmani finished cuffing Dad to the desk and moved on to Hoenekker.

Mom glared at Athmani. "If you sell those horns, you're just as bad as any poacher. You'll feed demand for more, which will lead to more dead rhinos. And for what? A little bit of money?"

"No," Hondo taunted. "A *lot* of money. Listen to yourselves, getting all worked up about some butt-ugly beasts. If you can't eat an animal, what's the use of it?" He turned to Athmani and asked, "Where are the *real* horns?"

Athmani nodded to a closet in his office. Hondo opened it. A large black duffel bag was sitting on the floor. Hondo unzipped it to make sure the horns were there, then zipped it back up and hoisted it onto his shoulder. He ripped Athmani's desk phone out of the wall so we couldn't use it, then turned to me and grinned. "You were clever to figure it out, kid. But not clever enough to stop us."

He grabbed the handcuffs that were already on my wrist, apparently thinking Athmani had put them on me—what twelve-year-old ran around wearing a set of handcuffs?—and clipped the other end to a desk leg. "Come on," he told Athmani. "The plane's waiting."

Athmani followed him to the door, then looked back at us with genuine sadness. "I really am sorry," he said.

Then he shut the door on us and hurried down the hall.

"Of course he's sorry," Hoenekker muttered. "If it hadn't been for Teddy, he'd have been able to disappear without a trace."

Mom, Dad, Hoenekker, and I were all cuffed to the desk, unable to go anywhere and without phones. However, I still had the key to my cuffs in my pocket. I quickly fished it out.

"Where'd you get that?" Dad asked, surprised.

"From Marge. They're her cuffs."

"So you can get loose?" Mom asked, relieved.

"Yes." I unlocked myself from the desk, then tried the key on Dad's handcuffs.

"It won't work," Hoenekker told me. "Every set of cuffs has a different key. Don't waste time with us. You have to stop Athmani and Hondo! If they have a plane nearby, they could be in Mexico in less than an hour."

I looked to my parents. They seemed to agree.

"Be careful," Mom warned. "Hondo has a gun. Do what you can, but protecting those horns isn't worth losing your life over."

"I'll do my best," I told her, then raced out the door.

Hondo and Athmani were already long gone. Both of them were strong men in good shape. They could probably run much faster than I could. I was still tired from all the morning's excitement, but I gave it my best, racing through the hall and then down the stairs.

I emerged into the lobby of the administration building, expecting to find the guard who'd been on duty there that morning. Unfortunately, he was gone. One glance at his desk indicated his absence was probably due to Pancake. The place was a disaster area. The orangutan had yanked out every drawer and dumped out the contents.

There was also a huge hole in the front window that had apparently been made by an orangutan throwing the guard's chair through it. The chair lay in the entry plaza, busted into pieces.

I ducked through the broken window and sprinted into the park.

Far ahead of me, Hondo and Athmani were nearing the front gates. Beyond the gates, I could see Hondo's car idling in the drop-off area. There was no way I could catch them. They had much too big a head start. The only security officer I could see was stationed in the booth at the employee entrance. He was too far away to hear me, but I yelled to him out of desperation anyhow. "Stop those guys! They stole the rhino horns!"

Inside the security booth, the officer didn't budge. Hondo heard me, though. He gave me a mocking wave good-bye.

And then I heard purring. Or at least I *felt* it. I turned and spotted the elephant herd heading back home after their morning walk, closing in on the front gates.

Something slammed into me, knocking me to the ground.

It was Large Marge. She was still coated in icing and various pastry fillings. Her hair stuck out from her head in sticky coils that, combined with the rage in her eyes, made her look like Medusa. "I told you I'd get you!" she snarled.

"Marge!" I yelled. "Athmani and Hondo are stealing all the rhino horns! If you stop them, you'll be a hero!"

"Shut up!" Marge knelt over me, pressing me flat on the ground. "I've had it with your shenanigans once and for all!"

Athmani and Hondo were almost to the front gates.

"I'll let you arrest me if you want," I pleaded. "But I need you to—"

Marge clapped a chocolate-frosted hand over my mouth and roared. "I. Said. Shut. Up!"

Only, the last word wasn't exactly "up." It was more like "Unggggggh." Because Pancake whacked her on the head with a fist as she said it.

Marge's eyes rolled upward, and she collapsed on the ground beside me. Her face splatted right into an elephant poo the keepers hadn't got around to cleaning up yet.

Normally, I might have rolled her out of it, but there were other things to deal with.

"Thanks," I told Pancake, then yanked the gun out of Marge's holster. "Cover your ears. This might be loud."

Pancake did exactly as I'd asked.

I fired the gun into the air again and again.

The elephants trumpeted in alarm.

"Oh no!" Bonnie cried. "Not again!"

I kept firing. I'd never shot a gun before. The recoil was bigger than I expected, so I had to use my other arm to steady it. I pulled the trigger until it clicked empty.

The elephants stampeded in the opposite direction from

me, right toward the front gates. Just as they had two days before, they left a trail of droppings and a river of pee, and they flattened everything in their path. The beautiful landscaping of the entry plaza was trampled within seconds.

Athmani and Hondo were right in the elephants' path. Athmani had the presence of mind to keep running, but Hondo flipped out. The guy already had issues with animals, and now the biggest ones in the world were charging right at him. He screeched like a little girl and froze in terror. As the elephants bore down on him, he whipped out his own gun and pointed it at the oncoming herd.

"Stop!" he ordered. "Or I'll shoot!"

The little gun probably wouldn't have made a dent in the elephants' thick hides, but they bore down on him before he could fire anyhow. The lead elephant swatted him aside with her trunk and he flew through the air like a well-hit baseball. He smashed through the front window of the FunJungle Emporium and landed in a pile of Henry Hippo Junior commemorative merchandise.

The elephants then plowed through the front gates, knocking them off their hinges like living battering rams. The gates crashed to the ground and were crushed beneath the elephants' feet.

Athmani reached the getaway car, but there was no time for him to get inside. The elephants stormed right over it. A steamroller couldn't have done a better job. The tires exploded and the windows shattered. By the time the last elephant got to the car, it wasn't much thicker than a sheet of tinfoil.

I was about to run after them all when I heard a strange wailing noise coming from nearby me. At first I thought it was an animal in pain, but then realized it was coming from Marge.

She was sitting up, wiping elephant poop and frosting from her face and crying. "I give up," she sobbed. "Whenever I try to stop you, I lose. No one cares that you're a menace, and look at what happens to me!"

"I'm not a menace," I pointed out. "The orangutan broke into the stores, not me."

"I know!" Marge bawled. "You're right, as usual. The great Teddy Fitzroy solves another crime while I end up covered in poo! It's not fair!"

I wasn't quite sure what to do. Up until that moment, I would have expected that seeing Marge soiled with poop and swearing off chasing me would be a dream come true. But now she seemed so sad and pathetic that I actually felt bad for her. I'd never seen an adult cry like this before, but I didn't really have time to deal with it either. So I gave her a quick pat on the back, trying to avoid touching any of the disgusting stuff on her, and did my best to be reassuring. "There, there," I said. "Things will get better."

Marge managed to stop crying and looked to me thankfully. "You really think so?"

"Well," I said, "they couldn't really get much *worse*." Then I raced off to see what had become of Hondo and Athmani.

I got to FunJungle Emporium first. Hondo was still lying there in the window display, unconscious after being coldcocked by the elephant. He was buried under a hundred stuffed hippos. The duffel bag lay in a pile of broken snow globes.

Bonnie ran up to me, angry as could be. "What on earth were you thinking with that gun? Someone could have been hurt!"

"Sorry," I said, unzipping the duffel bag. "I was trying to stop them from stealing *these*."

Bonnie gasped upon seeing the horns inside. Her anger instantly dissipated. "Are those real?"

"Unfortunately, yes." I looked out through where the front gates had been. With his getaway car flattened, Athmani was searching desperately for another way to escape, but the few other cars in the area were locked. Which left Athmani out in the open in the big, wide parking lot.

"Athmani was in on this?" Bonnie asked, aghast.

I pointed to Hondo. "It was his idea. But Athmani made it all happen."

The anger returned to Bonnie's eyes, but it was no longer

directed at me. "I'll handle this, then." She plucked the gun from Hondo's hand and stormed into the parking lot. "You get those hands up right now!" she yelled. "I have zero tolerance for poachers!"

Athmani realized he was caught. He froze and raised his hands in resignation.

Beyond him, far across the parking lot, a lamppost toppled as one of the elephants bumped into it.

"What on earth happened here?" someone demanded.

Pete Thwacker stood behind me. He was staring in shock at all the destruction around us: the busted front gates, the trampled landscaping, the flattened getaway car, and the broken display window with Hondo lying in the middle of it.

"The elephants sort of stampeded again," I said.

"Really?" An ear-to-ear grin blossomed on Pete's face. "This is fantastic!" he crowed. "Look at this awesome devastation! The tourists are gonna love it!"

EPILOGUE: RHONDA

"It's a girl," Doc said.

Everyone gathered outside Rhonda's house cheered. While the birth of *any* new rhino was something to be happy about, females were slightly more important to the survival of the species than males. Rhino pregnancies last sixteen months, only one baby is born at a time, and it takes at least another year to wean them. That means it can be three to four years between births, which is very slow for an endangered species. So the more females there are to make babies, the better.

"How's she look?" Mom asked.

"Healthy as can be." Doc flashed a smile, looking as happy as I'd ever seen him.

It was ten in the morning. I should have been at school, but when word got out that Rhonda was in labor, Mom had called my teacher and said I was having a special educational experience at home. After all, rhinos weren't born every day.

Dad was already inside the rhino house, documenting the birth with a video camera. The rhino keepers were gathered outside with us, waiting for the chance to see the newborn, as were Pete Thwacker, Kristi Sullivan, and a few other PR minions. J.J. McCracken was also there, though he didn't seem as imposing as he normally did. Instead, he was giddy with excitement.

Summer was there too.

I hadn't seen her much in the week since World of Reptiles. Although she wouldn't admit it, I was pretty sure she'd been avoiding me. The dozens of texts she normally sent me every day had dwindled to nothing, and instead of eating at our regular table in the cafeteria, she'd been AWOL at lunchtime. She'd also blown off the basketball game the previous Friday, as well as pizza afterward with all our friends.

It was all very frustrating. After everything that had happened at World of Reptiles, I was desperate to talk to Summer, but she obviously had the opposite reaction.

And now that she was here, she was keeping some distance between us as well, staying close to her father. Although every once in a while, when I looked her way, I got the sense that she'd just been looking at me herself.

Around the rest of the Asian Plains, everything looked almost exactly like it normally did. At the front of the park, the gates were being replaced (although Pete had argued against this, as it was excellent elephant damage), and work had begun to replace the chain-link fence along SafariLand with a hunter-proof wall, but both those projects were so far away we couldn't even see them. All around us, the various Asian antelope grazed the same way they always did, oblivious to the birth of the rhino nearby. Every few minutes, a monorail cruised past, full of tourists equally as unaware. No one even looked at the small crowd of people gathered around the rhino house. They were much more interested in the rhinos they *could* see out in the plains.

The hornless rhinos still looked odd to me, though Pete and Kristi's disinformation campaign had been a success. "Rhinoplasty for Rhino Awareness" had made the national news, and plenty of stories about how endangered rhinos were had run across the country. Almost no one, even at FunJungle, knew the truth about why the rhinos had really been dehorned—or that the park had nearly been swindled out of them. I figured the story would probably blow up once Athmani and Hondo went to trial, but Pete seemed confident he could keep a lid on it. J.J. didn't seem to care. "I don't give a dang how bad it makes the park look," he'd stated. "I'll do whatever it takes to make sure those con men go to jail for a long, long time."

"Can we see the baby now?" Summer asked Doc.

Doc's smile faltered a tiny bit. There were probably lots

of people he would have preferred to let into the rhino house first, but he couldn't say no to the daughter of the park's owner. "All right," he said. "But there are some rules. The mother and her baby are bonding right now. I need you to keep your distance and stay quiet. Not a word. And you can only stay in for a little bit. When I signal you it's time to go, you go—got it?"

"Got it," Summer agreed.

"Ditto for me," J.J. said, then looked at me expectantly. "Care to join us?"

I pointed to myself, surprised. "Me?"

"Of course. I think you've earned this, given all you've done for our rhinos. You too, Charlene." J.J. waved for Mom and me to join him.

I wasn't sure if J.J. was doing this because he really thought he owed me or because he was trying to make a good impression on my mother after forcing me to investigate a crime behind her back, but I wasn't going to turn down the chance. I hurried into the rhino house.

Mom followed me. She was still on crutches, but the cast was supposed to come off in a few days.

Summer seemed a little uneasy that her father had asked us to join them, but once we were inside the rhino house, she seemed to forget all about me. In truth, I forgot about Summer, too. For a few moments, at least.

The newborn rhino was adorable and awe-inspiring. She was slightly pinkish with enormous eyes, and like all the other rhinos at FunJungle except for her mother, she didn't have a horn. However, her rounded hornless nose looked cute, rather than strange. The remnants of her umbilical cord still dangled from her belly button. As we entered, she was getting to her feet for the first time. Rhonda helped her, nudging her lovingly, and then the baby took its first few wobbling steps.

Summer gasped with excitement beside me.

Dad had a bunch of cameras set up on tripods around the room, though he was also recording with a handheld video camera. He turned away from his work for a moment to grin at Mom and me, then went right back to filming the baby again.

The little rhino staggered over to Rhonda's side and began to nurse.

Doc signaled our time was up. Everyone seemed disappointed—I could have happily watched the baby all day—but we knew the deal and filed outside again.

"Well, that was certainly something special," Mom told me, beaming. "But now, kiddo, it's time to get you to school."

"Teddy can ride with Summer if he wants," J.J. offered.

Summer looked caught off guard, unsure what to do.

"You're sure that's okay?" Mom asked. She was still angry

at J.J. for how he'd dealt with me, although she had promised Dad she'd try to keep her cool around him.

"Of course." J.J. grinned. "Summer's heading that way anyhow. We're testing out a new bodyguard today." He pointed to the hulking man who'd been hired to replace Hondo. "I think we can trust him. He can't be worse than the last guy."

It had turned out that getting the rhino horns had been Hondo's idea from the start. In fact, he'd taken the job with the McCrackens only with the intent of figuring out how to get the horns; he had connections to a crime syndicate in Vietnam willing to pay millions for them. But while he'd figured out that it wouldn't be hard to kill the rhinos, getting away with the horns was more difficult. Then he'd met Athmani.

Athmani's job at FunJungle was only short-term. He knew that within a few months he'd be back in Africa again, and sadly, being on the front lines in the war against poachers was a rough life. It didn't pay well, and it was extremely dangerous. More than a thousand African park rangers had been killed by poachers in the past few years, and Athmani was looking for a route to a better life. The enemy had approached him many times in Africa, but he'd always refused them because he didn't want to harm any rhinos. Now, at FunJungle, he saw a way to get the horns while letting the rhinos live. With Hondo's help, he could make more in a few hours than he would have in an entire lifetime of honest work in Africa. The money was too tempting to resist.

"Which is exactly why poaching is out of control right now," Mom had told me. "You can't stop the slaughter by merely going after the hunters. You have to stop the demand. You have to educate people that they're paying millions of dollars and dooming animals to extinction for something that is medically useless. If we don't, your children might very well grow up in a world without wild rhinos."

Standing in the Asian Plains outside the rhino house, I could see two of the other Asian rhinos in the distance. Although they didn't have horns, they were going about their lives as usual. The SafariLand monorail had paused near them, and the tourists were piling up to take pictures. It seemed to me that, for any one of those people, a world without rhinos would be a much sadder place.

I noticed Summer was watching the rhinos too, smiling at the sight of them.

"You're cool with me riding with you?" I asked.

"Of course," she said. The first words she'd actually spoken to me in a week.

"You're sure?"

Summer bit her lip, then seemed to realize that she couldn't avoid me forever. She stepped away from the adults, indicating that I should join her.

"I know I've been acting strange lately," she said. "I just . . . I didn't quite know how to handle things after the other night. It was all kind of, well . . . embarrassing."

"It wasn't your fault that you almost fell into the crocodile pit. We thought Athmani was trying to kill us."

Summer shook her head. "Not that. I mean, that was scary and all, but . . ." She took a moment, trying to figure out what to say next. "I kissed you."

Now *I* wasn't quite sure what to say. So I didn't say anything at all.

Summer continued. "I need you to know that wasn't, like, a big deal, 'I'm in love with you' kiss. It was more like a 'thank you for saving my life' kiss. I was happy to be alive, and I didn't really know what I was doing."

"I'd figured as much," I said. Although the truth was, I'd secretly been hoping that kiss was the other kind.

Relief descended on Summer. But she still seemed nervous around me. "Whew. Oh, cool. I was worried that you might have had the wrong idea there. I mean, I didn't want to get in the way between you and Violet or anything. . . ."

"Me and Violet?" I asked.

"Yeah. In case you're interested in her."

"I'm not."

Summer took a step back. "But she's the head cheerleader. And she's gorgeous. And she likes you."

"I guess," I said. "But I like *you*."

The words hung there for a moment. I started to feel like an idiot for saying them, wishing I could take them back.

But then Summer blushed. And smiled a little. "You do?"

I felt myself blushing as well. "Yeah. You didn't know?"

"I thought you only liked me as a friend."

Another silence fell over us. Neither of us was quite sure what to say again, though I felt a lot happier than I had in the last week, and at the moment, it had nothing to do with the newborn rhino. Before either of us could figure out what to do next, J.J. called to us. "Hey, you two! You can talk in the car! You've got school today!"

Summer and I headed back toward him.

As we did, Kristi Sullivan asked, "Does anyone know what we're going to name the baby?"

"I think we ought to let Teddy have the honor," J.J. said.

Everyone turned to me, seeming to like the idea.

Even Mom seemed to have forgiven J.J. For at least a little while. "Any ideas?" she asked.

I turned to Summer. "What's your middle name?"

"Jade."

"I like it," I said, then looked to everyone else. "How about 'Jade'?"

Murmurs of agreement rippled through the group. Mom looked from me to Summer, then smiled knowingly.

"I'm kind of partial to that name myself," J.J. said. "Jade it is."

Summer blushed again. "C'mon. The car's parked all the way up by the front gates."

We set off through the Asian Plains, walking side by side. Somewhere along the way, we started holding hands. And we stayed like that all the way through FunJungle.

Rhonda Is Not the Only Rhino in Danger

It's not an exaggeration to say that rhinos could disappear from the earth in your lifetime. In the last fifty years, the number of rhinos on earth has declined dramatically. One subspecies, the northern African black rhino, has gone extinct, while there are fewer than one hundred Sumatran rhinos left in the wild—and fewer than fifty Javan rhinos. And in the year it took me to write this book, the number of northern African white rhinos dropped to *five* left in the entire world. Meanwhile, in recent years, cases of poaching have doubled in southern Africa. There's a human cost too: More than a thousand park rangers have died fighting poaching in the past decade.

And the saddest part of all this is that the slaughter is pointless. It is funded by people who think that rhino horn has curative powers, when there is no scientific proof of that at all.

As I pointed out in this book, how to best protect rhinos is a complicated issue. There are advocates for legalized hunting, dehorning rhinos in the wild, educating people so they won't buy rhino horn products anymore—and many other methods. But everyone agrees that the situation is critical. The rhinos need your help. Now.

For more information on what you, your friends, and

your school can do to keep rhinos from going extinct, visit rhinos.org and savetherhino.org.

Sadly, the elephants discussed in this book are being poached in the wild as well. Nearly one hundred a day are killed. You can find ways to help them at sites like 96elephants.org and awf.org.

And if you're interested in helping protect other animals as well as rhinos—or critical habitats—all around the world, check out the websites of these wonderful organizations.

World Wildlife Fund: worldwildlife.org
The Nature Conservancy: nature.org
Center for Biological Diversity: biologicaldiversity.org

Thanks!
Stuart Gibbs

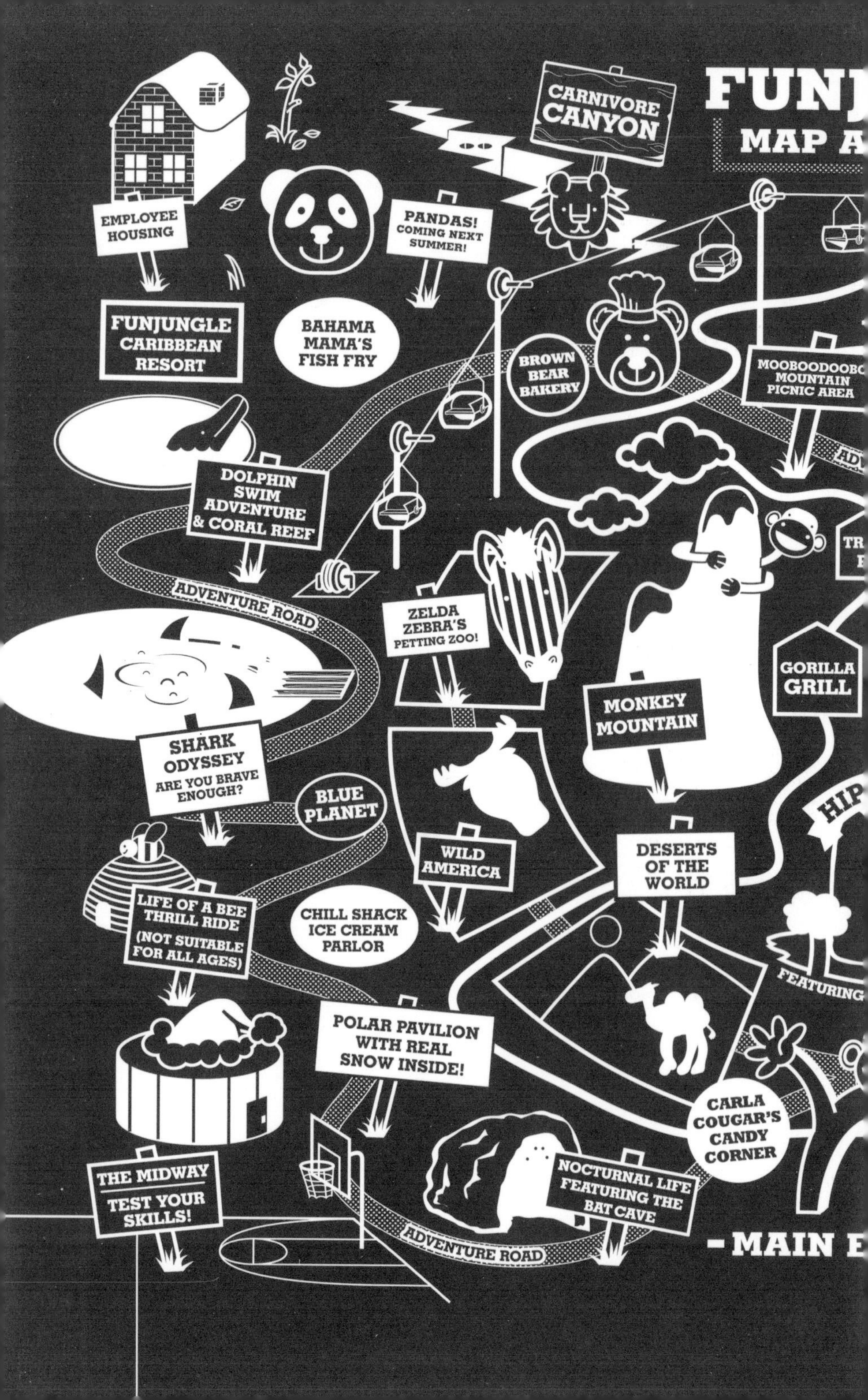
CARNIVORE CANYON
EMPLOYEE HOUSING
PANDAS! COMING NEXT SUMMER!
FUNJUNGLE CARIBBEAN RESORT
BAHAMA MAMA'S FISH FRY
BROWN BEAR BAKERY
DOLPHIN SWIM ADVENTURE & CORAL REEF
ADVENTURE ROAD
ZELDA ZEBRA'S PETTING ZOO!
GORILLA GRILL
MONKEY MOUNTAIN
SHARK ODYSSEY ARE YOU BRAVE ENOUGH?
BLUE PLANET
WILD AMERICA
DESERTS OF THE WORLD
LIFE OF A BEE THRILL RIDE (NOT SUITABLE FOR ALL AGES)
CHILL SHACK ICE CREAM PARLOR
POLAR PAVILION WITH REAL SNOW INSIDE!
CARLA COUGAR'S CANDY CORNER
THE MIDWAY
TEST YOUR SKILLS!
NOCTURNAL LIFE FEATURING THE BAT CAVE
ADVENTURE ROAD